A Touch of BLUE

A Touch of BLUE

Basalt Bay 2

Mary E. Hanks

www.maryehanks.com

Suzanne D. Williams Cover Design

www.feelgoodromance.com

Cover photos:

Fox One, Isniper, Huy Maiden, Aki 2007 @ shutterstock.com

Visit Mary's website:

www.maryehanks.com

To Ruthie

Thank you for loving my dad and being a

wonderful companion to him!

God bless your journey.

To Jason

My favorite walking partner and writing encourager.

You are still the one.

"And we know that in all things God works

for the good of those who love him,"

Romans 8:28

Chapter One

Blue Paxton pressed the gas pedal to the floor of his red Mustang convertible, clocking nearly ninety miles per hour around the seaside curves. He clutched the steering wheel tightly, the salty wind whipping his face and stinging his eyes. He liked driving fast, but this felt too dangerous! Who was the redhead in the SUV who had attempted to run him off the road? A deranged fan? An angry gallery worker? He didn't recognize her when she came alongside his car, shaking her fist at him.

He glanced into the rearview mirror for the thirtieth time or so and thanked God that he didn't see the black vehicle this time. Gram must be praying for him!

He had been undecided whether to push on toward Portland or stop at Basalt Bay—hardly a choice, considering the coastal town was so tiny. But since he preferred arriving at a gallery unannounced and had a few days free on his schedule, the rare decision to choose his next location was up to him. Should he pull into Basalt Bay, even if it wasn't very impressive? He'd get off the road sooner. If he kept going, the irrational driver might catch up to him again.

What would Alfie say if he chose Basalt Bay over Oregon's largest city? His business partner, who usually took care of scheduling, social media applications, and the financial side of their enterprise, would call Blue a fool for choosing such a mediocre place. Would he find anything worthwhile to critique there? His online fan base expected, no, demanded, to hear the nitty-gritty flaws and noteworthy intrigues about art and artists that he discovered wherever he went. Isn't that why they tuned in to *Blue's Art Clash*? That, and the prizes he doled out for giveaways, he thought mirthfully.

"Search for the dirt and the topics our audience craves," Alfie had told him a bazillion times. "That's what brings in the money and subscribers." He and Alfie didn't always see eye-to-eye, but Alfie Denver was a mastermind regarding business. After five years of podcasting about art and artists and his opinion about both, Blue was living the dream—driving his "Stang," podcasting on the road, and boldly analyzing galleries and artists wherever he wanted to go, or wherever Alfie sent him. What more could he want?

Someone to love?

He groaned, wishing the topic hadn't come to mind. How could he have a meaningful relationship while living on the road? It would never work! However, even though he appreciated his nomadic, successful lifestyle that his master's degree in Modern Art and Communications and Alfie's business prowess had helped him achieve, lately, he'd been yearning for a missing aspect of his life. He heaved a sigh and brushed thoughts about love aside.

A sign came into view. "Turn left for the best fish and chips on the West Coast!" The best, huh? He was hungry and ready to stop driving. Glancing in the rearview mirror again, he thought he saw a dark shadow. Was it the black SUV? He pushed hard on the gas pedal and veered left.

Last week, a local reporter sent him an email announcing an upcoming winter festival happening here—otherwise, Basalt Bay wouldn't have been on his radar. Now, a delicious fish dinner sounded fantastic. First, he'd check into a motel with decent Wi-Fi and then scope out the town. It might take, what, five minutes? He chuckled and then scowled at the red and blue lights flashing in his rearview mirror. *Welcome to Basalt Bay, Blue!*

Slowing down, he pulled to the side of the road and wished he'd kept driving to Portland. A law enforcement officer approached his car and peered down at him like a judge staring at a troublesome adolescent.

"What did I do, sir?"

"You were doing forty in a twenty-five!"

"Oh." He was glad Deputy Brian, according to the name tag on his uniform, hadn't caught him going almost ninety on the highway. "Sorry about that."

"Where are you headed in such a hurry?"

Should he explain why he pulled into town? If he mentioned the berserk driver, would the police officer let him off the hook? "A woman was stalking me or trying to cause an accident."

"Stalking you?" the officer asked doubtfully. "In Basalt Bay?"

"Back on the highway, a redhead in a black SUV was driving erratically, coming alongside me on a curve, backing off, then doing it again." Blue kept his voice modulated, but he was tempted to sound more dramatic like he did on his podcast so the officer would sympathize with him. "She almost caused several accidents. I did my best to outrun her."

"Outrun her?" The deputy's eyes shuttered nearly closed. "Folks have given me a lot of excuses for speeding, but this is the first time I've heard that one."

Heat bled up Blue's face. "I'm telling you the truth."

"What kind of problems are you bringing to my town? Are you in trouble with the law?"

"No, sir."

"Then, what?"

"It's a casualty of my line of work." That had to sound foolish and pathetic. The deputy didn't know Blue Paxton or his podcast identity from a criminal on a wanted poster.

"What kind of work are you in? Politics? Acting?"

"No. However, I am in the public eye, er, ear." He didn't elaborate. If this officer knew the art world, he'd surely recognize his voice. "The good news is I lost her before the turnoff."

"So a woman was chasing you?" Deputy Brian scratched his chin and nodded as if he'd solved the problem. "Disgruntled girlfriend? Ex-wife? Mistress?"

"Not even close." And Blue hated the grilling.

The officer sniffed the air and perused the back seat. "Have you been drinking?"

"No, I have not!"

"I imagine this souped-up Mustang must have cost a fortune. Hits top-notch speeds?" Blue's cheeks flushed, but he wasn't confessing anything to the officer. "Did you get a license number for this supposed stalker's vehicle?" *Supposed?*

"No. It was a black SUV," Blue said tensely.

"Needle in a haystack." Deputy Brian thrust out his hand. "License and registration."

"For what?"

"For driving fifteen miles over the posted speed limit."

"Yeah, but—" Blue bit back a groan and grabbed the documentation from the glove box. "I was hoping since the vehicle tailed me hazardously close, you might—"

"Let you off scot-free? Not happening."

Blue set his license and registration on the deputy's palm. First, a ruthless driver stalked him. Now, he was being ticketed for running for his life? Yeah. Well. He should have slowed down more before turning off the highway into this hole-in-the-wall. Chalk that up to another strike against small towns!

Deputy Brian glanced suspiciously between the license and Blue like he might be faking his ID. He had more facial hair now than when he got his last license, but otherwise he looked the same. "Bartholomew Paxton?"

"So my grandmother calls me," Blue said, still perturbed.

"The name doesn't ring a bell."

"Probably not." He'd gone by Blue since he was a kid and his sister, Desi, dubbed him that. "Are we done here?"

"Drive slower. And pay at the courthouse." The law enforcement officer dropped the paperwork and a pink slip on his palm, which Blue stuffed in the glove box. "You can file a complaint about the SUV in my office behind City Hall." He'd rather forget any of this happened. "Does your silence mean you aren't certain the woman was stalking you?"

"No! I'm sure of it." If he wanted to file a complaint, he would. But he wouldn't do so to prove he was telling the truth to anyone, this officer included!

Besides, he'd received threatening emails and calls before. However, the person who tried to run him off the road had taken vengeance, rage, or whatever emotion she felt to a new level. For some of those curvy stretches, he had feared for his life.

What would the driver do if she didn't find him up north? The nature of his live podcasts would expose his location.

Would she come back looking for him in Basalt Bay?

Chapter Two

"You are listening to Blue Paxton on *Blue's Art Clash*, and here's my recommendation—don't even bother attending Lyle Jeffers' exhibit!" The art critic's ranting grated in Sarah Blackstone's ears like fingernails against a chalkboard. Since she subscribed to Blue Paxton's podcast and tuned in regularly, she'd heard enough of his outrageous critiques to have a strong opinion of her own! Why couldn't the grumpy podcaster say one pleasant thing about Lyle Jeffers?

"A gallery with such poor quality of art isn't worth your valuable time and hard-earned cash," Blue said in a dramatic southern drawl. A whistle chimed in the background like a point tallied on a scoreboard. Sarah rolled her eyes toward the wooden rafters above her. "If you attend this forgettable art show"—Blue's voice returned to normal—"be sure to drop a note in the comment box and inform the director exactly how much of a waste of time you thought it was! Let your opinion about art be heard!"

Blue Paxton thinks too highly of himself and his jaded viewpoint! Yet, despite Sarah's aggravation with him and the bells, whistles, and theatrical voices, she adjusted her earbuds and continued listening while she got ready for work.

She applied makeup, straightened her chin-length brown hair, and checked her navy skirt and light gray sweater in the full-length mirror of her attic bedroom, occasionally groaning at Blue's comments. How could he say such awful things about a gifted artist? Even if Blue regularly reminded listeners that he was expressing only his opinions, Sarah had observed Lyle's charcoal drawings and considered them fine works of art. Of course, she felt loyal to all the coastal artists. While Blue Paxton didn't seem to have any loyalty, other than to himself.

As she descended the ship's ladder to the second floor of the project house and went down the regular staircase to the living room, she thought about how excited she was to be hosting the art demos for the town's first winter festival this week. She'd grab a homemade muffin and fruit for a quick breakfast and catch a ride to town with Bess. Thankfully, the mayor left for work at the same time. Otherwise, she'd have to schedule an Uber ride since she didn't have a car.

Unfortunately, Blue's voice still rambled in her ears. "In my view, Lyle's drawings are lifeless and unimaginative. Is the artist's head stuck in the sand when he creates?" If anyone's head was stuck in the sand, it was Blue Paxton's! Why was she even listening to him?

Ever since Paige Harper asked Sarah to work at the gallery and fill in for her during her childbirth leave, she'd been listening to every podcast she could access to learn more about contemporary art. She'd stumbled upon *Blue's Art Clash* because of its high ranking on an internet search—not because of Blue's affable demeanor! His podcast was popular and controversial, and since it originated from the West Coast, she couldn't stay current with the local market and ignore it. But his bold, sometimes heartless-sounding reviews stirred tremendous angst within her and made her want to hurl her earbuds across the room.

Instead, she dropped them into her tote bag as she rounded the corner to the kitchen, muttering, "He loves the sound of his voice way too much!"

"Something wrong?" Kathleen, Sarah's seventy-year-old housemate, and a mosaic artist, gave her an understanding look and lifted her steaming cup. "Want to join me for some chamomile tea? It's good for calming the nerves."

"No, thanks. While I could use something calming, I have to get to the gallery and prepare for today's event. We have a special speaker this morning, you know." Sarah winked.

"Ah, yes." Kathleen grimaced. "I am a bit nervous about that."

"You will do exceptionally well! I can't wait to hear your discussion on mosaics." Sarah hugged her, and then hurried to the fridge, pulled out the salad she prepared last night, and stuffed it in her tote bag.

"Is the demo the only thing bothering you, dear?" Kathleen gazed at her with concern.

"I was listening to Blue Paxton and got riled, as usual." They had discussed the man's rude dialogue about art before, so this wasn't a new topic.

"He has a way of getting under your skin, doesn't he?"

"He certainly does. I should stop listening to him altogether." She'd said that before, too.

"Perhaps." Kathleen's eyes twinkled. "But that's the reason people listen to him, right?"

"Because he's infuriating?"

"Exactly." Kathleen laughed melodically. "Whether or not you agree with him, he gets people thinking and talking about art. That's valuable. Granted, he provokes them, too. But if someone convinces folks to ponder the meaning behind an artist's work, that is a rare gift."

As in, Blue Paxton was a rare gift? More like he was a pain in the—

"God made us different," Kathleen continued, interrupting Sarah's ungracious train of thought. "Blue looks at art uniquely. He's abrupt and outspoken, but his show overflows with interesting content. And the art he gives away is spectacular!" Kathleen had a sage way of giving wisdom and grace in bite-sized portions.

"You are wiser and more understanding than me." Sarah picked up a banana nut muffin from a plate and fingered it. "I've been grinding my teeth over his critique. But you're right. People listen to his outlandish opinions for a reason." She popped a few more items into her bag. "I'm looking forward to your demo today."

"Even if I'm uneasy about it?"

"Even then. But why are you anxious?"

"My art is private and meaningful to me." Kathleen smoothed her hand over her chest. "How can I do it justice while conveying my deepest feelings to others?"

"You will be superb." Sarah gave her another quick hug. "Just share your heart like you've done with me a hundred times. Now I'd better get going, or I will be late. Has Bess come down?"

"I haven't seen her yet."

Lola, a younger housemate, entered the kitchen carrying her son, Micah. The toddler spread out his arms. "Sarah! Sarah!"

Not hesitating, she scooped him up and twirled in a circle. She loved this little guy's morning snuggles and curious questions.

"What's that? What's that?" Micah pointed toward the dining room window, and she obliged him by pointing out a half-dozen items. Like other mornings, she talked about the eagles, the squirrels scurrying around the tall tree, and the ocean where the fish and whales lived. Every moment spent with this sweet boy felt like seeds of hope were being scattered over her dreams for a family of her own, even though she was approaching her fortieth birthday and wasn't in a relationship.

"Let's go!" Bess Grant, the town's mayor, and Sarah's half-brother's mom, rushed into the room, waving her phone. "Sorry for the delay. I had to take a call. But we have to run now!"

"I'm ready!" Sarah kissed Micah's forehead and returned him to his mother.

She'd have to fly through her tasks at the gallery to open on time, but she didn't regret a second she'd spent holding Micah.

Chapter Three

Walking briskly from the City Hall parking lot toward the gallery on the other side of the road, Sarah adjusted her earbuds. Bess had been listening to an audiobook during the drive into town, so Sarah listened to an old episode of Blue Paxton's. Why did he have to exaggerate Peggy Donnelly's artistic flaws? Was he even being fair to the artist? If Sarah stood in front of him, she'd be tempted to tell him what she thought of his critiquing style or else slap some sense into him!

"If you were thinking of purchasing one of Donnelly's paintings, save your money!" Blue spoke like a car salesman in a TV ad. "You'd be better off buying some acrylic paint, dumping blotches on a canvas, swirling it around with your eyes closed, and then hanging your masterpiece in your living room!"

Unbelievable.

Sarah yanked the earbuds out of her ears and noticed a black-haired man with dark-rimmed glasses huddled in the gallery's entryway, shouting into his cell phone. "No! That isn't happening! I doubt there'll be anything worth—" His gaze clashed with hers. The most bottomless sapphire eyes she'd ever seen peered back at her. She felt momentarily stunned, her heart pounding. "Talk to you later." He stuffed his phone into his jacket pocket.

"May I help you?" she asked around a gulp. Was the tall man with a laptop-carrying-case strap slung over his shoulder here to work? She had too much to do to let anyone in early.

"Do you work here?" His voice sounded vaguely familiar. "Someone should have opened the joint by now." *The joint?*

"I'm the manager. But it's not time—"

"When are you going to open? Shouldn't you be preparing for the demonstration?" He tapped his wristwatch. "I've been waiting fifteen minutes. Time that would have been better spent doing anything other than standing outside this rundown gallery, waiting in the wind."

Rundown? Sarah bristled. Having been remodeled after two hurricanes, the building looked practically perfect. She took a deep breath, forcing herself to speak calmly and politely despite the tension creeping through her nerves. "I'm sorry for your wait, but we don't open until ten."

"It's almost that now!"

"But not quite!" And every moment spent with him was time she wasn't preparing to open.

"I'm sure others besides me would appreciate hot coffee before ten." The man thrust his hand over his pitch-black hair, eyeing her. "Are you regularly late? Is bad customer service what Paige's Gallery is known for?"

"Now, hold on!"

"Needlessly forcing people to wait outside?" he continued as if she hadn't spoken. "I find such behavior annoying and irresponsible." *He* found *her* annoying?

"But you're the one who's—" She stopped herself from saying something rude and condescending back. "Look. I'm sorry for the inconvenience. However, as I said, we don't open until ten." Ignoring his groan, she pulled a key out of her pocket and stepped forward. He didn't take the hint. Was he going to continue blocking her entrance?

The art demo attendees would be arriving soon, and Kathleen would need to set up her supplies. Sarah had to get inside and start the coffee, among other things. "I have work to do, so please step aside."

"I'm here for the art demonstration." He slid his bag's strap higher on his shoulder and peered at her through his glasses. "Will it begin at ten-thirty? Or is it starting late, too?"

"I'm not opening late! And yes, it will start at ten-thirty." She rushed forward with her key extended. Either he was going to move or get jabbed. He shifted slightly, allowing her to pass, but now they stood uncomfortably close, and their shoes stirred up sand that had gotten lodged in the entryway. He coughed like the dust was her fault, too.

"May I come inside?" He was close enough for his minty breath to tickle her nose.

"Come back in ten minutes."

"I promise to stay out of your way." His voice changed from grumpy to congenial.

"Sorry." The keys shook as she tried inserting one into the slot.

"What's the harm in—"

"I said no!" She bit her lip and felt it tremble. Less than a year ago, she'd been involved in a risky situation here at the gallery and wouldn't take any chances. This guy might plan to steal some art or try to harm her. "Please, come back later." *Or don't.* Unless he was going to buy something pricey, it would be okay with her if he never returned!

Suddenly, an SUV roared past them, its engine revving loudly. Gasping, the stranger wrapped his arms around her, his cold nose pressed into her ear. She shoved against his chest. "Let go of me!" He shushed her! "Don't shush me! Let go of me, now!" She kicked him in the shin, although not hard since it was a confined space.

He groaned and released her. "Why did you do that?"

"Why did you grab me?" She yanked her cell phone from her pocket to call 911.

"Sorry. It's just—"

"Just what?" Her finger hovered over the nine on the screen.

"Did you get a look at the SUV?" His voice hiccupped on the last word. She made the mistake of peering into his blue eyes, which were darker now, filled with fear or vulnerability. "Did you catch the number on the license plate?" He shuddered like something awful had happened.

"No. Why?" She lowered her phone. "What's going on? Are you in trouble?"

"The driver of that vehicle tried to force me off the road yesterday."

"Force?" She didn't care about him not getting into the gallery, but she cared about anyone being a victim of road rage. "Why would someone try to cause an accident?"

"Good question."

Uneasily, Sarah glanced down the road beyond Bert's Fish Shack and the old cannery, but the vehicle was out of sight.

"May I go inside? I need to get off the street."

She almost yielded to his pleading tone and softer expression. "Wait until the other attendees arrive."

"Why can't I come in?" He straightened taller and pointed at the sign on the wall. "It says you serve coffee."

"At ten a.m.! I know nothing about you. You might be an art thief or a kidnapper." Even saying "kidnapper" made her heart rate accelerate.

"I am not an art thief." He sounded offended. "I'm not going to harm you, either."

"Yet you grabbed me."

"Only to protect you." He lifted his shadowy chin.

"To protect yourself, you mean."

"Okay. That too. Are you going to let me in or not?" His shoulder sagged against the side of the building.

"Not." She slipped inside the gallery but left the door open a crack with her shoe against it. Recalling how afraid he'd looked and the heart-stirring she felt gazing into his moist blue eyes, she paused. "Give me one reason why I should let you enter without calling the police."

"Because I'm a trustworthy guy."

"That's hard to believe."

"Then let me in because I'm Blue Paxton."

"You are not!" What a joke! Yet her heart pounded.

"Oh, but I am." He gave her a dizzying smile.

"You are the arrogant podcaster every gallery worker on the West Coast despises and fears?" Heat fanned up her face. Maybe she shouldn't have said that.

The man stared at her with an insulted yet amused look. "It's me in the flesh."

It can't be Blue Paxton. She listened to an audio app, so she had no idea what he looked like. But how could the guy who cowered in her doorway be the mean-spirited podcaster who criticized Mack Cantor's oil paintings so severely the artist was said to be hiding in a hut in Alaska? *That* Blue Paxton would not shake in his boots because a vehicle made a loud sound. "Why would Blue Paxton visit a small gallery like this?"

"Go figure. Now, may I come in?"

If this was Blue Paxton and she refused to let him in, it would be a personal insult, and he'd probably speak rudely about her on tomorrow's podcast. Sighing, she opened the door, and he passed by her, leaving his wafting scent of musky deodorant and mint in the air. He smelled too good to be Blue Paxton. His eyes were too gorgeous to be Blue Paxton's. She closed and locked the door and flipped on the lights. "Welcome to the best little art gallery on the West Coast."

"That's a stretch of the imagination." Giving the gallery a scant glance, he strode to one of the tall tables in the café seating area and set his bag on the wooden surface. "I take my coffee black and extra hot."

The man's in-person behavior was as impolite as his podcast personality sounded. Nevertheless, she responded professionally. "I'll bring you some coffee shortly."

"No problem. I don't expect prompt service here, anyway."

Sarah gritted her teeth. *Then go somewhere else! How about leaving and never returning?*

Sorry, Lord. I know I'm supposed to be loving and kind to everyone. But why did Blue Paxton have to show up here today?

She nearly ran into the kitchenette, lamenting her situation. Why had she accused him of being an art thief? How could she MC today's event with Blue Paxton observing and judging everything she said and did? Poor Kathleen. She was already nervous about speaking, now she would have to give her mosaic presentation in front of the formidable Bold Brash Blue!

After taking a few deep breaths, Sarah focused on starting the coffee and heating the cinnamon rolls a bakery service from Florence had delivered yesterday. At least she could make a decent cup of coffee.

Blue's fingertips were already clicking rapidly against his laptop keyboard when she rounded the corner. What was he writing so vehemently? Was he condemning the gallery manager who didn't have the decency to open early for him? The same one who accused him of being a thief? She set his steaming cup on the table. "Black and hot the way you like it." *Ugh.* Did that sound as flirtatious to him as it did to her? Their gazes met. He quirked an eyebrow over one of those sapphire eyes.

"Say"—he squinted at her name tag—"Sarah, let's not mention the SUV incident to anyone, all right?" He took a sip from his mug and nodded as if surprised it didn't taste horrible. "I'd rather not sound like a paranoid lunatic." *Seriously?*

"Agreed. And let's not mention my reaction to your wanting to get inside the gallery early, either."

"Deal."

"Thank you." Although she was curious about the SUV and why Blue Paxton had hugged her, she felt relieved he wouldn't be mentioning the other stuff on his podcast.

"Sorry about hugging you," he said quietly. "It's all I could think of to disguise myself."

"At least you didn't try kissing me like they do in the movies." She groaned. "I didn't mean—"

"No, I didn't do that." His lips spread slightly, making his blue eyes shine brighter and Sarah's heart beat faster. It had been so long since she'd experienced anyone being vaguely flirtatious with her that she hardly knew how to react.

"Not that I wanted you to kiss me!" He'd better not say anything about her wanting him to kiss her in his podcast!

"I'll have to try that next time." He winked.

Oh, for Pete's sake! Face flaming, she scrambled back into the kitchenette. She agitatedly checked on the cinnamon rolls and refilled a bowl with sugar packets. The whole time, her mind spun with thoughts of how she felt staring into Blue's sapphire irises and what it would be like if he smiled widely at her with those velvety-soft kissable-looking lips.

Kissable? He might have the most luscious, curvy pink lips, the darkest eyebrows that made him seem mysterious, and the bluest irises in the world, but she'd never kiss a man like Blue Paxton!

Never!

Chapter Four

Sarah adjusted Kathleen's *Stormy Ocean* mosaic over a black velvet cloth to maximize the effect of the soft rays of light coming in through the window overlooking the bay. She'd already set out eight chairs facing the demonstration table, but how could she predict today's attendance? She'd advertised in the local paper and a news outlet, hoping some residents would attend. Something lured Blue Paxton here, but what? Since he often spoke disparagingly about small towns on his podcast, Basalt Bay's homey ambiance wasn't what appealed to him.

While she worked, Blue circled the gallery's perimeter twice, peering at paintings, sculptures, mosaics, and labels, tsk-tsking or groaning over each one. At Paige's beautifully framed sunset photograph, he huffed, "You've got to be kidding me," and strode quickly away. His reaction didn't bode well for his opinion of this gallery or Paige's art.

"It's ten o'clock," he said as if she needed a reminder. "Isn't it time to open? Or are you still running late?"

"I wasn't late!" How many times did she have to tell him that? Why did he keep needling her? Was he hoping for an argument he could discuss on his podcast? She took a deep breath and let it out slowly. There was no reason to fight with the art critic, but she couldn't forget her earlier thoughts about wanting to slap some sense into him, either. That would give him something to talk about on his show! She met his piercing blue eyes and opted for a less combative tone. "May I get you some more coffee before I open the door?"

"I'm here to work. Not schmooze."

"No schmoozing allowed. Sometimes people drink coffee while they work. Do you need anything else?" Ice water tossed over his head? Another kick in the shin? Anything to cool down the intense glares he'd been dishing her?

"Is this tiny space all you have? Is there an attic showroom? A hidden space? Why stay open if this paltry art display is all you can offer?" Blue shoved his black-rimmed glasses up his nose, his gaze flitting about the room dismissively. "Why did I waste my time coming here?"

"To avoid the black SUV?"

"Touché! No thanks about the coffee." He unfolded a copy of the Basalt Bay *Gazette* and held it up. "The headline says, 'Art Extravaganza.' I've seen better displays at county fairs."

A rush of irritation mixed with loyalty to her artists ignited in Sarah's gut. "I am proud of our gallery and the valiant efforts of our coastal artists. If you can't perceive the beauty, heart, and determination displayed on these walls, then you are blind!" Ignoring the heat crawling up her neck, she stiffened her resolve to speak her mind. "Our gallery has charm and a hometown character which far outweighs the building's modest but appealing space."

"I hadn't noticed," he said drolly.

"Stick around. Maybe you'll grasp its worth despite your unfounded ideas about small towns."

"Unfounded?"

She exhaled a hot breath. "I meant, I hope you'll be open-minded about today's presentation."

"That's why I'm here."

Blue Paxton wasn't known for being open-minded. He was unrelentingly opinionated about art, artists, and galleries. He hadn't been dubbed Bold Brash Blue for nothing!

Sarah unlocked the door and turned the Closed sign to Open. Callie Weston, a good friend and mentor in her sixties, entered first, grinning. "I'm so excited for Kathleen's presentation."

"Me too. I'm glad you could make it." Sarah greeted Kathleen and two others. "Hello! Welcome! Have a seat, browse the gallery, or order a drink while you wait."

"I'll have my regular hot tea." Callie waved back at her. "And when you have a minute, I want to show you a photo Ruby sent this morning."

"Okay. I'll be over in a minute." Sarah noticed Kathleen was carrying two heavy-looking canvas bags. "May I help with those?"

"Thank you, dear." Kathleen handed her one and leaned her cheek against Sarah's arm. "Any advice for me?"

"Take a deep breath and enjoy sharing your passion for creating mosaics." She led Kathleen to the table where she'd set up several of her mosaics without mentioning Blue Paxton being here. "I can't wait to hear everything you're going to say."

Sarah's gaze snagged with Blue's across the room, and his eyebrows lifted above his glasses. Was he sending her a message? What? That he would criticize Kathleen like he'd done with hundreds of other artists before her? Sarah felt a rush of irritation rise in her again. His rolled-up, baby-blue sleeves with flowery cuffs made him appear relaxed and approachable, contradicting his gruff demeanor. Why did he have to grimace at patrons like a judge presiding over a courtroom of scoundrels? Why did he act like he hated art galleries when he earned a living by talking about them?

The man was a puzzle. An enigma. At least she got her chance to tell him how she felt about her gallery, or rather, Paige's. But she felt some ownership in her role as the temporary manager here, too. And she loved Kathleen and felt fierce loyalty toward her. Blue's and her gazes parried again, this time like fencers clashing swords. If he said anything disparaging about Kathleen—*aaargh*—Sarah would tell him exactly what she thought of him and his lousy podcast!

"Is he an unhappy camper?" Kathleen nodded toward Blue, who was speaking vehemently on his cell phone again.

"He's Blue Paxton, the art critic," Sarah admitted.

"At our gallery?" Kathleen put her fingers to her lips contemplatively.

"This is a waste of time," he said into the device. "I shouldn't have come to this town. I doubt I'll stay for long." That was the best news Sarah had heard in a month! "There's so little art here. What will I talk about tomorrow?"

"Ouch." Kathleen swept her long white hair off her shoulder. "It's like having a teacher watching over us."

"Yeah. A mean one."

"Although"—Kathleen grinned—"he's not bad to look at. Hunky physique. Dark good looks."

"Kathleen!"

"I have eyes, don't I? The man's as gorgeous as Elvis!"

Had Blue heard that? Hopefully, he wouldn't think Kathleen was flattering him to get a complimentary review!

Chapter Five

After making sure the other guests were settled, Sarah stopped by Kathleen's table again. "How are you doing? Is there anything I can get for you before the demonstration starts?"

"Some water? And so you know, the Lord and I had a little talk. I feel much better now."

"That's great! I'm glad to hear it."

"In fact"—Kathleen's eyes sparkled—"I wonder if there might be something more happening here than meets the eye."

"Such as?"

"Nothing to worry about, dear. Just relax and be your lovely self." She made a praying hands gesture and smiled.

Relax? How was Sarah supposed to do that?

She rushed into the kitchenette to get bottled water and fix Callie's hot tea. When she returned, Kathleen stood next to Blue, one hand on his arm as if they were already friends. A soft smile spread across the man's attractive lips, and Sarah came to a dead stop, mesmerized. With him wearing such a pleasant, welcoming expression, he was gorgeous and a danger to her heart!

But he's Blue Paxton! Her thoughts jolted back to reality. She could not be attracted to him!

"Oh, thank you." Kathleen reached out and clasped the bottle of water from Sarah. "Are you all right, dear?"

"I'm okay." She cleared her throat, hoping her brain freeze would clear as quickly. Blue muttered something, and she asked, "What was that?"

"Another cup of black coffee would be great."

"Oh. Uh, sure. I'll deliver this first." She lifted the hot cup of tea and hurried toward Callie. Why was she acting all gaga in front of Blue? She had to stay focused on today's event—not on a handsome guest who might destroy her gallery with an unfortunate choice of words and her heart with his exquisite blue eyes aimed at her.

"Sarah, look!" Callie extended her phone screen from her front-row seat, showing a picture of her newest great-niece. "Lonna Aurora Cedars. One month old today! Isn't she the most adorable baby you've ever seen?"

Since Sarah loved babies, it was a timely distraction. "Aww. What a sweetheart." She leaned her head against the side of Callie's, sharing the sentimental moment of gazing at Ruby and Peter's baby. Ruby had been a remarkable influence in her life when she first came to Basalt Bay, and Sarah couldn't be happier for her. "What a proud great auntie you are!"

"I am." Callie sniffled and accepted the cup of tea. "Here I am, getting all emotional. I never used to cry."

"You have all the tender emotions of a loving great auntie. I'm happy for you. I wish they lived closer so we could all enjoy holding baby Lonna and watch her grow up."

"You and me, both. The thought of my nephew, a rugged Alaskan fisherman, doting on this little one gives me such joy." Callie sipped her tea. "Mmm. This hits the spot, even if I'd rather have a delicious cinnamon roll to go with it."

"Are you saying you want one now?" Callie followed a strict healthy diet, but whatever she decided to eat, Sarah would support her.

"I always want one. But I won't order a treat today. Maybe another day?"

"Whatever you decide." Sarah smiled, glad she and Callie understood each other. "I'd better get this show on the road." Otherwise, Blue Paxton would judge her as tardy and ill-prepared for the event. "After I grab a coffee for our art critic that is."

"Art critic?" Callie squinted at Blue. "Don't worry. You'll have him eating out of your hand in no time."

"I doubt that. But thanks for the vote of confidence."

"You've got this." Callie eyed her thoughtfully. "Paige trusts you with her gallery. You're doing a splendid job! Now lift your chin and show that critic the Sarah we know and love."

Warmth flooded her. "Thank you, Callie." The woman had been like a close family member to her for the last year. What would she have done without Callie, Kathleen, Ruby, and all the others who'd befriended her? "Duty calls!" She turned toward the kitchenette.

"Have you seen Teal lately?"

She glanced back, wondering about Paige's sister-in-law who was staying at the project house temporarily. "Not really. She came in late last night."

"Perhaps I should have a talk with her."

"Maybe." Since Callie kept track of the ladies at the project house, she probably would check in with the single mom of twins who had been trying to salvage her marriage. However, Sarah didn't have time to worry about that now. She had coffee to pour and bring to Blue.

A couple of minutes later, when she passed the cup of coffee to him, their fingers touched, and heat shot up her nerve endings that had nothing to do with the hot coffee. When he laughed at something Kathleen said, Sarah's heart did somersaults. A fuzzy sensation fogged her brain again. How did Kathleen manage to coax Blue into smiling and laughing in such a relaxed way? What would it be like to have him smile like that at her? *Ugh*. She was not going to fantasize about herself and Blue Paxton! How romance starved was she?

"Come over to the presentation area if you'd like." Kathleen waved toward the table filled with samples and mosaic tools.

"I'd love to," Blue said. "Thank you for the invitation."

Wait. He'd love to come closer to the artist's table? Why was he being so friendly to Kathleen when he was a self-professed aloof critic who distanced himself from artists and gallery workers? Didn't some attendants balk about that in the comments section of his website? Then again, what if some of the reports she'd heard in the artists' community were false?

What if Blue Paxton had a heart, after all?

Chapter Six

After twenty minutes of listening to Kathleen Baker share her passion for mosaic art, Blue had a good feel for the woman's talent and heart for her work. She spoke with an encouraging vibe, and her enthusiasm for her projects had drawn him in emotionally, which was rare. Daily, he listened to artists discussing their craft and explaining why they chose the medium or surface they did, yet seldom did anyone inspire him to consider a different viewpoint or appreciate the artist's journey the way this older woman did today.

Gram would undoubtedly approve of his positive response to the senior's philosophy. Kathleen's grandmotherly persona might have appealed to him the most—or else it was the twinkle in her eye when she talked about how she always reached for blue when she struggled to find the perfect color. In many ways, the white-haired woman reminded him of Gram. The two of them would surely hit it off, although Gram was more into gardening than art.

As Kathleen explained shading and movement, she held up a mosaic of ocean waves created from blues and greens and smiled warmly at her captivated audience. Everyone was facing the artist with intrigued, engaged expressions that looked exactly how Blue felt. How was he going to present Kathleen Baker as a fallible artist when he was smitten with her charm?

His podcast subscribers and Alfie expected him to critically analyze the art he found in each location. But how could he criticize the personal achievements of a septuagenarian making a living from her art when he admired her? She was an inspiration! The experiences she shared might even encourage older listeners to be more diligent and creative about their artistic endeavors. Yet could he forego his usual sharp-tongued wit and speak wholeheartedly in favor of Kathleen's work?

Alfie wouldn't like it! According to his business partner, Blue had to be factual, abrasive, and stay entertainingly in character while podcasting, or else he'd lose subscribers, and such a loss meant a substantial deficit in revenue. But did it really? Wasn't there room for the occasional motivational piece and high-fiving a deserving artist?

Blue and Alfie created his Bold Brash Blue image to grab attention and get people commenting about their podcast on social media—and it worked! After five years, their ratings were still climbing. But even with that, Alfie often badgered him about being more edgy, digging deeper, and doing things his way and only his way, and that chafed. Blue wanted some leeway when it came to subject matter and how he presented his artistic findings. Alfie disagreed.

Maybe this time, Blue would stick up for an artist, even if it meant going against his business partner's preferences. Kathleen impressed him with her humble yet courageous attitude about mosaics and her commitment to doing what she loved, no matter what. She demonstrated passion and kindness—he noted that in the first thirty seconds of talking with her. Her demo was well worth his time. In fact, he could listen to her for another hour!

He glanced at the pretty gallery manager standing near the café, and their gazes collided—that had been happening a lot today. Was she silently asking him not to speak negatively about Kathleen or the gallery? He hated it when other attendants had done that in the past.

What if that was a spark of romantic interest in her dark eyes? He looked at her again, and an electrical current shot through him. His heart pounded. *Man.* He had to be careful. He couldn't allow himself to be attracted to anyone affiliated with a gallery. Whatever he said in his podcast would upset her and they'd argue, which would be the end of any budding relationship. No. It was far better to keep his distance from artists and gallery attendants.

He homed back in on Kathleen, who was comparing shadows of broken glass to reflections of life and difficulties everyone had experienced. "Art replicates the beauty and grace of life." When she spoke of her mosaics reflecting herself and herself as a reflection of her art, Blue was fascinated. Perhaps he'd elaborate on that in tomorrow's episode.

He stood, planning to move to his laptop, but his foot clipped the chair in front of him, and he tripped, barely righting himself. "Sorry. Sorry," he muttered. The manager should have set the chairs farther apart for someone with longer legs like him to navigate. He might mention that in his show notes, along with her accusing him of being a thief. But then, recalling his promise to her, he knew he wouldn't go that far.

He intercepted the dark-haired woman's cool gaze, looking him over and, what, analyzing him? Was she irritated by his stumbling or how he was heading to his computer before Kathleen finished talking? When inspiration hit, he wrote. He felt her scrutinizing him all the way across the room, which was weird since he was the one who usually scrutinized others.

As soon as he dropped onto the chair at the tall table, he typed some quotes. No artist had yet to receive a perfect review from him.

But what negative thing could he say about Kathleen Baker? Her discussion didn't lack sincerity or authenticity. She explained her process in an engaging way. Was her work flawed? What about her color scheme? *Hmm.* He'd never had to think so hard to produce fault or the "nitty-gritty dirt," as Alfie often said, on any artist. Why was it difficult this time?

He thought of Gram and how she faithfully listened to his podcasts, and a smile curved his lips. If only one person existed on the planet who he wanted to please, it was her. She'd never said a disparaging word about his life, career choices, or his show. And at the end of every phone conversation, she always reminded him of her love and how she was praying for him. Thinking of her devotion got him a little choked up, and he swallowed hard to alleviate the emotion. It had to be due to that similarity he'd imagined between her and Kathleen.

His gaze meshed with the dark-haired manager's, and he wanted to assure her that everything would be okay and not to worry. He glanced at her navy skirt, ending at her knees, and then down the beautiful lines of her bare legs to her brown slip-on shoes. She appeared to be in her upper thirties with a nice figure and a sweet smile. He liked a woman who was close to his age. Too bad they got off to a bad start—or just as well, since she worked in this gallery.

He should take notes and stop ogling the woman in charge—what was her name? He let his fingers fly over the keys, purposefully forgetting everything and everyone in the room.

"Mosaic art isn't your thing, huh?"

He glanced up at the woman whose gaze he'd sought and avoided over the last hour. "I liked the artist's take on art soothing the soul."

"Treat her with respect, okay?" Up close, gold flecks shimmered in her brown eyes. "Be kind to her, that's all I ask."

Did she doubt his ability to be fair in his critique? Did she think he was a monster for telling the world the truth about the art he saw every day? If someone's art moved him, he'd tell the world that truth, too, no matter what Alfie said. But why was he silently defending himself? Why did this woman's thoughts about him ruffle his feathers? "Since I liked her presentation and she reminds me of my grandmother, I will be kind, but not because you told me to."

She blushed and nodded. "I'm relieved. If you broke her heart, I'd have to hunt you down."

He almost laughed at her teasing threat. But her defending the artist spoke volumes about her loyalty to the woman. She wasn't warning him to go easy on the gallery or her. She didn't want the mosaic artist to be adversely affected, which he applauded. And it made him more intrigued with this gallery manager.

Chapter Seven

Wearing a comfortable robe and pink slippers, Sarah poured a container filled with broken glass onto the work table in the corner of Kathleen's bedroom. Finally, it was time to relax and enjoy some art for herself. This was where Kathleen usually worked on her mosaic projects, and she generously let Sarah use the space and her supplies in the evenings.

Today had felt longer than usual with Blue Paxton hovering around and grumbling about the gallery's size and quantity of art, or lack thereof. All afternoon, Sarah had looked forward to unwinding and thinking of nothing other than whether to place a blue-green, periwinkle, or Mediterranean blue glass piece on the sixteen-by-twenty-inch wooden rectangle she'd been working on for a few weeks. Doing mosaic art was a slow process, but that was part of the enjoyment for her. While some vegged in front of the TV or read a novel for relaxation in the evenings, she enjoyed arranging broken pieces of glass according to her whim and mood.

A brief image of Blue smiling at Kathleen flashed through her thoughts. She liked picturing him happy and carefree instead of thinking of him as a grumpy podcaster who might ruin them all. In the morning, she'd have to grit her teeth and listen to whatever he had to say about her beloved gallery, Kathleen, and herself. What horrible things might he expose? Her shoulder muscles tensed. Her jaws felt tight and achy. She groaned. She wasn't going to get all worked up about tomorrow's episode or its speaker tonight! She was supposed to be relaxing.

She took several deep breaths and exhaled slowly after each one. Then she worked on her ocean scene for ten minutes without thinking a single thought of Blue. But as she placed a bluish-green piece of glass on the board, her brain started working overtime again.

Why did Blue have to be so handsome and fascinating? Why did he gaze at her with so much perplexity, curiosity, or, at one point, she was confident, attraction in his deep blue irises? While her heart had skipped and fluttered every time their gazes met, it took only one thought of what he did for a living and what she did for a living, and she knew she could never fall for him.

However, it had been ages since anyone had flirted with her or made her heart flutter—not since before Jeremy died two years ago—so she felt inept at figuring out what was attraction and what wasn't. Surely, she was blowing Blue's faint flirtations—if they even were flirtations—out of proportion due to her romantic barrenness. But what if she wasn't? What if he, too, had felt some sparks between them?

Was it possible?

Even if the tingles she'd felt were only physical attraction, did that mean she was ready to fall in love again? Was she emotionally healed enough to move past her widowhood and grief—enough to flirt with another man? She took a deep breath and held it, waiting for a negative feeling or a twinge of heartache to come over her. It didn't. Maybe she was ready to move forward and love again. Not with someone like Blue, but with someone.

She rearranged pieces of broken porcelain on her board, uncertain which hue to choose for a darker portion of water. What had Kathleen said? Choose a hint of blue? *Blue. Blue. Blue.* She pictured his soft smiling lips, the little crease in his chin, and the way his sapphire eyes sparkled with unexpected warmth and groaned again.

"That doesn't sound good." Kathleen entered the room with two cups of steaming tea and set one beside Sarah's workspace. "I thought you'd like something hot and calming like chamomile." Her eyes twinkled like she knew what Sarah was thinking.

"Thank you. I could use something calming." Sarah sipped her tea and fingered a couple of turquoise fragments of glass.

"Mind if I join you?" Kathleen waved her hand toward an empty chair.

"Please do. I'd like the company." Anything to get her thoughts off Blue Paxton would be greatly appreciated. "I'm struggling over which colors to use for the water."

"Let it come naturally." Kathleen sat down slowly. "You have a lovely assortment of hues. Start with one you especially like. Then let your emotions and thoughts flow through your fingertips, so to speak, and pick up the pieces that catch your eye."

"What if I pick the wrong colors?"

"There are no wrong ones, my dear. Let the art express your sincerest feelings." But what if her most authentic feelings were about Blue tonight? She bit her lip and felt it tremble. Kathleen reached across the table and patted her hand. "What's troubling you? Do you want to talk about it?"

"Not really."

"If you change your mind, I'm here." Kathleen picked up some glass pieces and arranged them on the table. Shortly, she'd created a dark wave with moonlight shimmering across it.

"That looks amazing! How did you work those colors together so easily?"

"Lots of practice. And I went with what I feel in here." She tapped her fingers over her chest. "Darkness brings out the beauty of light. Just like some of our most troubling times and deepest questions bring joy to the surface of our hearts." Kathleen smiled, and her face glowed with wisdom or experience. "Try it. Pick complementary shades. When in doubt, you can always choose blue." She winked.

Ah, yes. *Blue.* Planning to pick a teal color, Sarah snatched up two yellowish-green ones, a few navy pieces, and two skinny black fragments instead. When she set them closely on the board, they fit together like a puzzle. "The opposite hues work so well."

"It's lovely, my dear. A perfect combination of light and dark."

Hot and cold. Easy and difficult. Her and Blue.

"What if I'd chosen something else?" Squelching thoughts of Blue, Sarah glanced back and forth between the colors she'd chosen and Kathleen's. "I like yours too. What if I'd gone with different colors?"

"That would have been fine." Kathleen smiled. "Every color or shape changes the picture, like in life. Imagine the daily decisions we make. Each turn in the road alters the picture of our story, and that's okay!"

Boy, had her story changed. She'd been a wife for nine years. Had expected to have kids. Was wishing her marriage would improve. Then Jeremy died, and everything became instantly altered. Horrifically so. But at least she could think of his passing without choking up now. She saw herself as a woman who'd grown stronger over the last year. She felt so thankful to the Lord for everything He'd done to bring her to this place of having more peace and purpose in her life.

When she'd wandered into Basalt Bay, she would never have imagined being invited to live in the house where her grandmother had lived and experience the inner healing she had since then. She couldn't have envisioned the love she'd feel toward Kathleen, Callie, Ruby, Lola, and others. She couldn't have foreseen herself running an art gallery, even temporarily. Yet the Lord Jesus, in His love and grace, had brought all this together, piece by piece, like a beautiful mosaic. *Thank You!*

She felt more relaxed now. "I needed this. Thank you, Kathleen."

"Of course, my dear."

Sarah added more navy pieces, noticing how closely they matched Kathleen's eyes, which made her think of Blue's sapphire irises, so she searched for a similar hue.

"Art is soothing and peaceful, isn't it?" Kathleen took a few sips of her tea. "Yet it's also challenging and complex, taking all our attention and determination."

"Like a dichotomy?"

"Like you and Blue?" Oh, she had to bring him up! "Or is he the one you don't want to discuss?" Kathleen's eyes twinkled.

Sarah felt the heat of a thousand-watt bulb on her face. She and Blue were like oil and water, salt and sugar, mountains and desert. She glanced back and forth between the navy and soft blue tones she'd picked up. "He is unusual."

"And very handsome!" Kathleen's voice rose playfully.

"Kathleen!"

"Well, he is!" After a moment, she asked, "Are you afraid of falling for another man, Sarah?"

Was she? She'd gone through and come out of a black hole of grief and wandering. Jesus's love had brought her into a new season of life. Hadn't she been praying for a fresh start and a family of her own? "I'm not afraid of falling in love." Saying the words felt freeing and hopeful.

Chapter Eight

As soon as Sarah awoke the following day, she sat up and grabbed her phone, her heart pounding at the thought of listening to Blue's review. She took a deep breath and tapped the app icon, but she didn't start the episode immediately. Was she prepared to hear Blue's assessment of her gallery and Kathleen? Of her? She skimmed the episode title—"A Darling Ignites a Fire in Basalt Bay." *Darling?* Her nerves strained, she tuned into the podcast.

"I almost walked out the door seconds after stepping inside Paige's Art Gallery," Blue said in his usual commentator's voice. "The tiny gallery isn't much to brag about, but that's exactly what locals did! They boasted about their tiny gallery by the sea like it was the best thing since the invention of ice cream!"

What? Was he going to say only positive things?

"Here are a few comments I gathered from yesterday's mosaic demonstration." He used a different voice for each comment—"'I love Paige's Gallery;' 'I'm attending every demo this week;' 'Our town is small, but it boasts great heart where our artists are concerned,' Sue Taylor, fundraising chairperson for the winter festival, said."

Blue cleared his throat lightly. "I heard 'great heart' mentioned several times during my visit to this art gallery in the middle of Basalt Bay, Oregon."

Sarah gnawed on her lip, waiting for the ax to fall because it surely would. When had Blue Paxton ever critiqued a gallery or artist without bashing their technique, style, or color scheme? What if he told the world she had accused him of being a thief? She clutched her fingers around a fistful of her comforter and squeezed.

"I had mixed feelings during yesterday's event, so I have a diverse review, unlike my typical first-day critique. The darling I'm referring to in today's show title is"—Blue paused dramatically—"the quaint mosaic artist, Kathleen Baker."

Sarah exhaled a breath.

"This septuagenarian wears a winsome smile, has the gentlest, most polite mannerisms, and talks about art in a way that makes you want to sit back and listen for an hour or two." Blue's voice got deeper. "Her engaging, often humorous explanations of the mosaics she loves drew me in like I haven't been captivated in ages."

Oh, Blue. Thank you!

"Kathleen Baker pulls the observer into her worldview of experiencing life through art, summarizing a theory that art comes from everyday life." He chuckled. "She went so far as to say that life is reflected and even encapsulated within an artist's work. Deep thoughts, my friend."

Yes! Sarah thrust her fists upward. Blue was giving Kathleen a raving review! She was so happy she could kiss him! She wouldn't. *Silly thought.* But she was so ecstatic, she could.

"The senior artist was a wealth of knowledge and a ray of sunshine," Blue continued. "I felt as if a stream of motivation flowed from her into our minds and hearts. Did the other attendees experience the breathless inspiration I did?" He felt breathless over Kathleen's presentation?

Sarah whooped.

"I'm embarrassed to admit this, but Kathleen Baker almost had me on her hook." *Almost?* Sarah settled down her enthusiasm. "I was tempted to return to my motel room and start cutting up glass. Perhaps make a mosaic of a cute seal."

He sighed.

"How could a tiny gallery by the sea obtain such a talented artist and philosopher? Kathleen threw a wrench into my plans of unapologetically critiquing the Basalt Bay gallery in a harsher vein." Blue's voice went softer. "Instead, she challenged me to reevaluate my view of mosaic art because she values taking broken glass and creating something unique and meaningful." The background lacked any of its usual bells and whistles. "Who would have thought Blue Paxton had it in him to celebrate an artist?"

Who indeed? Sarah took a gulp of air and scooted to the edge of her bed.

"Although her name escapes me, the gallery manager warned me that I'd better be nice to the mature artist or else."

A flush of humiliation prickled Sarah's skin. Was she so unmemorable that he couldn't recall her name?

"As if someone in their seventies couldn't take a tough critique? Come on," Blue said in a mocking tone. "I perused a half-dozen mosaic creations by Baker with colors that were too bright for my taste." He spoke less confidently, as if grasping at straws for something negative to say. "Some of the mosaic scenes had ostentatious colors which could have faded to gray imperceptibly, creating more realistic oceanic hues and wave movement."

Oh, brother. Why did he have to dig up something negative about Kathleen's work that didn't matter?

"If you go by the art demo in Basalt Bay today, here's what you'll find in the minute gallery." What did he expect in a town of eleven hundred? "A minimum crowd of locals will attend. Don't blink, or you'll miss the whole thing!"

Groaning, Sarah pounded her fist against her pillow.

"Honestly, it's hardly worth the time or money it takes to get from where you are to here. Except"—his tone changed again, sounding like he was emotionally affected—"there's one distinctive thing you won't want to miss. It's what surprises me every time I experience the heart of a true artist. That rousing interpretation of art is worth whatever time and money it takes to experience it. It's the difference between seeing chocolate in a photo and tasting it for yourself. Yesterday, I found an unblemished, authentic gem in Kathleen Baker and her mosaics. If you missed it, I feel sorry for you."

Sarah closed her eyes and dropped backward onto the bed. "Thank You, Lord!"

Blue rambled on for a few more minutes and announced the winner of a pastel painting giveaway. Then he ended the episode with a rundown on the winter festival activities, including the watercolor artist Gracie Parker, who would be presenting today's demo at the local gallery.

Sighing, Sarah sat up and closed the web connection. Had Blue taken her threat about being kind to Kathleen seriously? Or did he experience the same sparks she felt around him, causing him to be more pleasant? Not a chance! Blue Paxton would never change his mannerisms for her.

Still. Whenever she thought of him, warm fuzzies sizzled through her middle, her heart pounded, and she anticipated seeing him again like she might die if she didn't. How could she feel so intensely about Blue already? *He is an art critic. He's not for you!* Too bad her heart and head weren't jiving with her self-lecture. How was she going to get through another day with him hovering around the gallery and gazing at her with his sapphire eyes?

Did he really forget her name? How could he remember all the stuff in the art world yet forget that vital piece of who she was?

Chapter Nine

Sarah was prepping a to-go cup of coffee and gathering lunch supplies when Kathleen strolled into the project house kitchen, humming a tune. She seemed in fine spirits. Had she listened to Blue's podcast?

"Good morning." She hugged Sarah. "Ready for another day at our 'tiny gallery by the sea?'" So she had heard Blue's critique!

"Yes, I am. What did you think of this morning's episode? I hope your feelings weren't hurt."

"Are you kidding? Blue made my day!" Kathleen filled the tea-kettle with water, set it on the stove, and hummed a few more notes.

"So, you weren't offended?"

"Not in the least. Some folks might be encouraged to stop by the festival and experience it for themselves because of what he said." She smiled. "Wouldn't that be grand?"

"Yes!"

"And the booths open tonight." Kathleen nodded, her eyes glowing.

"Thirty-five of them!" Sarah was keeping track since she was the Caring Society secretary. "The town is abuzz with activity."

"I can't wait to learn what everyone else has been working on." Kathleen pulled a cup from a shelf and dropped a tea bag into it.

"And the silent auction will be a fun finale."

"Here's hoping we raise a ton of money for all the women needing our help in the coming months." Kathleen squeezed Sarah's arm lightly. "With our mosaic contributions, we're pitching in too."

"Yes, we are." A feeling of satisfaction over their achievements rushed through her. It had taken a lot of work by a group of dedicated people to pull it off, but thanks to the newly formed ladies' group, the first winter festival and silent auction were happening. *Lord, please help us make a lot of money for a worthy cause.*

Lola entered the kitchen with Micah on her hip. "Look who's awake!"

"Sarah! Sarah!" Micah reached for her.

Even though she needed to hurry and get out the door, she couldn't ignore the toddler's outstretched arms. "Hey, buddy!" She scooped him up, and he giggled.

Kathleen patted his back. "Good morning, sweet boy!"

"Where's the bird?" Micah pointed toward the dining room window. "Where's the squirrel?"

"Let's go take a look!" Before pivoting to the window, Sarah glanced at Lola. The young mom looked worn out, and the day was just starting. Raising a two-year-old on her own had to be challenging. "How are things going?"

"So-so. I have an interview at Bert's." She didn't sound eager.

"Aren't you excited about it?"

"Not really. It isn't a position I'll love. But I have to get Micah and me on stable footing. We can't live here forever." Lola shrugged. "I will do my best and thank God for whatever job He sends my way."

"What's this about not living here forever?" Kathleen hugged Lola. "You and your darling boy are welcome to stay with us for as long as you want."

"I second that!" Sarah added.

"Thank you." Lola glanced back and forth between them. "You both have been so kind. I am grateful for your hospitality and support." Lola kissed Kathleen's cheek. "But I must find a job to provide for my boy. I am independent. And I need to make money to pay for my divorce." She whispered the last word.

Sarah knew her separation and divorce were difficult subjects for her. But by all appearances, Lola was doing better emotionally than a month ago. "Are you okay?"

"I will be. Now, it's time for breakfast. How about a waffle, Micah?"

"Waffle! Waffle," he said without the "w."

"You've got it!" Lola hurried to the freezer and opened the door.

"Bird! Bird!" Micah chanted.

Sarah had one more thing to say to Lola. "If you're serious about needing funds for a lawyer, the Caring Society should be able to help cover it."

"Thank you. But I'd like to do this myself."

"I understand. But I hope you'll consider reaching out to our group. That's what we're there for." Sarah brought Micah into the dining room, giving Lola a few minutes to get things ready. She pointed out the window at an eagle in flight, a fishing boat in the distance, and a cloud resembling a dog. Micah chattered animatedly about all three.

A longing for motherhood and the what-ifs that occasionally plagued her rushed through her now. What if she and Jeremy had gotten pregnant? What if she'd had a child during the two years of being alone? Would she have coped with her grief better? What if she met someone who wanted children? An image of Blue came to mind, but she rejected the mental picture. As mesmerized as she felt around him, she wasn't pondering him in the same context as pregnancy and parenthood. But was there still time for her to have a kid?

Lord, help me trust You and not fret. I know You are working in my life. I am declaring good over my life and that of my future family.

She kissed the side of Micah's head, enjoying the baby scent of his warm skin and shampoo. Between holding him and the times she got to rock her three-month-old nephew, Tanner, she'd thought her desire to be a mom might be satisfied. If anything, they intensified her longings, which were increasing as she approached her fortieth birthday.

"Are you all right?" Lola took Micah from Sarah's arms and settled him into his high chair. They'd shared plenty of late-night conversations about their previous relationships and sympathized with each other's losses.

"I'm okay. Just remembering some unfulfilled longings." She rubbed her arms to comfort herself and ward off the memories.

"About your husband?" Lola peered at her.

"Yeah. And what might have been."

"We make a fine duo. You pine for your husband while I am still angry with mine."

"I'm not pining for him so much now. But not having a child from our marriage? That still bothers me." Sarah heaved a sigh. "How are the talks going with your counselor?"

"Pastor Sagle lets me vent." Lola set Micah's plate on the high chair tray, and the boy put several bites of food into his mouth. "If he didn't, what would I do with my bitterness?"

"I'm sorry."

"Me too. But what can I do?"

"Pray?" Prayer had been Sarah's greatest comfort during the last year. Even today, prayer was her first line of defense.

"Mmm. Yes. Lots of prayer."

"We have to run!" Bess rushed through the room, her grayish hair flapping slightly as she waved her keys.

"I'm ready!" Sarah grabbed her to-go cup and tote bag. "It's going to be a long day."

"One you'll get to enjoy with your podcaster, no?" Lola's eyes sparkled. "Kathleen mentioned how handsome he is and how he couldn't stop watching the lovely gallery manager."

Sarah coughed. "I think Kathleen is the one who has a crush on him."

"What about you? Do you have a crush on this Blue?"

"Oh. Uh. Hey. I've got to—" Sarah dashed out the door without answering, but Lola's question lingered in her thoughts.

Did she have a crush on the art critic?

Chapter Ten

Blue ducked into the alcove where sand had accumulated overnight and groaned. The gallery was still closed? Why wasn't the manager here yet? After his upbeat podcast this morning, there would be more curiosity seekers showing up and the person in charge should be prepared!

The click of heels alerted him to someone's approach. Turning, he saw the dark-haired woman he met yesterday hurrying toward him. Her friendly smile mellowed some of his frustration.

"Sorry to keep you waiting. Although I'm not late."

"Right." But wouldn't she have been here prepping a half hour ago if she were on her game? Had she heard his podcast? Perhaps she didn't even know he gave Kathleen a positive review.

Tomorrow, he'd return to his normal critiquing style. His listeners and Alfie expected a strong follow-up show, which they were going to get. He'd rather avoid another call from Alfie like the one he received this morning, telling him how much he hated his "sugary" review.

Blue followed the perky manager into the dark gallery, then waited while she entered her code and switched on the lights. Once the place was brighter, he walked to the table where he sat yesterday and set up his laptop. From this perch, he could watch Gracie Parker's demo without interacting with her or anyone else. That should help him remain aloof and unbiased. Aware of the gallery waking up, he heard the quiet rumble of appliances, smelled the fresh scent of coffee, and noted the warm lights coming up in various nooks, highlighting paintings and sculptures that invited him to come closer.

He took a stroll around the gallery as he did yesterday, reading the labels of each piece. He ignored the sunset photograph and skimmed past a garish oil painting of a crimson sky over the ocean. However, a large acrylic painting of a lighthouse with gales of wind and sea beating against it caught his attention. The painting was realistic enough that he felt as if he were standing right there on the rocks with sea spray pounding against him, his feet bracing against the boulders as the biting gale assaulted him. *This one is good!*

He leaned forward, adjusted his glasses, and read the title. *The Storm?* How boring! He could think of more fitting names. *Escape to the Lighthouse. Bludgeoned by the Waves. A Terrifying Rescue.* Eh. Sometimes simple was better. Paige Harper was the artist. Was she—

"Paige is a local artist and one of the gallery owners," the manager said. He hadn't heard her approach.

"I wondered about that."

"I'm Sarah, by the way." She extended her hand as if they were meeting for the first time, a soft smile playing on her pretty face. *Sarah.* He clasped her warm hand. "I forgot to mention I'm the temporary manager while the boss is on parental leave." She gave him a business card with her name and phone number listed on it.

"Sarah Blackstone." How had he forgotten that? He rarely felt embarrassed, but he did now. And her introduction meant she had heard his podcast. He handed her one of his cards, too. "A temp, huh?"

"Yeah. But managing is growing on me." Her grin widening, she pivoted away, holding his business card. Would she notice his name and number on it like he noticed hers?

Sarah opened a closet door and pulled out a broom. Soon, he heard her outside sweeping the sandy entryway. He should be busy writing ideas for his upcoming podcasts or studying some of the styles of other contemporary artists. Then why was he so distracted with everything Sarah was doing?

Gracie Parker arrived with tote bags and a plastic tub filled with art supplies in her arms, her energy high by the sound of her giggling and chattering. Flashing a flirty grin in his direction, she rocked her penciled eyebrows. "If it isn't the illustrious and handsome Blue Paxton!" She pursed her cherry red lips like she was about to whistle at him. "You can critique my art any time you'd like." She winked as if she meant something far different than art and sashayed toward the demo table, swinging her hips. Yeah. He'd have to watch out for her.

He focused on a pamphlet he'd found on the table. Gracie Parker, a long-haired blond, had been doing watercolor paintings for hire since high school. Considering how young she looked and acted, it hadn't been all that long. He skimmed over the boring data that read like so many other pamphlets.

Would Gracie's spiel be as dull as dry cereal without milk? He'd listened to enough painting lectures to last a lifetime. That's why Kathleen's fresh, optimistic discussion about mosaics had interested him so much. If Basalt Bay boasted a lineup of artists with half her enthusiasm, he'd have difficulty finding anything to criticize. He'd become a starving art critic! He'd have to sell his Stang to survive! But sadly, if he found two artists as engaging as Kathleen in a row, he'd eat his hat—or swim in the ocean in a dolphin costume! He chuckled. No doubt, Alfie would like to use that for one of his publicity stunts.

Sarah set down a mug of black coffee and a giant cinnamon roll dripping in cream cheese frosting on his table. Before he could say thanks for the mouth-watering dessert, she walked away. Why did she keep doing that?

Three bites into the pastry, he was in sugar paradise. If all else failed, he'd give five stars to the cinnamon roll and whoever created the divine sugar buzz! He took a sip of hot coffee, glad for the morning dousing of caffeine and its lack of sweetness. He set the cup down as Sarah dropped into the seat opposite him with a mug clutched in her hands and a cute blush on her cheeks.

"I want to say thank you for being kind and thoughtful toward Kathleen this morning."

"Oh, that." He wiped his lips with a paper napkin, uncomfortable with her scrutiny.

"She's a warm, loving person. I hated the thought of you being mean to her."

"Mean?" His job was to challenge contemporary artists to improve their craft and deliver their most genuine selves in their work—not to be mean. Although he had to admit, with the way Alfie badgered him to be more critical, and how he'd gone along with it, he might come across as less than kind sometimes. "Kathleen Baker is a unique artist who inspired me. For the record, I'm gut-wrenchingly honest."

"Honest. Right." Her eyes lit up with those gold flecks that made him want to stare into them all day. "Maybe not so tactful?" she muttered, more to herself than him.

"Perhaps." He gulped at the rare feeling of vulnerability he was experiencing sitting across from Sarah Blackstone. He wouldn't forget her name again.

"Speaking the truth is a trait we have in common, although our understanding of honesty might differ." Her lips widening in an easy smile and her gaze shining directly at him gave him a heady feeling, taking the sting from her words. "She got to you, didn't she?"

"Kathleen?"

"Mmhmm." She sipped her coffee.

He appreciated that Sarah was being friendlier and seemed more comfortable around him. "Maybe she did. Although that won't happen today." He couldn't let himself see only the good in another artist.

"I'm sorry to hear that." Sarah glanced over to where Gracie was setting up the demo table, allowing Blue a chance to peruse her unnoticed.

Sarah's dark brown hair flipped inwardly, barely touching her chin. A few errant strands made him want to stroke them back behind her ears. He admired her chocolaty eyes that sparkled with happiness or joy yet seemed to hold mischief, too. He liked a woman with a spunky attitude.

Was she married? She didn't wear a ring. Was she dating anyone? He bit back a groan. Why was he asking himself these questions? *Remember your rule? No dating gallery workers!* Besides, once he critiqued Gracie Parker, Sarah probably wouldn't speak pleasantly to him again.

"Are you going to add more chairs?" He nodded toward the eight chairs facing the demonstration area, trying to focus on why he was here.

"Should I?" A slight frown crossed her soft-looking pink lips.

Realizing he was staring at her mouth, he forced his gaze on her eyes, dark pools of liquid emotion, and felt himself drowning in them. "I, uh, well, can't say for certain." He cleared his throat. "But since I have a following because of the podcast, more people may come today." He didn't want to sound boastful, and she wouldn't be impressed by his subscriber count, anyway. What would impress her? His saying something positive about this gallery? Or giving a thumbs-up to Gracie? He couldn't do that, but another idea came to mind. "I can help put out more chairs." He'd never offered to do that at any other gallery before. What was with him? Gram would say it was about time he started acting gentlemanly.

"Thanks. I'll manage." Sarah stood, strode toward the presentation area, and pushed a few chairs closer to the table.

He followed and shuffled a couple of chairs, too. "Worked here long?"

"Almost a year." She slid another chair forward. "I love working in a cozy gallery like this and being acquainted with the local artists and patrons." He nodded, enjoying listening to her. "Getting to wrap up the pieces as they go to their new homes, where they will be treasured and cherished for generations to come, is like helping with a special gift that keeps giving every day."

Sarah was special herself. Was she a gift that would keep giving? Whoever became her husband had better be worthy of such a treasure. He grinned at his play on her words. Of course, he couldn't tell her what he was thinking. He didn't even know why he felt affected by her. It must be due to those thoughts he'd been harboring about missing a relationship because of his traveling lifestyle. Yeah, that had to be it.

"Do you have any more chairs?" he asked, deflecting from his thoughts and longings.

"Over there." She pointed to a corner where three chairs leaned against the wall.

"You'll need more." At her surprised look, he tried not to sound like a know-it-all. "I'm serious. You might have a houseful."

"Then the others will have to sit at tables in the café or stand."

"What if there's more than that? Shouldn't you be prepared?" As soon as he saw her tense expression, he wished he hadn't been abrupt, but the damage was done. "I'm worried you might be swamped, that's all."

"If it happens, so be it."

"Don't say I didn't warn you."

"I won't." She squinted at him.

Why did he have to make things worse? Was he covering his feelings about her beneath an emotional barrier? He groaned. *Stick to your rule, Paxton. Keep your distance from gallery personnel and artists.* His insides roiled as he returned to his more companionable laptop. Maybe he should write a review about how the temp manager arrived almost late each morning and didn't take his advice concerning increased attendance.

However, he couldn't say one negative thing about Sarah. He pictured her glistening eyes with gold flecks, soft smiling lips, and how she thanked him for being nice to Kathleen and was tempted to give another positive review so she would keep smiling at him. If he were a painter, how would he paint her? Sparkling, mysterious, dark eyes. Smooth pink lips with the right touch of shimmer. Rose blossom cheeks. When her lips spread in a warm smile, his heart pounded a wild drumbeat he feared everyone could hear. Although he wasn't an artist, he was creative with words.

The beautiful Sarah Blackstone greets every patron as if they are the stars of the art show—not mere observers. If every gallery worker had her flair for welcoming guests and communicating from the heart about her passion for art, our nation's galleries would be filled with patrons.

Even how she expressed her love for working in this gallery and sending customers home with a perfect art piece was appealing. He imagined his podcast as a blank canvas he could fill with anything. How could he make it artistically worthy of Sarah's praise? Now, he was getting carried away with sappy nonsense. Yet he felt a distinct yearning to get this woman's attention and make her see him as more than a harsh podcaster.

What would it take for Sarah to see him as a decent guy? A heartwarming review? Complimenting the gallery she loved? He couldn't risk stirring up Alfie's wrath by sharing another inspirational piece too soon. He had to dig up the gritty truth about today's artist.

With Gracie's flirtatious behavior toward him, that shouldn't be too difficult. But would doing so create more distance between him and Sarah?

Chapter Eleven

Sarah took a quick look around the gallery, ensuring everything was ready for Gracie's presentation. Several easels displayed nautical watercolor scenes at the demo area, and the table held a variety of brushes, paints, and tablets. Surely, they wouldn't need more than eight chairs. Blue's warning was purely precautionary, right?

She heard laughter and a knot tightened in her chest. Gracie and Blue had been swapping humorous tales about artists' mistakes for the last ten minutes. The younger woman's tinkling laughter at everything he said and his deep-timbred chuckle grated on Sarah's nerves. Was he attracted to the younger woman?

But why should it bother her if they hit it off? She wasn't jealous of them. No? Then why were intense emotions tightening around her throat like a noose? Why did she long to be the one with whom Blue was laughing? She groaned inwardly. Why was she wasting time and energy entertaining conflicting feelings about Blue Paxton?

She strode into the kitchenette to make sure the pastries were ready. Thankfully, the bakery delivery service had increased her order on short notice.

"Sarah?" Gracie said in a sing-song voice. "Did you see the lineup outside?"

"There's a lineup?" She bolted past the café table where Blue sat, his muffled, "Told you so," annoying her. She unlocked the door and swung it open. A group of ten adults were waiting and more were coming across the street. "Come in. Welcome!" She smiled at Callie, Kathleen, Sue Taylor, a few others she knew, and some she didn't.

Callie hugged her. "I'm so excited about the out-of-town visitors. Aren't you?"

"Absolutely." However, she could do without one out-of-towner who was causing her emotional stress.

"I can't wait to chat with you about Sue Anne. Are you ready for her arrival?"

"Almost." Sarah had nearly forgotten about her birth mother's eventual arrival, thanks to all the winter festival preparations. When this week was over, she'd have more time to contemplate her upcoming meeting with Sue Anne. "Give me another day or two, and I'll be ready."

"Certainly. When you have a minute, I'd like some peppermint tea." Callie bustled toward one of the few remaining chairs.

Sarah directed the others to the demonstration area.

"Any more chairs?" Blue asked over her shoulder.

She gulped at his nearness and musky scent. "Uh. No. That's all we have."

"I'll make a few calls."

"But—"

He pulled out his cell phone and strode to the door. Sarah didn't have time to follow and find out who he was calling. She dashed toward the kitchenette, where a line was forming. Today, she wished she had an assistant!

She took drink and pastry orders and hoped Gracie was self-reliant enough to start her session independently. Sarah worked out a routine of preparing two hot beverages, delivering them, and then taking two more orders and distributing them to guests. At some point, Blue and Samantha, the mayor's secretary, hauled in folding chairs with "Basalt Bay City Hall" written on the bottoms. Sarah didn't know why Blue was helping, but she was grateful. Hopefully, he wouldn't mention her unpreparedness in tomorrow's episode, but she didn't have time to worry about that now.

As soon as everyone was seated, Gracie began her talk, and what she said sounded interesting, though Sarah caught only snippets. At one point, she observed Blue staring intently at the speaker. Was he captivated by the subject matter or the flirty young blond? The way his masculine lips curved upward made her wish he'd bestow one of those rare smiles on her. A few times, when she glanced at him and caught him gazing back at her, her heart pounded an earthy, intoxicating rhythm. But why was she so attracted to him?

The hour-long demonstration, including the Q and A, flew by fast with Sarah busily taking orders and delivering drinks and pastries. By the time Gracie finished speaking, and most of the attendees had left, she longed to drop into a chair, put her feet up, and drink a cup of hot coffee herself. Unfortunately, clean-up tasks took precedence over relaxation. *Soon,* she promised herself. She hustled around the tables, picking up discarded napkins, wiping tabletops with a damp cloth, and listening to Blue and Gracie talking. Most of it sounded informational, not personal, but Sarah wanted to scooch closer and participate in the conversation.

"I liked how you presented watercolor painting so anyone could go home and try it, even me," Blue said. Would he give her a favorable review, after all?

Was Gracie giggling and gazing adoringly at him so he'd talk positively about her on his podcast? Was her flattery a ruse, or was she genuinely attracted to him? Sarah stacked a couple of chairs and cast discreet glances in their direction.

"So you approve?" Gracie asked in a teasing tone.

"Approve of—?"

"My art. What else would I mean?" She nudged Blue's arm and tittered. "Why don't we talk some more over lunch? Or we could drive to Florence for dinner. What do you say?" She batted her eyes at him. *Good grief!* She was blatantly flirting with him!

"I don't know." Blue tugged his finger beneath his shirt collar, casting a panicked look toward Sarah.

What? Couldn't he decline a date request on his own? But since she loathed the idea of him and Gracie going anywhere alone together, she capitulated. "Hey, Blue, did you want to talk with me about the gallery? Maybe chat over a business lunch?" She grimaced apologetically toward Gracie.

"You're right. We should talk shop."

Gracie extended her lower lip in a pout. "Don't you want one of my paintings for a giveaway, Blue?" She purred his name.

"I sure do. My listeners will appreciate it, too. Thanks."

"Well, then—"

"Gracie," Sarah interrupted. "Can you tell me more about your ocean scenes before you go? They are such favorites here."

"I guess." Before moving, Gracie peered at Blue with a yearning expression, like she was silently imploring him for something. A great review? Or for him to treat her romantically?

Did every female artist and gallery attendant fall all over themselves, kissing up to Blue, so he wouldn't say something disparaging about them on his podcast? Did Gracie feel desperate and willing to do anything to acquire his good opinion? Sarah ushered her back to the demonstration area, resolutely telling herself, *I would never beg and cajole Blue Paxton into giving me his approval.* Not even for a kiss? *No!* Her neck and hairline burned.

After Gracie explained some concepts about her watercolor paintings, Sarah helped load her belongings into her car. Then she returned to stack chairs while Blue typed on his laptop.

"Let me help with those." She hadn't heard his approach. "You should have someone around to assist with coffee and setup during busy times."

"That sounds nice. But there are usually only one or two customers in the gallery at a time, and I can manage." She thought of something playful. "You aren't applying for a coffee-making job, are you?"

"Not on your life!" A brief smile crossed his mouth, which sent sparklers lighting up her romantic feelers. "No one's ever asked for my help with coffee before."

"It takes talent." She shook her head, eyeing him mischievously.

"What kind of talent might that be? A pretty smile?" Was he flirting with her now?

Heart pounding, butterflies dancing in her stomach, she felt so aware of interacting with a man she found attractive. But instead of saying something flirty back, she said, "It might take fortitude not to dump coffee on a guy who's being a little rude or pushy."

"Ouch." He grabbed his chest dramatically. "I concede I may come across as abrupt occasionally."

"Occasionally?" She grinned.

"Hey, now. I treated Kathleen decently after you asked me to, didn't I?"

"True. But you could work on your people skills." Even though she was being bold, her words came out breathily.

"So I've been told." Blue set a couple of chairs along the wall, gave her another heart-stirring smile, and then returned to his seat as if their teasing and smiling didn't mean anything.

And they didn't, right? Besides, why would she be attracted to a man she'd previously found despicable? Of course, that was before she met Blue Paxton "in the flesh." But still. She was reacting to him way too quickly.

Later, she finally got to sit down with a cup of coffee and relax. She'd taken a couple of sips when Blue stopped by her table, the strap of his laptop briefcase slung over his shoulder. "Care to close shop and get lunch with me?"

"If this is about Gracie—"

"It'll give us a chance to talk about the gallery. I appreciated your helping me out of a jam earlier. Staying here longer gave me time to jot some notes."

"All good, I hope."

"I wouldn't say all good."

She sighed, already dreading his next podcast. "Do you have this problem everywhere you go?"

"What's that?"

"Women fawning over you."

His cheeks darkened. "Not everywhere."

"It is a problem, though?"

"You have no idea." He rubbed the back of his neck. "What's your story? Why are you living in Basalt Bay, working in this tiny gallery?"

"Like I'd tell you. You might reveal my secrets."

"Your deepest mysteries are safe with me," he said huskily, his blue eyes gleaming. "I can keep my mouth shut when I want to."

"Not if telling serves your purpose. Your mouth is too—" *Ugh.* Why did she mention his mouth, which was spreading in a wide, appealing smile? And why did she have a sneaky longing to touch his lips with her fingers and discover if they were as soft as they looked? Would his slight facial hair tickle her skin during a kiss? *Where did that come from?* She swallowed hard. "I should probably—" Run? Do anything other than being mesmerized by Blue Paxton?

"I find myself wanting to talk with you, Sarah." The air whooshed from her lungs, and all she could do was stare at him. "You're easy to talk with. You don't flirt with me." Not even when she was gaping starstruck at him? "I live on the road. I don't make friends easily. Rarely date."

With artists like Gracie trying to impress him, he didn't date? Then again, with his curmudgeon online attitude, it was more understandable.

"Would you go to the festival with me tonight instead of lunch?" He smiled even more generously, which was her undoing. "Not as a date," he added quickly, shuffling back and forth. Why was he acting nervous? On his podcast, he sounded like the most confident man on the planet.

And the bigger question—why was he such a temptation to her? She was generally level-headed and cautious. Was her attraction to him only because he was the first man she'd been drawn to since Jeremy? Or was it because opposites attracted, and their magnetic fields were careening towards each other? If that were the case, shouldn't she resist the gravitational pull?

"Based on your delayed response, I gather you aren't interested. No problem."

"I work in an art gallery. I'm loyal to the artists," she said, reminding him of their conflict of interest. "You are an art critic. Isn't there an unwritten code that we shouldn't—"

"Socialize? Date? Don't worry. I don't plan to pursue you."

Shocked by his bluntness, she said, "Good to know," and marched toward the kitchenette. She was a fool for craving his attention! The sooner he left the gallery and Basalt Bay, the better!

Mid-stride, she froze. This was exactly how she used to respond to conflict, by pulling into herself and stomping away from confrontation. After Jeremy died, she vowed never again to be someone who couldn't explain her thoughts and feelings to a man. She turned back abruptly, and despite her rapidly pounding heart, declared, "Right there, what you said about not pursuing me was rude and insensitive." Blue's jaw dropped. "Don't tell me what you don't plan to do with me. I have a list of things I don't plan to do with you."

He sputtered and coughed. "I didn't mean anything snarky. I don't date anyone related to the business, not just you. Nothing can happen between us, that's all."

"So you said!" She should be glad the arrogant man didn't plan to pursue her. Yet how dare he dismiss her like that!

He thrust his fingers through his black hair before meeting her gaze again. "Would you be willing to introduce me to some people at the festival so I can get a few quotes?" He sounded far from eager to hang out with her now. "We could grab dinner at one of the booths as business acquaintances."

Right. Business acquaintances. Not someone she'd imagined kissing. Not someone who caused her heart to race. "I work until five. I'm free afterward," she spoke as formally as he had.

"Great. See you later?"

"Sure."

With his hand on the doorknob, he glanced back, his moist sapphire eyes aimed at her for several long seconds. Then he exited.

Sarah exhaled, relieved he was gone, yet conflicted. If Blue Paxton wasn't interested in her and didn't want anything romantic to happen between them, why did he stare at her with such longing or indecision?

God, should I even care about a man like Blue? She waited for an impression that would guide her away from spending the evening with him.

None came.

Chapter Twelve

With five minutes left until closing, Sarah paced from the bay window to the door and back again. She'd dreaded and anticipated seeing Blue and hanging out all afternoon. Now he was arriving any minute. But why was she having mixed emotions? He'd told her that he didn't date gallery workers. This wasn't a date. So why was her heart pounding at the thought of seeing him again?

She stared out at the dancing whitecaps, captivated by the movement of wind and sea, and knew why she felt such turmoil. Strolling around the festival with Blue as business associates was one thing. Hanging out with a man she was already attracted to was vastly different. And what was with that look of longing, or whatever, in his gaze before he left the gallery? Had he been trying to tell her something, like he was interested in her but couldn't do anything about it? Or was that wishful thinking on her part?

She strode back to the door, flipped the Open sign to Closed, and her phone rang. Was Blue calling to cancel? She had given him her business card with her phone number. "Hello?" she answered without checking the screen.

"Is this a good time to talk?" It was Sue Anne.

"Hey. Sure. I can talk. However, I'm expecting someone, so I may have to cut our conversation short." She glanced out the front window but didn't see Blue. A group of people were crossing the street, heading toward the booths in the City Hall parking lot. The whole area sparkled with Christmas lights casting a welcoming glow over the lot.

"That's okay. I'm over my bout with pneumonia," Sue Anne spoke quietly. "Callie asked me to stay with her this weekend."

"This weekend?" Sarah cringed. She didn't mean to sound so alarmed.

"Is that too soon? I should have asked you first. I'm sorry."

"No, that's all right." She tried to sound less intense. "I'm glad you're feeling better and planning a trip west."

"Me too." Sue Anne's breathing was a little raspy. "I'm sorry I had to postpone my plans. I hope my being there during the tail end of the festival won't be too big of an imposition."

"Not at all." The extra weeks had given Sarah time to prepare her heart for meeting her birth mother. But was she truly ready? "Are you planning to stay with Callie and James? You'd be welcome at the project house. We have a spare guest room." After a silence, she asked, "Sue Anne?"

"Sorry. I was thinking about how I don't want to barge in where you and"—she gulped—"Bess live, what with the festival and all. I want us to have time to adjust and feel comfortable with each other."

"That sounds good to me, too." Sarah sighed, relieved.

"How do you think Bess feels about my coming to town?" That seemed like an odd question. Was Sue Anne worried about her old relationship with Bess's ex? "Do you think she minds now that she's aware of the past?"

"I can't say how she feels. That's something the two of you should discuss."

"Of course. You're right."

Blue stepped in front of the window and lifted his hand in greeting. Sarah's heart lurched as she met the blue-eyed, complicated man's gaze.

"Just a second. The person I've been expecting is here." She unlocked the door. "Hey. Come in."

"Thanks." Blue stepped inside, looking casual and smiling as if there wasn't any tension between them. "Are you ready to go?"

"Almost. I need to finish this call. Give me a minute?"

"Sure. I'll wander over here." He nodded toward the large window.

Sarah's gaze trailed him and the relaxed way he walked. "If you'd like to stay with Callie, that's okay," she spoke into the phone. "I work at the gallery down the street from her house, so you can pop in any time. We'll have plenty of opportunities to talk."

"That sounds perfect. About Bess? Sorry for asking again."

Blue stood facing the window, his hands in his jacket pockets. Hopefully, he wasn't paying any attention to this conversation.

"Bess is a great person," Sarah said. "She treated me nicely and like family even after we found out Edward was my biological father. I doubt she holds a grudge against you."

"Okay. Thank you."

"You know Paul Cedars lives across the street from Callie and James's house, right?"

"Callie has reminded me of that more times than I care to admit."

Sarah chuckled. "With her matchmaking, I believe it."

"Matchmaking?"

"If you want, I can run interference." Blue glanced at her curiously, but she continued, "I can't promise success since Callie excels at what she does."

Sue Anne groaned. "I'm going to have a stern talk with my old chum."

"You do that! If staying across the street from Paul becomes too awkward, you can come out to the project house." This time, Sarah meant the invitation more sincerely. "You'd love Kathleen. She's the sweetest person I've ever met."

"She sounds delightful. I'm eager to meet all your friends."

"What day are you coming?"

"Would the day after tomorrow be too soon?"

"No. That's fine." She and Sue Anne had chatted over phone conversations and texted, so they weren't strangers. However, a face-to-face meeting would be different altogether.

"That way I'll catch the festival's final days—Callie insists!"

"And we must do what Callie says."

"Don't I know it?" Chuckling, Sue Anne said goodbye.

"Sorry for the delay." Sarah motioned toward the door. "We can go now."

"No problem." Blue crossed the room. "Sounds like you have an unexpected guest arriving."

"Yeah."

"May I escort you to the festival, Sarah?" Hearing him speak her name softly, butterflies raced up her middle, though she tried stuffing them down.

"Of course." As they exited the gallery, she had a playful thought, and since Blue deserved a little razzing, she asked, "You are familiar with how it is in small towns, right?"

"Which part are you referring to?"

"Raised eyebrows, judgmental nods, whispers behind your back?"

"Ah. Right. People might talk about us?"

"Talk. Point. Gossip." She fought a grin. "They might even exaggerate about us getting married!"

"What?" His dropped-jaw expression was extremely gratifying! "All because we're walking around together?"

"That's right. So, keep your distance, Mr. Paxton!" She wagged her finger at him. "And stay away from mistletoe!"

"There's mistletoe at this winter festival?"

"You'd better believe it."

Chapter Thirteen

Strolling around the booths, looking over the vendors' wares, and chatting with Sarah was entertaining and a surprising experience that made Blue want to prolong their evening together. She was intelligent, beautiful, empathetic, a good listener, and easy to converse with as they shared stories and laughter. He was grateful for their easy companionship despite his blundering comment about not pursuing her. He'd thought it was best to be upfront with her, but his remark may have been insensitive and premature. Considering how pleasant the evening was going, he was having second thoughts about his policy against dating gallery workers.

It had been years since he'd been around anyone other than Gram without feeling pressured about what he should or shouldn't say on his podcast. Sarah hadn't mentioned anything to make him think she expected him to speak well of the gallery or any local artists on *Blue's Art Clash*. His podcast hadn't even come up.

They talked about the various arts and crafts and the delicious scents of food coming from some of the stalls. And being with her made him feel like a regular person—like he wasn't Blue Paxton, the podcaster, which was a relief in this instance. She spoke naturally about her faith, how grace-filled and loving God was, and how she wanted to be like that, too—things he hadn't thought much about in years. He admired her genuineness and how she expressed herself so well. She told him about the profits from the festival going to a local charity for women in dire circumstances, and he heard her passion for the cause in her voice. The more they talked, the more attracted to her he became.

The twinkling lights above invited them to the next booth and the next. At each one, the friendship and jovial chatter of the vendors made him more aware of the small-town vibe, but he didn't resent it like he usually did. Maybe that was because the interactions seemed authentic, and the event was for a good cause. He could embrace such camaraderie and generosity among neighbors, since it made the festival atmosphere more welcoming and almost magical.

Was his feeling of belonging and being part of something meaningful due to his present company? A few times, he thought about holding Sarah's hand or settling his arm over her shoulder. What would she say if he did? Considering what he said earlier, would she think he was too forward or insincere?

They walked side by side around the City Hall parking lot twice, although the feat wasn't much to brag about since the booths were crammed together into a compact space. Many of the sellers greeted Sarah by name, but a few raised eyebrows were aimed in his direction. Did some of the citizenry assume they were dating as she'd suggested? Would that be so bad?

At a food stall, a female server waved fervently at him, grinning and acting like she knew him. Who was she? The sign above her read, "Bert's Fish Shack." Oh. Right. Wasn't she the server who introduced herself and asked him out at the diner? He hadn't taken her suggestion seriously and didn't recall her name.

Sarah gave him a quizzical look. "You know Lucy?"

Lucy. "Not really. But she asked me on a date during breakfast."

"I bet she did." Sarah chuckled like she knew of the woman's flirtatious behavior.

"I didn't do anything to encourage her." He held up his hands.

"I'm sure you didn't." Yet she still chuckled merrily.

They continued exploring the booths and talking with crafters. He liked how Sarah's dark eyes sparkled toward him whenever he spoke as if she thought everything he said was important. At other times, she widened the space between them like she was guarding herself from getting too close. Was that because of what he'd said about them not dating? Did she sense he was becoming more interested in her?

He'd be here for another day or two, and then he might never see her again. So why was he even toying with thoughts of them getting closer? His throat constricted with an undefinable emotion. Was it longing? Missing Sarah already? How was that possible? He heaved a sigh.

"Is the festival that awful?" She looked amused.

"Just mulling over some things."

"Getting your ammo lined up for a full offensive attack on the Basalt Bay art world?"

He snorted. "Not quite."

"You're not going to—" Sarah stopped suddenly and, gazing upward, her eyes widened. His gaze followed hers. Above them, a red bow with a cluster of mistletoe dangled from a string of lights, swaying in the wind as if dancing.

"Are you kidding?"

"Don't blame me," she said indignantly. "I warned you, didn't I?"

"Yeah, you did."

Their gazes met, and with the holiday lights casting a glow over Sarah's face, a jolt of attraction hit Blue with lightning-bolt intensity. They'd known each other for all of two days, but he already felt more connected to her than he had to anyone else in ages. The sounds of country music and laughter faded. Sarah licked her soft-looking lips like she might be anticipating a kiss, and he was so drawn to her and to her lips. She smiled softly. Was she inviting him closer? Should he kiss her? Wouldn't it be reckless of him to kiss a business associate?

If he kissed her like he longed to do, like he'd already thought of doing, it would mean revealing how he felt about her and becoming vulnerable. It would rip off his mask of indifference and his declaration that he wouldn't pursue her. Yet standing here under a sprig of mistletoe, exposing his heart to this woman was exactly what he wanted to do.

Despite his indecision, Sarah moved toward him first, brushing her lips tentatively across his. The sweet delicateness of her mouth, barely touching him, took his breath away and made him long for more of her kisses. He drew her into his arms like it was the most natural thing to do, and she fit perfectly against his chest. He kissed her slowly, tantalizingly, as if tasting sweet dark chocolate for the first time and delighting in it. Their kisses became more intense and insistent, like they were both starving for romance and longed for a closer emotional bond with each other. They lingered beneath the mistletoe for several delicious minutes, kissing and making memories he'd cling to in the days ahead.

Snickering and handclapping brought Blue to his senses. Sarah's eyelids fluttered open, and their gazes met briefly before they faced a group of people gathered around them. Sarah's cheeks reddened. He tucked her under his arm, leading her away from prying eyes. "Are you okay?"

"I'm okay." Yet she still blushed. "I didn't mean to get so carried away."

"No? I did."

"You meant to kiss me so passionately?" Her mouth fell open, drawing his attention to her lips again, making him long to kiss her some more.

"I like you, Sarah. And I liked kissing you." He touched her cheek with the back of his knuckles, smoothing them down her warm face. "I'll always remember us kissing under the mistletoe. That was a first for me."

"Me too."

"I'm sorry to say, it doesn't change anything." He hated bringing up anything negative after sharing those sensational kisses, but he had to tell her the truth. "I don't see how a relationship could work between us." He softened his voice, hoping to lessen the awfulness of his words. He wished things were different between them and their situations, but they weren't.

"Don't worry. It's not like I expect a proposal or anything." She stepped back from him, creating a chilly barrier, or his words had done that.

"That's good because I can't give you one. Our lifestyles are too different."

"No kidding." She sucked in a stuttered breath. "The two of us are like night and day."

"Sarah—"

"Don't." She lowered her gaze and shook her head, halting his attempt at an explanation. But then, she lifted her chin and pegged him with a look. "You'd better not blab about our kissing to your online audience. Don't you dare tell them I swooned at your charms!" She thought she swooned? While the idea pleased him, he was the one who melted at her feet.

"I wouldn't be so cruel."

"You'd better not be. Otherwise, my sister-in-law will take you down in our town's *Gazette*." Even though she spoke teasingly, he tensed. "Our newspaper doesn't have the reach your podcast does, but Ali will put you in your place, Mr. Paxton." His heart plummeted at her formal address. "Now, shall we continue our tour as if the other stuff didn't happen?"

Like he could forget their kisses? "Uh—"

"If you want to say good night and leave town in the morning, I understand." She waved toward a booth where two older gentlemen stared at them, frowning as if they'd observed their interaction and disapproved.

"I'd like us to continue hanging out together if that's okay." He'd prefer the evening didn't end on a sour note. But how could they salvage their companionship after the way they kissed like lovers, and then he ruined everything?

"Let me introduce you to some friends who specialize in wood-working." Sarah hooked her arm with his and led him toward the booth with the two older guys. "James and Paul, this is Blue Paxton. This is Paul, my sister-in-law's dad. James is my friend's husband."

"It's nice to meet you both." Blue shook the men's hands.

"How do you know our Sarah?" Paul emphasized "our."

"We met through the gallery."

"Blue is here to critique the artists, the gallery, and me." Sarah made a wry face. Blue wanted to assure her that he wouldn't say anything personal about her on his show, but now wasn't the time.

"I'm watching you, bub," Paul said. *Bub?*

"Don't worry, Paul. Blue and I don't agree about much, but I can take care of myself." She thought they didn't agree? They agreed perfectly while they were kissing.

"Even so. Sarah is one of our own, and we look out for each other in this *small* town." So Paul had heard about his grudge against tiny towns?

"Are you interested in any items made of wood?" James smiled affably.

"Sure. I like handcrafted products. But since I live out of a suitcase, I don't collect nonessentials."

"Nonessentials?" Paul scowled like the word offended him.

"For living on the road, that is. Occasionally, I pick up gifts for my grandmother."

"So your work brought you to Basalt Bay and Sarah?" James peered back and forth between them. "Anything you want to tell us?"

"James—" Sarah shook her head.

"I'm here to report on the artists and the festival, that's all."

Sarah winced, and Blue wished he'd said that differently.

"Then you ought to stay away from mistletoe!" Paul said grouchily.

"Well, I, uh—"

"Your listeners might be interested in hearing about two senior citizens who recently started a woodworking business together." Sarah was obviously trying to rescue the conversation, but her suggestion surprised him. She hadn't promoted anyone else all evening. "Aren't their pieces impressive?" She tipped her head toward an Adirondack chair and gazed at him as if expecting him to agree.

"Yes. Fine work, gentleman." He ran his hands over the lines of the wood, inspecting their workmanship. "That headboard looks intricately made, too."

"Thanks, I guess," Paul muttered.

"We'll see you guys later." Sarah smiled fondly at the two. "Hey, James. Where's Callie?"

"Inside City Hall. She's watching over the silent auction items."

"I'll check on her in a bit."

Sarah introduced Blue to several other artisans along the way, and he enjoyed observing her interactions with them. How she encouraged each one about their artistic endeavors gave him another glimpse into her personality and heart for people. It made him scrutinize himself, too. In all the times he'd interacted with artists, had he ever encouraged any of them the way Sarah was doing tonight? He was always hunting for flaws, things to criticize and critique, and searching for areas where an artist didn't bring their most authentic selves to their work. But what if he were to look for the positive attributes instead of the worst? Would he find anything worth talking about on his podcast? He groaned. Alfie would have his head!

Over the next half hour, a few times, Sarah gazed earnestly at him like she was asking for his affirmation about other products. He was tempted to speak reassuringly of an artisan's work so she would think well of him and smile at him again. But whatever survived between them after their unbelievable kisses and tomorrow's podcast, he hoped it would be based on honesty and friendship—not because she despised him.

Chapter Fourteen

"Shall we head inside?" Sarah paused outside City Hall and glanced at Blue, who had one hand tucked in his jacket pocket and nursed a to-go coffee cup in the other. Now that she'd kissed him like he was the last man in Oregon, reverting to chatting like they were only business acquaintances was challenging and disappointing. But she was going to have to act like he was Blue Paxton, the podcaster who ate artists for breakfast, because that's who he was! Why had she cozied up with him and forgotten that fact? "Or are you ready to call it a night? You still have to prepare for tomorrow, right?"

"Yes. But I do my best writing after midnight."

"One of those burn-the-midnight-oil writers?"

"Exactly. Now you know a personal detail about me." Their gazes met, and her throat felt as dry as sandpaper. They kissed passionately, so she already knew a personal detail about him—he was an incredible kisser—and she'd never be able to forget how wonderful and special she felt in his arms. "Look. I'm sorry for being a jerk earlier and saying I wouldn't pursue you. I was afraid—"

"I'd use my attraction for you to twist your arm about talking nice about my gallery?"

"Something like that." He glanced at the ground as if the topic made him uncomfortable. She wasn't letting him off the hook that easily!

"Here's something you don't know about me. This is the first time I've gone out with anyone since my husband died two years ago." She blinked fast to avoid moisture from filling her eyes. "Our kisses tonight meant something to me, even if they meant nothing to you."

"I didn't say they meant nothing. Sarah—"

"Just don't ruin it for me, okay?"

"I won't." He stopped walking. "Your husband died?"

"Christmas Eve, two years ago."

"That's horrible. I'm so sorry." He clasped her hand in a sympathetic gesture.

"Thanks." She pulled away. Holding hands with him would make her want to kiss him again. And kissing him again would lead to wanting more kissing, followed by expecting promises that were never going to happen. "I only mentioned it to say I'm out of practice regarding romance. When you asked me to join you tonight, even though you said it wasn't a date, it felt like one. But don't worry. Your words cleared things up for me."

"I'm sorry for being abrupt." Sighing, he peered up at the sky. "Dating anyone in the business makes everything complicated."

"Understood. So why ask me out in the first place?"

He met her gaze again. She liked how he looked directly at her, like he was seeing her for who she was. "Something about you intrigues me, Sarah. Kissing you was unforgettable. Even though I have to put on the brakes, I am very attracted to you."

She appreciated his honesty and vulnerability. "That's how I feel, too. Kissing you felt like I was kissing a guy for the first time."

Unfamiliar with any man other than her late husband gazing at her with such affection, it brought out more honesty in her. "I like you, Blue. Even if a relationship can't work between us, it feels good to acknowledge that."

"I like you too." His Adam's apple bobbed. "While I don't feel at liberty to kiss you again, that doesn't mean I don't want to." They shared a mutual desire, then.

"What now?"

"I'd still like to get to know you better." A soft smile widened his lips. "But you should think about how a relationship with a traveling boyfriend might work."

Boyfriend? "I may be unfamiliar with dating, but I'm pretty sure referring to yourself as a boyfriend on a first date is off-limits." Why was he discussing that, anyway? Talk about sending mixed signals!

"No doubt. I'm out of practice, too." Blue's cheeks turned ruddy. "Is there any way we could start over and pretend this conversation never happened?"

"And forget about our mistletoe kiss?" A smile crossed her lips that felt like it came straight from her heart. "No way!"

"Yeah. Let's not forget about that." He held out the crook of his arm. "May I escort you inside City Hall, Sarah?"

"You should know that couples get married there." She gave him a playful nudge, and he coughed hard. "If we walk around town with our arms linked and smiling like we're gaga over each other, people will talk. Some already observed us kissing."

"True. I'm willing to take the risk if you are." His inviting smile convinced her to slide her hand around his arm.

"Don't say I didn't warn you."

Blue chuckled, and the sound was like water trickling over the parched desert of her heart. She would be content if he stuck around and laughed with her for the rest of her life. Well, not quite content. She'd experienced Blue's thrilling kisses, so she could never be satisfied with anything less than feeling his heart beating against hers. Was it wrong to still wish for that?

Chapter Fifteen

When Sarah arrived at work the following day, she was steaming mad. Back at the project house, she'd listened to Blue's podcast with her jaws clenched so tightly they still hurt. He had acted like his usual Bold Brash Blue, railing about Gracie Parker's "mediocre attempts at art." But when he implied that the artist had offered romantic advances as collateral against a negative review, that was too much! Sarah wanted to shut off the app and never speak to him again!

Even though she had observed Gracie's flirtatious behavior, she felt it was wrong of Blue to discuss the artist's conduct during a podcast. But that was the nature of his business—sensationalism, stirring up emotions, getting people gossiping about it on social media. All for what? A few more clicks and comments?

Despite her annoyance with how he spoke about Gracie, she continued listening, because hearing Blue's voice felt too intoxicating to shut off. And she hoped he'd say something redemptive about Gracie's work to justify her continuing to listen, but he didn't. He concluded that Gracie's art fell dismally short of contemporary standards and lacked the depth needed in today's market.

Groaning, Sarah forced herself to focus on prepping everything for today's demonstration, but doing the tasks wasn't enough to make her forget Blue's podcast or their tender kisses from the night before. Why had she succumbed to them so easily? Was it due only to the mistletoe? Or had she secretly wished for a romantic interlude with him? How could she be attracted to a man who lacked compassion and common decency in his work ethic?

She was so hypocritical! Even now, if Blue walked into the gallery and took her in his arms, she'd kiss him like the sky was falling and they had one last chance to kiss before the end. However, afterward, she would tell him what she thought about his blatant rudeness toward Gracie and give him the coldest shoulder anyone had ever been given.

How was Gracie doing? Had the harsh review offended her? She wasn't the type to hide out in a hut in Alaska, but should Sarah call her and— What? Apologize for Blue's arrogance? His honest opinion? She could say he didn't know everything there was to know about watercolor paintings, even if he thought he did, and that the critique was solely from his perspective. But would that appease her?

Lane Baxter, usually a friendly and chatty fellow, arrived and quietly unloaded his boxes and small sculptures in the demo area. No doubt, Blue was at fault for the artist's subdued attitude. Had Lane heard this morning's podcast and feared what the critic might say about him and his sculptures?

Lane's teenage son, Mason, trailed behind his dad, carrying a box. His slumped shoulders and begrudging look said he wasn't pleased to be here. Since Lane had assistance, Sarah returned to the kitchenette and prepped the cinnamon rolls and blueberry muffins she'd ordered.

So far, Blue hadn't shown up. He arrived early on both previous days, so maybe he wasn't attending today's demonstration. Perhaps he received angry feedback about his podcast and was spending time responding to the comments. What if she wrote a furious social media commentary about her perception of today's episode?

She sighed. It wasn't her place to comment on an art critic's view, not even Blue Paxton's! It was her job to remain polite and impartial. She had to gracefully accept negative reviews, even if they frustrated her to no end and didn't reflect her feelings. However, soothing ruffled feathers would be at the top of her priority list, starting with Gracie's.

"Sarah?" Lane called.

"Yes?" She leaned around the corner of the kitchenette.

"Those lights came loose." He pointed at a string of fairy lights dangling from the wall. "Do you want me to fix them?"

"That's okay. I'll take care of it." She hurried to the closet and grabbed a small ladder. As she climbed to the top rung, intense rapping at the door made her pause. Was that Blue?

"Is it the critic?" Mason scowled. "I'll tell him what I think of—"

"Mase. Cut the sarcasm."

"But Dad—"

"The guy was just doing his job."

"A lousy job. You heard what he said about that artist!"

"Take it easy." Lane palmed the air. "Want me to open the door, Sarah?"

"Would you?" She needed to finish securing the string of lights and still had other tasks to accomplish before guests arrived.

"Thanks," Blue said as he entered.

"No problem." Lane locked the door, then returned to the demo table.

Blue met Sarah's gaze across the gallery with a cautious look. Was he worried about how she'd react after the way he kissed her like Romeo and then spoke rudely about one of her artists? When he smiled softly, her heart fluttered, and the cold shoulder she intended to give him dissipated. They all needed grace sometimes. But did Blue realize how rude he sounded this morning? Did he feel any remorse about it?

He dropped off his laptop bag and strode toward her. "Need a hand?"

"No thanks. These should stay in place now." She climbed down the ladder, stiffening when she felt his hand touch her back, guiding her. She didn't want Lane and Mason to assume they were a couple or that she approved of how Blue spoke about Gracie. She stashed the ladder in the closet and returned to the kitchenette without interacting with him.

"I see you aren't gearing up for maximum attendees," he said while setting up his laptop.

Why would she? Ten chairs were too many. Other than Callie and Kathleen, would anyone else show up?

"After your critique of Gracie Parker, I doubt we'll have much of a turnout." Sarah shrugged toward Lane. "I am looking forward to hearing you share about your sculptures."

"Let's hope a few diehards attend." Lane glanced at Blue as if silently asking what the art critic thought. That was dangerous territory!

"That's what I'm counting on," Sarah said.

"It can't be all that bad." Blue made a scoffing sound. "You might be surprised by how a gut-honest assessment of art brings people flocking to the showroom."

"I doubt your opinion about Gracie's work did our gallery any good." Sarah hated throwing a pall over the room with Lane and Mason present, but she didn't back down.

"You'll see," Blue said.

Yes, I will.

"I think my dad's art is cool!" Mason clenched his fist. "Lots of others think so, too."

"I love your dad's sculptures." Sarah slipped her hand around the crook of his arm, tugging the teenager away from Blue. "Can I get you a hot drink? How about a cinnamon roll or muffin?"

"Do you have hot chocolate?"

"I sure do. Lane?"

"I have my water bottle. Thanks."

"If you change your mind, it's on the house." She glanced at Blue. "Anything for you?" Her job description included being polite to everyone in the gallery, but she wasn't feeling very accommodating toward him. She should never have set her lips against that man's.

"Coffee. And it's almost ten." He tapped his watch. Was he itching for an argument?

"Right." She hurried to the prep area, fixed Mason's hot chocolate, and topped it with whipped cream. Then she poured a cup of hot black coffee for Blue, tempted to stir in five heaping teaspoons of sugar to sweeten him up, or to annoy him. "Here you go." She set the steaming drink on his table with a clink.

"Thanks." He didn't meet her gaze. Did he sense the frosty air in the room or that he was the cause? He deserved every second of discomfort or misery he might be feeling.

Sorry, Lord. I know I'm supposed to be kind and gracious to everyone.

"Here's the hot chocolate." She handed the mug to Mason.

"Thanks. Can I have one of those cinnamon rolls later?"

"Absolutely. I'll set one aside." She hustled over to the door before Blue reminded her it was time to open again. When she pulled the door back, she was surprised to find a dozen guests waiting. "Welcome! Come in! Thank you for coming!"

"It's cold out there." Callie shivered as she moved past Sarah.

"Sorry." She patted the older woman's shoulder.

"You're still here?" Callie asked Blue.

"As you can see, I am."

A few others shot grumpy looks his way. They must have listened to his podcast yet still showed up to support Lane and the gallery.

"Haven't you done enough harm with your contempt?" Callie questioned in an irate tone.

"If this paltry turnout is all my words evoked, it wasn't contemptuous enough!"

"I'll have you know—"

"Callie." Sarah patted her arm. "Let's keep this discussion friendly, hmm?"

"Fine." Callie lifted her chin toward Blue. "I heard about your shenanigans last night." *Uh-oh.* Was she talking about their kiss? "Step out of line again, and I'll—"

"Let's find you a seat before they are all taken." Sarah helped Callie get situated in the front row and was thankful she didn't mention anything else about last night. "I hope you enjoy Lane's talk." She returned to greeting guests and saw more scowls thrown in Blue's direction. She prayed he wouldn't come down too harshly on Lane, or there might be a riot!

As she introduced Lane to the group, a woman with a scarf covering the lower half of her face strode into the gallery and stood at the back. The redhead's green eyes searched the crowd like she was hunting for someone. Then she squinted harshly at Blue. Did she know him? Over the next half hour, while Sarah served coffee and pastries, she observed the out-of-towner still staring at him. Was she angry about today's podcast, too?

Later, Sarah heard the woman whisper, "Hi, honey. Over here. Remember me?" She finger-waved at Blue. Was she a fan? Someone from his past? Sarah's gaze swung toward Blue. He was either ignoring the whispers or didn't realize the woman was trying to get his attention.

Sarah caught parts of Lane's discussion during some lulls in orders. She enjoyed his explanation about how he gathered objects wherever he went—camping trips, the beach, cross-country vacations—and how he kept a box in his car to drop off stuff like a progressive art receptacle. "I've often found unusual pieces that later became part of my most valuable sculptures. Looking for found items is like an adventurer or a treasure hunter continually on a hunt for gold or the next artifact."

A few exclamations of "Ah," and "Isn't that something?" filtered through the room.

The mystery woman didn't make any other comments. However, her jade eyes remained trained on Blue, while he faced forward, glued to Lane's lecture—or maybe he wasn't. His fingers raking through his hair and a sickly look on his face seemed the opposite of attentive. Was he more aware of the woman than he was letting on?

"This is the first found-object sculpture I made as an adult." Lane patted the head of a four-foot, weathered silver farmer wearing a hat and holding a rake. The vintage sculpture was made of tarnished metal pieces, and age discolorations added to its unique look. "It's been in my garden for years, but I still love it."

He went into detail about how he'd formed the sculpture. He didn't have a smooth public-speaking voice, but his pleasure in making sculptures was evident, and hearing about his journey toward becoming an artist was inspiring. Would Blue notice that?

Lane asked for volunteers, and several came forward to make their own miniature sculptures. Sarah would have enjoyed participating if she hadn't been the host. When Lane segued into his Q and A, she glanced back to check on Blue. Surely, he had some questions.

His seat was empty. The woman was gone, too.

Had they left together?

Chapter Sixteen

After Lane finished his presentation and most of the attendees were gone, Callie cornered Sarah. "That man left before I got to tell him what I thought of what he said about Gracie! Where'd he go, anyway?"

"I have no idea." Sarah was embarrassed Blue had departed without talking to Lane, but there wasn't anything she could do about it.

"When I see him again, he'd better watch out!"

"Callie," Kathleen said calmly, "let's pray for the man instead of judging him too harshly. Don't you think he might be troubled and needs our prayers?" Was Blue troubled? Did Kathleen know something about him that Sarah didn't?

"I know he's arrogant and says harsh things about artists." Callie crossed her arms staunchly. "No one should listen to him."

"Yet people do." Kathleen chuckled. "Didn't you tell me you were trying to keep your fervent opinions to yourself? I think Blue may need our understanding more than our gossip."

Callie's shoulders sagged. "I have been trying harder to watch what comes out of my mouth. But I was tempted to be judgmental about him. I only want to defend Gracie and Sarah."

"Of course you do. But let's not discount Blue's character, either. He may turn out to be an okay fellow yet." Kathleen winked at Sarah. "Are you all right, dear?"

"I'm all right. I wanted to give him a piece of my mind, too." She smiled at Callie. "I need more grace in my heart like Kathleen has."

"Like Jesus does, dear."

"Yes. Like Him. I've been upset about Blue's podcast ever since I heard it this morning." She felt the heat of regret burn through her. "Now that he left so abruptly, I wonder if I'll ever see him again."

"Have a little faith." Kathleen squeezed her hand gently, and then linked arms with Callie. "Let's give Sarah a few minutes to herself, shall we?"

"Love you." Callie smiled tenderly at her.

"Love you both."

Lane stopped beside Sarah with an overflowing box of supplies and partial sculptures in his arms. "Thank you for asking me to speak today. I'm honored to have the opportunity to share about my work with such a supportive group." He was a pleasant man and a widower, someone Sarah related to on various levels. Why couldn't she be attracted to him instead of pining for someone like Blue Paxton?

"You're welcome. The honor is mine. And ours." She waved toward Callie and Kathleen, who stood in front of Gracie Parker's watercolor display. "I'm sorry Blue didn't stay long enough to speak with you. I'm sure he had questions."

Lane shrugged. "He probably didn't like my presentation."

"I don't know about that." What could she say? She couldn't defend Blue's actions when she didn't understand them herself.

"You're doomed, Dad." Mason carried another box, heading toward the door. "What'll that podcaster say about you?"

"Who knows?" Lane shrugged. "Maybe there was an emergency, and he had to leave."

Sarah hadn't considered that. Why didn't she pause to think the best of Blue or even pray for him?

"I guess we'll find out in the morning," Mason said in a voice of doom.

Lane tipped his head toward Sarah. "Anyway, thank you for the opportunity."

"You're welcome. I have cinnamon rolls for you guys when you're done loading up."

"Yes!" Mason pulsed his fist, nearly toppling the box.

"We appreciate your kindness." Lane carried his things out the door, and Mason followed him.

Sarah said goodbye to Callie and Kathleen and then boxed up the two frosting-laden cinnamon rolls. Mason ran in and grabbed them. "Thanks a million!"

"You're welcome."

She cleaned the counter and tabletops, mulling over Blue's departure. Did an emergency come up? Did he take off because of the stranger who called him honey? What if he left town without saying goodbye? She recalled Kathleen's words—*"Have a little faith"*—and spent a few moments praying for Blue.

Later, when things were slow in the gallery, Sarah decided to call and check on Gracie. "How are you doing?"

"As well as can be expected in the aftermath of Blue Paxton's critique. He thinks I'll donate a painting to his show now? He can think again!" Gracie muttered a swear word, then cleared her throat. "I have received support from friends and fans calling and texting to offer condolences."

"I'm glad to hear it. I wanted to say I'm sorry for what Blue said. I'm sure he didn't mean it personally." Sarah had to be careful. While she wanted to offer Gracie her sincere support and friendship, she wouldn't badmouth Blue to appease her.

"Not personally? It was personal to me! He tore my art to shreds!"

"I'm sorry. I just wanted to check and make sure you're doing okay."

"Thank you." Gracie sniffed. "You'll be interested to hear I received a commission to do five paintings."

"Five? That's amazing! Congratulations." So Blue's negative review hadn't been all bad?

The call ended, and Sarah fixed herself a cup of tea before sitting down at one of the tables. With an hour left before closing, she was relieved to have a few minutes to herself. If Blue was still in town, would he be at the festival this evening? He'd already attended three of the art demonstrations. Was it time for him to move on to another location?

And who was that woman who stared at him throughout Lane's demo? An old flame? Were they somewhere together, now, making up?

Chapter Seventeen

Blue leaned back in a rickety chair in his semi-darkened room at the inn and pressed his fingers against his temples, begrudging his situation. He hated being stuck in a bathroom-cleaner-scented room, hiding from that woman, who he was sure had tried to run him off the road the other day. Alfie told him to lay low and wait for the stalker, or whoever she was, to leave town. How long would that take? Alfie said he didn't want negative publicity, but Blue knew better. His business partner thrived on publicity, negative or positive. What was really going on?

At least, Alfie promised to try to find out if the redhead's presence had anything to do with a disgruntled artist Blue critiqued in the past. Was that what his life had come to? Hunkering down in a vintage inn, hoping a deranged artist or gallery worker didn't come after him? Sitting alone and miserable? He heaved a long sigh that hurt in his chest.

He should have called Sarah and explained why he rushed out of the demo. What must she think? That once again he was rude and self-centered? He hardly heard any of today's found-object discussion after that woman's whisperings, so he didn't have a detailed outline or even a simple plan for tomorrow's podcast. What was he going to do? If he ran an old episode, it would be an affront to Lane Baxter. But so would a poorly done commentary.

His phone rang, but he silenced it after "unknown" flashed across the screen for the seventh time today. He wanted to answer and yell at whoever it was to stop pestering him or he would call the police.

The walls of the archaic room were closing in on him, making him stir-crazy. Why hadn't the owner modernized the prehistoric relic? The toilet barely flushed. He'd taken three cold showers since he arrived. If anyone deserved a negative review, it was the owner of this motel! Although, admittedly, the place had a decent internet connection. If not for that, he didn't know what he'd do, other than leave town immediately.

The phone rang again, and he dismissed it. But when his gaze flicked over Sarah's name, he swiped the screen, glad he entered her information into his contacts. "Hello?"

"You are alive," she said blandly.

"I am. I need to explain some things. Maybe apologize?"

"That sounds like a good starting place." She sighed. "You left so fast I wondered if you got enough material for your podcast."

"I didn't. Did you notice the woman in the back of the gallery?"

"The one with the scarf around her face? Yes."

Sarah didn't demand answers like some women he'd been associated with in the past would have done, especially ones he'd kissed. However, in the following silence, he guessed she was waiting for an explanation, and she deserved one. "Shall we meet and have dinner?" he asked, although Alfie wouldn't like him leaving his motel room.

"What's going on?"

"I think that woman is the same one who tried to run me off the road the day I came here." He slipped on his shoes. "That's why I left the gallery abruptly. I hoped to lure her away from you and the others. She might be dangerous!"

"Is she a fan? An old girlfriend?"

"No. It seems she's out for revenge, but I don't know why."

"Have you made some enemies, Blue?"

"You have no idea."

"Okay. You've piqued my curiosity."

"Will you have dinner with me?" He'd love to spend more time with her before he left town. Thoughts of their time together last night and their kisses hadn't been far from his thoughts all day. "I have to warn you—there's a possibility the woman might be at the festival and follow us."

"Are you worried about me?"

"Something like that." He wanted to tell her how much he'd been thinking about her. But it would sound flirtatious, and he still couldn't fathom how a relationship could work with her being tied to a small town like this. Besides that, and his nomadic lifestyle, she was affiliated with a gallery he was currently critiquing! Since he kept things edgy and entertaining for his podcast audience, anything he said in his show might make her furious with him.

How could that end well?

Chapter Eighteen

"Why do you speak so gruffly about artists?" Sarah asked as soon as she and Blue sat down at a table near Bert's booth, waiting for the chili and rolls they ordered. It was far from a private place to talk, but she was determined to get some answers. "Don't you see how much effort and bravery it takes to complete a piece of art that people will view and criticize?"

"Sure. I get that. But you have to understand my online persona is my brand. It's a role I play. Nothing more."

"A role?" Did he hear the contempt in her tone? "Nothing more?" He had to be joking.

"Think of it as if I'm playing a character in a theatrical production while I'm podcasting." Blue shrugged like his role-playing wasn't a big deal and didn't damage people's self-confidence about their art. "It takes a lot of hype and drama to get my audience engaged and commenting. I've succeeded by being a convincing character."

"So, online, you become a different Blue Paxton?"

"So to speak." He looked at her uneasily.

"Then why does your character talk so curtly about the artists and galleries he's critiquing?"

"It's part of the biz, Sarah."

"Crushing people's hopes and dreams is part of your business?" How shallow could he be, especially if he was only playing a role and didn't genuinely care about the artists? "There's got to be a more honorable way of making a living."

They stared at each other for several long seconds without speaking. She was pushing this topic hard, but she had strong feelings about it.

"What's this really about?" Blue frowned.

"There are some things I just don't get about you." She saw Bert delivering an order to someone. His laughter reached her, as did the sounds of muffled conversations around them and the instrumental music of "Jingle Bells" coming from the sound system. Sue Taylor walked by with a clipboard, probably noting how the event was going.

"That's okay. I don't understand everything about you, either." Blue smiled like he was relieved to be transitioning away from her questions.

"Do you want to understand more about me?" Her tone came out softer than she meant it to.

"If we aren't talking about *Blue's Art Clash*, I do." He leaned forward, eyeing her. "If you think I've been gruff in my podcasts from here, you haven't heard anything yet."

She leaned forward, too, their noses almost touching. "I've heard enough of your podcasts to know how impolite you can be toward artists. What I don't understand is why, when I've seen your more *charming* side."

She didn't mean to say it flirtatiously, but when he grinned at her with an endearing look, she found it so appealing that some of her irritation faded with the last rays of sunlight coming across the ocean. Why ruin the evening with talk that could only lead to more disagreements and awkwardness? Blue would be leaving soon. She might never see him again. Shouldn't she enjoy their brief time together? But she wouldn't let her guard down and forget who he was and what he did for a living!

Lucy set two bowls of steaming chili and rolls on the table and smiled at Blue. "Here you go. Enjoy!" She winked at him and walked away, swaying her hips. Sarah rolled her eyes. Mercifully, Blue didn't watch the server's departure.

"Would it be possible to enjoy a meal together without us clashing over my business?" He took a bite of chili, his gaze little-boy pleading.

"'Clash' is part of your podcast's name, isn't it?" She picked up her spoon and twirled melted cheese into the beans. Steam rose with a spicy scent. "Where does the harsh critic and the man I've kissed part ways?" Her face warmed, but she held his gaze. "Are you the same man or not?"

"That's a tough question. Some days, I'm in a fog about where one version of me begins and the other stops." He tugged his roll into two pieces. "I guess there's some crossover."

"Do you like the man who is part good and part mean?" He winced, and she felt bad for being so blunt.

"The pertinent question is, can you like a man with a day job that riles you, even if you also find him attractive and charming?" He brandished one of his broad grins, which brought her focus to his lips and her traitorous thoughts to what kissing him and being held in his warm embrace felt like.

"Who said I find you attractive?" The catch in her throat had to give her away.

"Your lips must have whispered that to me when we were kissing last night."

"Blue—" She spooned chili into her mouth like she was starving.

"You told me I could expect complete honesty from you," he said like a challenge.

She swallowed hard and set her spoon down. "Fine. I'm slightly attracted to you."

"Slightly?" One of his eyebrows lifted. "I doubt a woman who kisses a man like you kissed me feels only minor attraction for him."

"Give it a rest, will you? Besides, it's difficult to be attracted to a man who's divisive toward people I care about."

"Divisive?" He dropped his spoon into his bowl. "I tell the truth as I see it. Yes, I push an edginess that gets folks worked up. Would you rather I lied?"

"No. But isn't there a way to critique an artist politely, at least with a shred of compassion? And use some tact?"

"Certainly. But who'd listen if I said"—his voice turned sugary sweet and sarcastic—"Sally's seashore oil painting is the most disgusting thing I've seen! But let's pat her on the back, and she might do better next time." He took a long drink of his clear soda. "Even you must see that would never work."

"Even me? Thanks, Blue." She picked up her roll and nibbled on it, stewing. He might have a valid point, but she wasn't conceding. "Can't you recognize an artist's efforts and applaud that? Look at how respectfully you spoke about Kathleen's work."

"You asked me to be nice to her," he said smugly.

"Like you would do anything because I asked you to."

A lazy smile crossed his lips. Was he also imagining their kiss? How quickly her thoughts jumped to their time beneath the mistletoe. She shoved her partially eaten food away, her appetite gone.

"You want honesty?" His smile vanished, and he pushed his bowl forward, too. "You're comparing Kathleen's A-plus discussion with Gracie's C-minus yawn-worthy lecture. Those parallels are night and day." Was his podcast character and the real Blue crossing over now? "If I applauded every artist's effort, I would be out of a job. People return to my podcast episodes because I am bold and honest about how I perceive art. What I say are my opinions, and I stand by them!"

Before she could respond, Paul Cedars stepped up to their table, grimacing at Blue. "You're still in town?"

"Yes, sir." Blue glanced at the older man warily.

"I've got my eye on you." Paul jabbed his finger at him.

"Thank you, Paul," Sarah said. "Everything is fine here."

"Just making sure." He squinted at Blue again before trudging back to his booth.

"Why does he mistrust me so much? I didn't insult *his* art."

"And you'd better not. That outspokenness of yours is why people put up walls. Perhaps it explains why the mystery woman is gunning for you."

"It might at that." He reached for his bowl.

"Are you admitting you're wrong?"

"I wouldn't go that far." He ate a few bites of his food.

Sarah ate some more of her chili, not wanting it to go to waste, and listened to the sounds of laughter and visiting going on around them. Everyone else seemed to be having a wonderful time at the festival.

Blue linked their fingers across the table. "Thank you for letting us try again despite our differences."

She tugged her hand free. She hadn't agreed to anything other than eating a meal with him. "Do you have enough information about Lane's demo for your podcast since you didn't stick around for the whole thing?"

"Weren't we going to avoid discussing work?"

"Were we?" She gathered their mostly empty bowls and napkins into a pile. "If you want to ask Lane anything, call him. I'm sure he'll talk with you about his sculpture process."

"Thanks. But—" He clicked his fingers. "Did you listen to his presentation?"

"In between serving coffee and pastries, I did."

"Then why don't you come on my show and do a Q&A with me in the morning?" He grinned like it was a brilliant idea.

"Why would I do that?"

"You don't like how I assessed Gracie's paintings, right?"

"No."

"Then let's find out how you would review an artist's work. You have an opinion about Lane's presentation. Why not share your thoughts with my audience?"

"I'm not a public speaker." She preferred quiet interactions with patrons—not talking to thousands of listeners via a microphone and Wi-Fi and not sitting in a motel room alone with Blue. "I'm not comfortable doing a podcast with you."

"How do you know unless you try? It'll be a breeze. Come on. Be a pal," he said coaxingly.

"So, we're pals now?" Since when? Since they kissed?

"Aren't we?" He blinked slowly, gazing at her lips as if he were thinking the same thing.

"That other woman called you honey," she said, changing the subject. "Why?"

"I don't know. It felt creepy. I didn't like the feeling of being stalked."

"I can relate to that." Should she tell him about her experience? "I was kidnapped earlier this year."

"You were kidnapped? Sarah. I had no idea. Were you injured?"

"Not really." She'd worked through most of the emotional trauma by prayer and talking about it with Kathleen and Callie. "It was scary, but I try not to dwell on it. Why do you think that woman is following you?"

"That online personality gets me into trouble sometimes. Threatening mail, that sort of thing." He clasped her hand again. "You're sure you are okay?"

"Yes." She withdrew her hand again. "Shouldn't you go to the police?"

"Maybe." He shuffled on the bench like he felt awkward with the topic. "About being on my podcast?"

How would it be to chat about art with Blue on his show? She'd get to spend more time with him. And she could say positive things about Lane's work. "If I join you and you don't like what I say, remember you invited me to share my thoughts."

"Deal." He stuck out his right hand, and she shook it slowly.

Only later, while she was getting ready for bed, did she question her decision. Sue Anne's arrival would already make the next day emotionally charged. Now, she was going to be Blue's podcast guest?

Chapter Nineteen

Blue had everything set up and ready to go before six a.m. He arranged two chairs facing the microphone on the corner table, double-checked the volume control and USB hookups, and made sure the mic and headsets were working. All he needed was for Sarah to arrive and fill the airwaves with her lovely voice. He had to admit he was anticipating sparring with her a bit. She wouldn't mind a short debate about Lane's work, would she?

When the quiet knock came, he bolted for the door and opened it. Sarah entered carrying two to-go cups. "Welcome to my studio, such as it is."

"Thanks." She handed him one of the cups. "I thought you might need this."

"Definitely." He took a sip of hot coffee and sighed. "Thank you."

"Sure." Sarah removed her coat, her gaze flitting around the minimal space. Did she feel awkward being with him in such close quarters or about going on air?

He felt in a bit of a sticky situation himself. Even though he hadn't engaged well with Lane's talk, a few creative ideas were circling in his brain that would add drama to this episode. However, since Sarah had expressed disapproval of his shows, if he ramped up today's dialogue, would that be off-putting to her?

"It's almost time to start." He took another drink of coffee, savoring the flavor.

"Is this it?" Sarah nodded toward the corner table covered with electronics. "I thought it might be more ostentatious."

"I keep it simple for working on the road. However, the equipment is top-notch."

"I would think so." She clutched her cup so tightly her knuckles were turning white. "How will this work?"

"You're going to do fine." He smiled, trying to be reassuring. "I'll begin with my usual opening and introduce you as my guest expert."

"Expert has a nice ring to it."

"Yes, well." He shuffled his shoulders, feeling some tightness building. The possibility of Sarah taking offense or being mad at him following the show was causing him to have second thoughts. Had he made the right decision in asking her to join him on his podcast? Last night, his idea sounded so appealing.

"Do you celebrate Christmas?" Her off-topic question caught him by surprise, but with the holidays approaching, he understood why she asked.

"I don't avoid celebrating Christmas. But I think it should be enjoyed with family and friends." He waved his hand toward the left chair, inviting her to sit down. The clock was ticking. "I haven't spent the holidays with my grandmother in several years. What about you? Do you celebrate Christmas?"

"I did until my husband died." She sat at the front edge of her chair. "Then I was too disheartened to appreciate the joy of a baby being born in a manager or a host of heavenly angels singing glory to God in the highest."

"Right. And now?" He dropped onto his seat and handed her one of the headphones, wishing they had more time to share experiences, especially since she brought up her husband's death. But he had to get the podcast started.

"I'm more hopeful about the future. I feel ready to celebrate life again." The soft smile she gave him curled his toes. Did she mean she was feeling more positive because of him? *Man*, he hoped so.

* * * *

Sarah adjusted the headphones over her ears, her heart pounding like she'd run a mile. As Blue gave his opening remarks, her mind whirred with thoughts of how she planned to say positive things about Lane's artwork, even if Blue didn't like her one-sided view.

"Listen up, folks! Sarah Blackstone, the beautiful gallery manager from Basalt Bay, Oregon"—he winked at her—"is in the studio with me to discuss the work of local found-object sculptor, Lane Baxter. Welcome, Sarah." He tapped an icon on the computer, and the sound of handclapping followed.

"Thank you, Blue," she said after the background commotion subsided. She waited for his next segue.

"Why don't you tell us about yourself? What's your favorite part of working in an art gallery?"

"Oh. Um." Why was he asking about her? She was supposed to be talking about Lane. Blue spun his pointer finger, making a keep-talking gesture. "Hello. I'm Sarah Blackstone, the temporary manager of Paige's Art Gallery in Basalt Bay. My favorite part of the job is meeting artists and fans of their work." She took a quick breath. "It's an honor to assist locals and visitors with choosing works of art that will complement and enhance the styles of their homes."

"You speak quite eloquently about your job."

"Thank you." She appreciated his agreeableness but wanted to get to the important segment of the podcast. "Hearing Lane Baxter talking about finding unique pieces for his found-object sculptures and observing his demonstration was quite inspiring. It made me proud of him and all he has accomplished in his field."

Blue's eyebrows quirked. Was he surprised by her taking the lead? "How so?"

"I was impressed with his journey of searching for rare pieces of wood and metal to use in his art." Warming to her topic, she said, "Each finished sculpture he makes is like a treasure chest filled with history, art, rare parts, and his individualized touch. Lane also likes to use recycled products, making his sculptures mostly green."

"Really?" Blue frowned. "What if someone disagrees with the philosophy of a found-object sculpture being a treasure? What if they say roadside trash isn't art at all?"

"Excuse me?" Sarah gripped her chair arms. "Lane carefully searches for the perfect item to use in his art scheme. What you call trash might become someone else's masterpiece."

Blue pressed his lips together like he was fighting a grin. "Are you telling me if I were to dig through a heap of junk and gather nails, a shoe heel, buttons, a can, etc., and then randomly glue them together, I would have a work of art that a savvy connoisseur would pay hundreds or thousands for?" He tapped an icon, and the honking of a goose sounded.

"I'm not saying you can do all that, Mr. Paxton." She squinted a warning at him. She was here at his request. He'd better act hospitable. "The found-object sculptor, Lane Baxter, has a keen eye for discovering objects that work well in a home or office setting. His taste is impeccable."

"Impeccable?" Blue coughed.

"That's my viewpoint, anyway," she said dryly. "Aren't you always telling listeners that your point of view is what matters? Since you graciously invited me on your show to share my thoughts about Lane's work, I'd say my view is all that matters today."

"You've got me there. But, Ms. Blackstone, are you saying you doubt my artistic abilities?"

"Would you say you have an artistic eye, Mr. Paxton? Do you sympathize with artists? Empathize, even?" She was pushing it. Getting on Blue's bad side wouldn't help her cause or that of local artists. Still, she asked, "Are you an artist?" She knew he wasn't.

"I have a Modern Art and Communications degree. I've visited hundreds of galleries, museums, art shows, and exhibitions." He lifted his chin. "Even though I am not an artist, I have a good, if not exceptional, artistic eye."

Exceptional? Her temper flared before she could tone it down. "If you have such wisdom and enlightenment about artists, what about the human spirit that fuels them? What about allowing kindness and compassion to guide you as you highlight artists whose hearts bleed into their work?"

"Well, I, uh—"

"How can you know an artist's thoughts without taking their perspective into account?" Sarah barely took a breath. "Why not ask him what makes his heart pound as it does when he envisions a new creation? Why don't you inquire why the painter defied expectations and chose a complex color or painted a flower black? Why speak harshly about someone whose life's work is at stake when you have no idea what brought him to that point?" Heart pounding, breathing raggedly, she couldn't believe how fiercely she spoke to Blue with an invisible audience listening. *What have I done?*

She and Blue stared at each other for several seconds of dead air.

"The point is," she said when he didn't speak, "Lane inspired me by sharing how he seeks uncommon items to create projects that make us ponder their beauty, rarity, or even the piece's humor." Blue cleared his throat, but she kept talking. "He painstakingly puts pieces together, making shapes he's planned or ones that materialize as he uses his most creative energies. None of his artwork is thrown together. None of it is garbage!"

"I get your point." Blue glanced at his cell phone. "Well, folks. It sounds like I've invited someone to *Blue's Art Clash* with some opinionated art clashing of her own!" He tapped another icon, and a cymbal clanged. He shook his head like he couldn't believe how badly this had turned out.

Sarah's emotions plummeted. Had she overstepped? Offended him?

Blue skimmed a list of questions like he was trying to find his bearing. "How did the, uh, audience react to Lane's discussion?"

"Most were engaged."

"Didn't some leave before the session ended?"

"The ones who were interested stayed." Her feelings of loyalty for Lane rose up in her again. "Some even participated in creating a small found-object sculpture for themselves."

"I didn't notice that."

"Isn't that because you left early?" She gulped. She didn't mean to be unkind. "Otherwise, you might have found your true calling as a found-object sculptor," she said in a softer tone.

Blue stroked his brow and stared at the wall, causing more dead air. Then he asked some trivial questions about the festival and gave closing remarks. Sarah couldn't wait to escape the look of shock or hurt she'd seen in his gaze. While Blue was focused on his laptop and technical stuff after the show, she set her headphones on the table, slipped into her coat, and left without any goodbyes.

She was proud of how she stood up for Lane and his art. But maybe she shouldn't have voiced her opinion so boldly. Would Blue ever speak to her again?

Chapter Twenty

Much to Sarah's relief, a decent crowd attended the fourth art demonstration later that morning. Even though Jeff Parsons didn't bring a pottery wheel or a kiln, he'd prepared a colorful PowerPoint presentation and aptly explained the process of turning clay into a work of art. He brought samples of his pottery projects—bowls, cups, vases, and a cake stand—and invited attendees to come by his studio and spend time creating a bowl or vase for themselves, free of charge. "Through the hands-on experience, you'll better understand the pottery-making process and, hopefully, come to love it like I do."

Sarah was surprised that Blue even showed up. They hadn't interacted since he arrived, other than a nod when she dropped off a cup of black coffee at his table. He appeared more engaged with his laptop than Jeff's discussion. Was he bored with the presentation? Disinterested in pottery? Or was he brooding over this morning's podcast and what she said?

Should she apologize? He'd asked her to share her thoughts, which she did. However, she said too much about Blue's typical commentary instead of sticking to the topic of Lane's artwork. What should she do now?

The pottery lecture wasn't as inspiring or participant-friendly as the other demos had been this week. But Jeff's enthusiasm about his craft and the pleasure he got from making usable art convinced Sarah he had the heart of an artist. Did Blue see that? Or was he here only to find fault?

By his quick departure at the end, without talking to the artist or Sarah, she had her answer. At least he wouldn't be asking her to sit in front of a microphone with him again. But even that troubled her. Her desire not to ruin their new friendship prodded her to try to clear the air. She sent him a brief text.

Sorry if I overstepped.

There was no response.

She stayed busy all afternoon with customer inquiries and packing up purchases. But even with her busyness, her thoughts weren't far from the two people she felt some inner upheaval about—Blue and Sue Anne. While she alternated between worrying about Blue leaving town without talking with her and running into him at the festival and what she'd say to him, Sue Anne would arrive at the gallery within the hour. It had been thoughtful of Callie and James to offer to drive to Eugene and pick her up at the airport. Callie and Sue Anne were, no doubt, having a delightful time catching up during the trip back.

How would it be meeting her birth mom for the first time? They'd talked on the phone, so it wasn't like Sarah didn't know Sue Anne at all. Still, this meeting would be embedded in her thoughts and heart forever.

She still had unanswered questions about why her parents hadn't told her that she was adopted and whether her brother, Ryan, had known about it. Since her parents had passed away, and Ryan didn't answer the emails she sent inquiring about the adoption, she would probably never know. Perhaps some heartfelt conversations with Sue Anne would ease her concerns about the past.

Was there any resemblance between her and her birth mother? She hadn't noticed any similarities in the photos she'd seen of Sue Anne. Callie said she saw a familiar trait she should have detected sooner. What was it? Sarah's eyes or smile? Would she and Sue Anne have anything in common to discuss? Or would there be uncomfortable silences with both trying to drum up something to say?

She was in the kitchenette putting supplies in the cupboard when she heard the familiar jangle of the door. Was Sue Anne here already?

"Sarah?" It was Blue!

She rushed around the corner and found him standing by a café table, hands stuffed in his jacket pockets, hair wind-blown, and his gaze fixed on the window or the golden sunset streaming across the ocean. "Did you forget something?"

His disheartened expression tugged on her heart. "Uh, no." He pushed his glasses up his nose and faced her. "I got your text. Do you have time to talk?"

"I wish I did. But I'm expecting someone."

"Someone?" His eyebrows shot up like he thought she meant a guy.

"A friend, or rather, some friends are stopping by in a few minutes." She didn't want to discuss her life story with him. Still, she felt a need to apologize again. "Blue, I—"

"Are you upset with me?"

"About you asking me onto your podcast and then acting irked with me for standing up to you? I am a little annoyed about that." She smiled to soften her words, but her need for honesty felt like she was creating a wider gap between them. "I am sorry for speaking so strongly about my perception of your critiquing process. I didn't mean to be bold, brash Sarah!"

Blue sighed like her words brought him relief. "I was taken aback, is all."

"I've heard it's good to keep a man guessing." Some euphoria filled her when he smiled despite the initial awkwardness between them.

"Is that what you were doing?"

"Not really," she said truthfully. "But you came back here. That must be a good sign."

"Maybe." His shoulders lifted, then fell. "I don't know what I'm doing here. Other than I had to see you again."

"You won't be in Basalt Bay much longer, then you'll leave and forget all about me." Why prolong the agony?

"I won't forget you." His softly said words were like warm honey flowing over her. She would never forget him or his kisses, either.

"Still, our paths won't cross. I have a commitment tonight, so I can't spend time with you."

"I understand." He met her gaze with a yearning look before turning toward the door.

"I can't manage anymore complications right now," she said quietly.

"Is that how you see me?" He stood stiffly, his hand on the door-knob. "As a complication?"

"I don't want to get into how I think about you or what I con-sider a complication after our shared emotional podcast today." Her intake of air rattled in her throat. "But what I'm about to face super-sedes everything else right now."

"I didn't realize it was so serious." He pivoted back, concern etched on his face. "Are you okay?"

"I will be. But I have to get through this on my own."

His gaze shifted to one of Paige's paintings. "For what it's worth, my business partner loved the show. Alfie said we should try again and call it *Sparring With Blue*."

"I thought our sparring was a catastrophe."

"You and me, both. But you never know what will jive with an audience. I hope we can talk before I leave town." Then he was gone.

I hope we get to talk again, too.

Chapter Twenty-one

Sarah grabbed a damp cloth and wiped down all the tables even though she'd already done it earlier. Why did Blue have to come by and make her long for more time with him? Was he implying they needed to discuss personal things like a relationship before he left, or did he want to talk about how the podcast had gone? And why did his partner like the episode when it felt like a giant flop to her?

Sighing, she tried focusing on what she had to do for the next day's event. Lexi Ferris was going to present pencil sketching tips. Would a smaller crowd show up? Was Blue going to stick around and talk to her? He'd already been to four demos. It seemed likely he'd move on to another gallery soon. Still, she hoped he'd stay a little longer.

The gallery door opened, and the chime sounded. Sue Anne, a slim woman with grayish-blond hair, entered, followed by Callie and James.

"Hello. Welcome to Basalt Bay! I'm Sarah." She smiled at Sue Anne, and her birth mother smiled back.

"Hello. It's so good to meet you in person."

They shook hands, and she was glad Sue Anne didn't push for a hug right off.

"I'm happy for you both to meet finally!" Callie said enthusiastically.

"I've waited a long time for this." Sue Anne's hazel eyes shimmered with unshed tears. She didn't have Sarah's darker features, but her gentle smile and shining eyes were comforting and seemed almost familiar. Was Callie right about them having some similarities?

"Would you like some coffee or tea?"

"Haven't you shut everything down?" Callie glanced toward the serving counter.

"I have. But I don't mind getting a few things going again."

"We had drinks and munchies on the drive, so I don't need anything," Sue Anne said.

"Lots of food and drinks at the festival." James shuffled his feet like he was anxious to get going.

"So this is the gallery where you work?" Sue Anne gazed around the room admiringly.

"It's where I hang my hat on most days."

"It's lovely." Sue Anne strolled toward the far wall, her slim figure swaying like a leaf gliding in the wind. Sarah recalled Callie talking about Sue Anne and Paul dancing together as young adults. "You must be proud to work at such an inspiring place."

"Yes. That's how I feel! Paige entrusted me with its care while she's on childbirth leave. I'm honored to fill her shoes temporarily."

"And she is so pleased with your work." Callie turned toward Sue Anne, who'd come back to stand by them. "Wait until you see the mosaic Sarah made for the silent auction."

"I'm a beginner, but I hope to get more proficient at it." Sarah wondered what Blue would think of her amateur efforts. Given the chance, would he critique it harshly? Or say no one should waste their money bidding on it?

"She's being modest," Callie said.

"I look forward to seeing what you've done." Sue Anne patted Sarah's shoulder, leaving a warm spot where her fingers touched.

"I have to get over to our booth. No doubt, Paul is beside himself, doing everything alone." James tugged on Callie's coat sleeve. "Want to walk with me? Or are you coming over with the ladies?"

"We'll be over soon."

"Sounds good." James kissed her cheek. "I'll catch up with you later, doll." He winked, and Callie's cheeks brightened. Sarah's heart warmed to see the newlyweds acting so affectionate.

"Silly man," Callie muttered as he moved toward the door, his limp barely noticeable. "But he's mine, and I sure do love him."

What did Sue Anne think of her friend's dreamy-eyed gaze at James? Did she still miss her husband? Being widowed was something Sue Anne and Sarah had in common.

"How did sales go today?" Callie asked.

"Great. I sold seven pieces, including two of Lane's sculptures."

"That's fantastic! I'm glad the festival is helping business perk up."

"Me too." Sarah grabbed her coat and tote bag.

"I hope the silent auction greatly benefits our Caring Society," Callie said.

"Amen," Sarah whispered.

"Callie told me all about the ladies' group and their activities." Sue Anne glanced at Callie with a pleased expression. "What a great idea to band together and be a strong presence in each other's lives and the community."

"It makes you want to stay and be a part of it, doesn't it?" Callie nudged her arm. Was she pressuring Sue Anne to move to Basalt Bay?

A tight feeling stretched across Sarah's chest as she put on her coat. Whatever was going to happen between her and Sue Anne needed to transpire naturally—not because Callie was pushing them toward a mother-daughter connection of her choosing. She had half a mind to tell Callie that herself.

"I don't know about moving here." Sue Anne shook her head. "But if I lived here, I'd want to be involved with your group. It sounds like the perfect thing to help me feel useful again."

"Exactly. Even more reason for you to set up residency here."

"Callie—"

"Sorry. I'm just eager for us to be close again. I hope you'll be convinced to stay before your visit ends." Callie embraced her. "It's so good to see you, Sue Anne."

"You, too. But Sarah and I have a lot of catching up before I'd consider such a life-changing move."

Sarah exhaled a breath she hadn't realized she was holding.

"Eventually, you'll have to run into my rascal brother." Callie's eyes sparkled.

"Now, Callie. What Paul and I experienced was forever ago." Sue Anne set one fist on her hip. "I fell in love and married another man. We had a good life. I have no interest in stirring up anything with Paul. You understand that, don't you?"

"Well, I, uh—"

"If you asked me to come to Basalt Bay, hoping I'd have a romantic interlude with your brother, you are mistaken!"

"Even with how you two cared for each other?" Callie asked woefully.

"I used to feel many things I don't anymore. I thought I loved Edward Grant! Look how badly that turned out." Sue Anne swiveled toward Sarah. "I didn't mean having you turned out badly."

"That's okay. You can't help who you fall in love with, right?" Just like she couldn't help it if she fell for Blue, even if that was a big if.

"That's right." Sue Anne linked arms with her, and they walked toward the door. "I hope you'll let me hang around here so we can get to know each other. If I ask too many questions, tell me to stop." She sent Callie a faux stern look. "Unlike some people, I can let a matter go if I'm asked to."

"I like helping my friends live their best lives, that's all."

"Callie Weston! On the drive over, you mentioned Paul to me twenty times! I am content being single. I like my life as an independent woman!"

"Here, I thought I was holding in my enthusiasm."

Sue Anne and Sarah laughed, and Sue Anne hugged Callie. "You are a sweetheart for all you've done to look after my girl. I'm thankful the Lord led her to Basalt Bay."

"I'm grateful He led me here, too." Sarah appreciated Sue Anne's and Callie's comments about her, but she was ready to go to the festival and leave their nostalgic reminiscing behind. "Shall we head over to the festival? As James said, there's lots of delicious food to try."

And maybe she'd get the chance to see Blue.

Chapter Twenty-two

Blue passed several booths without seriously looking at any of the vendors' crafts, his thoughts rehashing his discussion with Sarah. She hadn't said she wouldn't talk with him—only that she had something important going on. Was one of the people she was waiting for the unexpected guest he'd overheard her talking about on the phone two days ago?

What if she was so upset about how the podcast turned out that she didn't want to see or talk with him? He chewed on that thought until he remembered how she'd told him if she ever wanted to say something to him, she would. He appreciated that kind of truthfulness in another person.

He also liked how Sarah apologized for being so fervent on his show. At first, he was surprised by how boldly she defended Lane's work. He rarely interviewed guests and always set the tone for each episode, so her taking the lead disarmed him. But then he recognized how courageous it was of her to take him on. Kind of sexy, too. He grinned. Surely, he'd get the chance to talk with her before he left for Seattle tomorrow.

"Hey!"

Hearing the gruff male voice, Blue whirled around. One of the older guys from the woodworking stall followed him. Paul, was it? "Did you need something?"

"I thought your time of flapping your jaw about the good folks of our community was over!" He thrust his finger eastward. "Road's that way, bub." *Bub again?*

"Now, Paul." James came alongside him. "This is Sarah's friend."

"Troublemaker, more like. Sarah is better off without him."

Blue bristled, ready to verbally defend himself, but then his shoulders sagged. He had to agree with Paul's rude but true assessment. Sarah was better off without him. However, was he better off without her? He'd known her for only a few days, but what would his life be like without her? He hated the thought of finding out. "I didn't mean to offend anyone putting on this festival. Sarah told me about the proceeds benefiting local women in crisis and what a great cause it is. That kind of support for women and single moms means a lot to me."

A supportive group like that would have made a world of difference for his mom and their family thirty years ago. After Dad left, Mom struggled to make ends meet, and even though Gram sent weekly allowances and pitched in with rent money, food was scarce. Mom finally built up the courage to go to the church they attended and ask, or beg, for assistance, but a grumpy church guy said they couldn't help any woman who abandoned her husband.

Abandoned. A bitter taste in his throat made Blue want to gag.

Mom had come home sobbing, and he discovered the reason only when he heard her talking about it on the phone to Gram. After that, he wouldn't go near that church or any other religious building. He'd carried a grudge about it for a long time. Maybe still did.

"Is something wrong? Are you okay?" James asked in a kind tone.

Blue swallowed with difficulty and faced the men. "Do you ever listen to my podcast?"

"Not much." Paul crossed his arms. "It disgusts me."

"I'm sorry to hear that." Blue had endured his share of criticism about his podcast, so he didn't try to defend it. "Would you like to come on my show and discuss your art? You could tell folks why you like woodworking and how you got started." Wasn't that what Sarah encouraged him to do—dig deeper into the heart behind the artists' work?

Paul staggered backward. "Why would we do that?"

"No, thanks." James shook his head.

"You could describe how smoothing a piece of maple or cedar feels in your hands." Both men squinted at him like he'd lost his mind. "If you invited people to your booth during the podcast, some would come. And even if I exposed how you shouted at me to leave town"—he glanced sternly at Paul—"if I gave your work a nod, some art enthusiasts would line up to see it." Although he sounded a bit pompous, it was true.

"Like you're that powerful?" Paul clenched his fists at his sides. "When did you say you're leaving town?"

"Simmer down." James patted his shoulder.

"Don't tell me to simmer down!" Paul rolled up the sleeve of his right arm like he was getting ready to belt Blue in the nose. "I'm about to throw this smart aleck on his ear."

"Some folks would buy your wares just because I discussed them on my podcast," Blue continued as if the man hadn't insulted him. "You might double or triple your sales."

"You hear that, Paul? We could double our sales!"

"I don't believe it."

"All you have to do is sit in front of a microphone for a few minutes and talk about your process for making something out of wood." He tried to make it sound easy.

"I wouldn't do that in a million years." Paul turned his back to Blue.

"Okay. If that's how you feel about it." He started to walk away, then paused. "Are you certain you don't want to be on my podcast?"

"I think it's safe to say we aren't the type to do that." James shrugged apologetically and then smiled at a customer. "How can I help you, ma'am?"

"Any chance you know where Sarah is?" Blue asked.

"Nope." Paul shuffled into the woodworking stall.

"Will you tell her I'm looking for her?"

"Nope."

"Thanks, anyway." He strolled down the row of booths, barely noticing the homemade quilts, candles, and jams. One stall displaying pastel paintings caught his eye, but he didn't stop for a closer look. He wanted to find Sarah—needed to see her. But if he caught up with her, what would he say? *I'm crazy about you. Want to kiss under some mistletoe?* Yeah, right. *In your dreams, Blue.* He sighed.

He thought about his call to Gram earlier and how he'd updated her about how things were going in Basalt Bay. He hadn't mentioned Sarah. But talking with his grandmother improved his mood. And her saying she was praying for him touched his heart.

He'd also taken care of paying his fine this afternoon, so his speeding ticket wasn't hanging over his head. There wasn't much holding him in this town besides his need to talk with Sarah.

It was nearly time to return to the motel and contemplate what he would say about Jeff Parsons' unimpressive presentation on his next podcast. He had nothing against the idea of turning clay into a beautiful, valuable piece of art. But why couldn't the potter have drummed up something creative to say about his craft? What was he trying to say through his art? *Anything?*

After today's blasé lecture, if he skipped tomorrow's sketching demo and headed north, would anyone miss him? Would Sarah?

Chapter Twenty-three

"That was delicious!" Sue Anne wiped her lips with her paper napkin. "I haven't enjoyed tacos that much in a long while. I loved the spicy kick."

"Bert is a terrific cook." Sarah ate a couple more bites of her chicken taco with extra cheese and hot sauce and listened to the holiday music coming across the sound system.

"Do you know who I saw at James and Pauly's booth?" Callie gave Sarah a significant look.

"Who?" She glanced over her shoulder but didn't see anyone unusual.

"Blue Paxton!"

"Blue was there?" Sarah's heart hammered in her ears. She took a more extended look toward the woodworking booth without spotting him. "What was he doing?"

"I think I'll go find out." Callie shoved away from the outdoor table. "I'll be right back."

"Who's Blue, and why is Callie agitated about him?" Sue Anne asked.

"Have you ever heard of Blue Paxton?"

"No. Would you like to tell me about him?" Sue Anne smiled as if she were eager to hear everything about the man in Sarah's life.

"He's a guy I met on the job this week—an art critic and podcaster." There wasn't any reason to mention that she'd already kissed him or how much she enjoyed it. Hopefully, the heat of a blush spreading up her cheeks didn't give away her feelings.

Sue Anne nudged her arm. "And you like him?"

Her first impulse was to deny it, but her usual honesty kicked in. "Yeah, except he can be opinionated and rude."

"And handsome?" Sue Anne grinned.

"That too."

They shared a laugh.

"Do you want to find love again, Sarah?"

"I do." Suddenly she wanted to be more transparent with Sue Anne. "I've grieved and bawled my eyes out for Jeremy and what I lost when he died. But I feel ready to move on and live my life to the fullest—not to say Blue is a candidate for love, marriage, or a future with me."

"I understand. It's been two years since you lost your husband, right?"

"Two years that have seemed like ten, and at other times, a month or days."

"I get that. How does Blue make you feel?"

"Alive. Womanly. Romantic." Sarah smiled and sighed at the same time. She glanced around the area to see if he was anywhere nearby. *Where are you, Blue?*

"Well, then." Sue Anne's eyes sparkled. "I'm happy for you."

"We're not a couple. It's just—"

"He makes you feel things you haven't felt in a long time?" Sue Anne nodded as if she understood.

"Yes. Very much."

"I think admitting you're ready to move forward is a sign of your healing and hope for whatever lies ahead." Sue Anne smoothed her palm over the back of Sarah's hand. "Take it slowly and enjoy love again, hmm? If not with Blue, then with someone else who makes you feel happy."

After the kiss they'd shared and their time spent together, Sarah couldn't picture herself being with or kissing anyone other than Blue. But even how she'd come to feel so strongly about him so quickly was a mystery that boggled her thoughts and made her want to pray about it much more. Ready to turn the spotlight away from herself, she asked, "What about you? I heard what you said about Paul."

"It's odd how past mistakes can bother you decades later. I'm not saying you were a mistake, but my choices?" Sue Anne groaned. "I let people bulldoze over me—Edward, Mom, medical professionals, even Callie. I wish I would have stood up for myself."

"Did you love Edward? Was he nice as a young man?" Sarah had difficulty imagining that since he was in prison.

"I remember him as being charming." Sue Anne glanced toward the booth where Callie was talking with James and Paul. "Back then, I was fascinated with any man's attention. Paul was handsome and a good dancer. Who knows why I wound up with Edward?" She turned away from the booth, nearly bumping over her water. Had her gaze met Paul's?

"Did Paul love you?"

"It was so long ago, it's hard to say. We had fun together." Sue Anne got a far-off look. "Then Edward swept me off my feet. After my parents found out about my pregnancy, they sent me away to have you in secret. I had to live with a stern aunt. What a nightmare!"

"I'm sorry." Sarah felt sympathetic for the young woman in that situation. Thankfully, modern culture was more accepting of a single young mom keeping her baby, and of grandparents pitching in to help.

"I wished I'd found a way to keep you." Sue Anne's smile wobbled. "I always knew a dark-haired darling was living her best life and carrying part of my heart in hers somewhere. I prayed I'd get to meet you eventually."

"And here we are." The meeting Sarah had dreaded and dreamed about was going better than she'd anticipated. She was grateful Sue Anne was a kind and thoughtful person and hoped she had inherited those traits.

"Thank you for this." Sue Anne clasped her hand, then released it.

"I'm glad we got to meet." Sarah stacked their paper plates and cups. "Discovering my relationship with Edward Grant, however, was disheartening."

"Callie filled me in on his crimes. I can't believe the man I thought I loved turned out like that." After a pause, Sue Anne asked, "You have two more brothers, right?"

"Yes. And two sisters-in-law, a baby nephew, and more extended family who I dearly love." Sarah picked up the paper products and tossed them in a nearby garbage can. "Shall we check on Callie?"

"Sure." Sue Anne strolled beside her. "Getting to know each other will take time, but I hope someday you will include me in the list of people you dearly love."

"That sounds good to me, too. And I hope the years ahead will be happier for you."

Sue Anne gave Sarah a quick hug. Hanging out with her birth mom and even receiving her hug didn't make Sarah feel like she had a new mother, but Sue Anne seemed like the type of person who might become a good friend.

"You're never going to believe this." Callie met them, slightly out of breath. "Blue tried to get Pauly and James to go on his podcast and talk about their wood products. He said they'd sell more goods if they did." She snorted like she didn't believe a word of it.

"He might be right," Sarah said.

"What?" Callie's eyes bugged.

"Blue Paxton knows about art and how to get people stirred up about it." Sarah touched Callie's arm. "I think it's a great idea. I hope the men will go along with it."

"How can you say that?" Callie clutched her chest.

"Don't get upset," Sue Anne said soothingly. "Let's hear her out."

"Blue is a well-known podcaster. Whether he speaks negatively or positively about an artist, there's more interest in that person's artwork in the following days. Sometimes that equates to greater sales." Sarah shrugged. "With art, you must accept all the opinions, good and bad."

"I don't think James and Pauly are ready to find out if the man's views matter a nickel." Callie squinted back toward the guys. "Can you see James being interviewed by a city slicker who hates our town?"

"Not really."

"Me either." As if that settled it, Callie dusted her hands. "Let's head inside City Hall, where it's warm. I want to introduce Sue Anne to Bess."

"Oh. I, uh—"

"It will be fine." Callie drew Sue Anne toward the tall building, and she acquiesced.

Sarah followed them, peering at each of the booths they passed, searching for Blue. Had he seen her when he spoke with Paul and James? Was he avoiding her? She told him she didn't have time for him this evening, but she really wanted to see him.

As she was about to enter the front doors of City Hall, a commotion drew her attention, and she paused. To the right of the building, a redheaded female was yelling something in a slurred voice, and a crowd was gathering around her. Wait. Was she talking about

Blue? Curiously, Sarah followed the group to find out what was going on.

"Blue Paxton is a dirty, lying cheat! You can't trust anything he says! He's lower than a rattlesnake. As dirty as they come." The woman laughed raucously. Was she the same person who'd called Blue honey at the gallery? "He's a rat in sheep's wool. A venomous spider waiting to strike. A lowdown, stinking skunk." She belched noisily.

Why were these people interested in a stranger's rantings and rude behavior? A few had their cell phones aimed at the woman, recording her, which probably meant this was going to be bad publicity for Blue. How could Sarah deflect their attention away from the spectacle this woman was making? Had anyone called the deputy?

"Hey, everyone!" She moved through an opening in the crowd and got in front of them. "Why don't you all head back over to the booths and check out the great items our vendors have made? Be sure to try Bert's delicious tacos. I had some, and they are amazing!" A few bystanders nodded. Others met her gaze with defiant looks.

"Blue Paxton is a fraud!" the woman shouted. "Don't listen to him."

"Can I help you with something?" Sarah turned toward the redhead. "Do you need assistance? Or an Uber ride to a motel?"

"This isn't about you, gallery woman. So back off!" She flailed her hands. "Just wait until that clueless podcaster sabotages you, too!" What was she talking about? "You'll rue the day you met the villainous blue shark! Blue Paxton stinks!" Why was she verbally attacking Blue?

And where was he?

Chapter Twenty-four

"Hello," Blue answered as soon as he saw Sarah's name cross his phone screen. "I've been looking for—"

"Get over to City Hall now!" she shouted above the noise of a disturbance.

"What's going on?"

"Just get here as fast as you can!"

"Okay. I'm on my way." Was Sarah in danger? He took off sprinting toward the most prominent building in town. Nearing City Hall, he cut across a grassy section where a cluster of people were congregating around someone who was shouting. Was that female yelling something about him?

"Blue Paxton thinks he's such a genius about art?" She was talking about him! "He knows nothing! He's a horrible podcaster who exaggerates the truth. He's a heartless cad who ruined her!" *What?* Who did he supposedly ruin? He drew closer, trying to see who it was and find Sarah.

"I'm sorry for whatever you're going through." That was Sarah's voice! "You must have been hurt or experienced a tragedy to feel this badly. If only you'd—"

"Stay back! You know diddly-squat about me."

Blue peered around some people, trying to spot Sarah. There she was! The redhead was swinging her arms, nearly hitting her. It was the same person from the gallery! And she looked like the one who tried to run him off the road! What should he do? Call 911?

"I don't know anything about your situation, but I'd like to help," Sarah said. "Do you want to get a cup of coffee and talk?"

"Why would I want to talk with you? I don't want coffee. I want justice!"

Justice for what? Blue tried to figure out who she was and if he'd seen her before, other than during the road rage. Had he ever had dealings with her at a gallery? Why did she sound so vicious toward him? Was she an outraged podcast follower? A relative of some artist he'd critiqued?

"Why don't we sit down, and you can tell me all about it?" It was nice of Sarah to try to intervene and bring calm to the situation, but it might be dangerous.

"I don't want to sit down. These people need to hear me. It's my view that matters!"

Blue cringed at the familiar words. He navigated around the crowd, looking for an opening to get closer. How was he going to draw Sarah away from the woman discreetly? Some people had their cameras pointed at her, which meant there'd be more negative publicity in his near future. But all that mattered right now was making sure Sarah was safe.

"There he is!" someone shouted. Like a choreographed dance, about twenty cell phones pivoted toward him, and he groaned.

"It's Blue Paxton!"

"Is what she says true?"

"Do you have a comment?"

He wanted to yell at them to put their phones away and stop recording this unnewsworthy event. Videotaping public figures was part of the social media frenzy he hated. Nevertheless, Sarah had called for him to come promptly, and he was here. "Are you okay?" he asked as he approached her.

"I'm okay." Yet her gaze flicked nervously toward the group. "We need to disperse the crowd."

"We should leave. Come on." He clasped her hand. "The deputy can take care of this."

"You!" The ranting woman lunged forward, fists raised. "You are a beast!"

Blue tugged Sarah behind him, not releasing her hand. He wasn't going to let anything happen to her.

"You are a horrible person. You should be ashamed of yourself!"

"Why are you yelling things about me? Who are you?"

"Don't play the innocent, Blue Paxton." She said his name like it was foul, then took a swing at him. He lurched backward, bringing Sarah with him. "He harassed my grandmother!" She jabbed her finger at him, her eyes rolling like she couldn't see straight. "He caused her to be put in the hospital."

"I did no such thing!"

"Liar! He's worse than a mouse, er, louse." She laughed like her confusion was hilarious.

"I think you should go somewhere and sober up," someone in the crowd shouted.

Others agreed. "Yeah, that's right."

"Go sleep it off!"

"Get a life!"

"I think Blue Paxton should resign. He's a coward and a deceiver!" The redhead's nostrils flared. "Turn yourself into the cops."

"I don't know what this is about, but it isn't the place to air your disgruntlements." Blue took another step away, keeping Sarah close to him.

"After what you did to my grandmother, you think you're guiltless? You think you'll get away with your wrongs?"

"I don't know what you're talking about." He'd never harassed anyone's grandmother. He loved and respected Gram too much to do anything like that.

"How dare you injure my family and not own up to it!" Her family? Who was she? "You deserve to rot in prison."

Murmuring and comments spread through the crowd, becoming a rumble. This woman's unfounded accusations were breeding discontent, and Blue didn't want that happening in front of cameras. "We have to go, Sarah."

"I think we should stay and get some help for her."

"Help?" the woman screeched. "Like Blue Paxton paying me a million dollars to shut my mouth?" She was trying to cause him trouble! "How about him admitting he was wrong and telling the world he adores my family's gallery?" Her family's gallery? So this was about his podcast!

More grumbling traveled through the group.

"I'll show him what folks in Basalt Bay think of creeps like him."

"Let's throw him in the bay. That'll teach him."

Blue needed to get Sarah away from the mob. For both their safety, they needed to run now. But before he could lead her away, she released his hand and faced the crowd. "Everyone, please put your phones away and go enjoy the festival! Isn't that why you came here tonight?" Some bystanders lowered their phones while others continued aiming theirs. "Please stop recording and show some compassion for this woman." A few more lowered their phones as a siren approached.

"Let's leave this to the police." Blue tugged on Sarah's arm. "We've got to go."

"Yeah, run, weasel!" the redhead yelled.

"Don't you want to find out what this is about?" Sarah asked quietly. "Shouldn't we stay and discover who she is and why she seems so broken?"

Broken? An attention-seeker or someone out to extract money from him seemed more likely. "Not with video cameras pointing at us. I have to go." He hated leaving her here, but he couldn't make her come with him if she was determined to stay.

"Go then." She smiled faintly. Did she wonder if what the woman accused him of was true? "I'm going to stay and help if I can. It's the least I can do."

He bit back a groan and nodded, almost agreeing to stay, too. But then, contemplating Alfie's reaction and how all this was going to affect their business, he whispered goodbye and reluctantly slipped into the crowd and out of the spotlight. However, the woman's allegations rang in his thoughts all the way back to the motel.

They were still accusing him as he packed his bag.

Chapter Twenty-five

Sarah prepared for work the following day, only half-heartedly listening to *Blue's Art Clash* due to Blue's bland critique of Jeff's pottery presentation. She'd never heard him speak so disinterestedly before. He sounded more like a teacher giving a mild evaluation of a student's project than a critic giving a thoughtful analysis of an artist's work. His lack of censure and criticism, and the absence of his usual bells and whistles, made Sarah nervous. Had Blue pre-recorded the episode and then left town?

Please don't leave without saying goodbye.

An ache spread through her at the thought of never seeing him again. It wasn't like she knew Blue all that well, yet she longed to know him better and understand him better. She had enjoyed the times they talked and laughed together and would never forget their kisses beneath the fairy lights and mistletoe. Would he leave and forget about her? She groaned. Why did she care so much? Why was she having such strong feelings about never seeing someone with whom she disagreed philosophically and maybe morally, anyway?

She put on some rosy lipstick and blush, pondering the things that happened last night. She'd felt for Ingrid's emotional troubles when she shouted those accusations against Blue. She didn't believe what she said, but something had caused her to lash out like that. Sarah paid close attention when the woman told Deputy Brian her name was Ingrid Glasser and she was the granddaughter of Evelyn Glasser, an artist from Bend, Oregon. Sarah was familiar with the older woman's abstract oil paintings, although she'd never seen any of them in person.

Why was Evelyn's granddaughter in Basalt Bay, railing against Blue Paxton? Hadn't he critiqued the Glasser Gallery a while back? She faintly recalled hearing one of his episodes based in Bend. Was it possible he criticized Evelyn's work too severely? Was that why Ingrid was angry with him and why she talked about her grandmother having been hospitalized? Thinking of her claims reminded Sarah of a few of her own frustrations with Blue.

Shouldn't he have stayed and talked with Ingrid if he bore even a tiny amount of blame for saying something rude or insensitive about her grandmother? There must have been something he could have said to reassure her, even if he didn't want to assume any liability. Yet he'd rushed off into the night. Although, with all the phones aimed at him, she couldn't blame him too much. He was a public figure, and someone had recently tried to run him off the road. While the group around Ingrid didn't seem violent, who knew how serious things might have gotten if she kept shouting? In her inebriated state, Blue couldn't have a rational conversation with her, anyway.

Still, seeing anyone in such emotional anguish brought back thoughts of the pain Sarah experienced when she was homeless, alone, and feeling lost in the world. Did Ingrid feel that way last night?

Sarah grabbed her sweater and tote bag and hurried down to the first floor. Today was the last day of the winter festival, which included a sketching demo by Lexi Ferris and the silent auction winners being announced this evening. Would Blue attend any of the festivities? Or had he left without a backward glance? That possibility hurt, but she couldn't dwell on it. Too many tasks awaited.

Lord, please give me Your peace, no matter what the day holds.

Her phone buzzed, and she answered without checking the screen. "Hello?"

"It's Sue Anne."

A little disappointed that it wasn't Blue, she greeted her birth mom pleasantly. "Is everything okay?"

"Everything is lovely. Callie is planning a full schedule for me." Sue Anne chuckled like her friend amused her. "I thought I'd check with you and see if there's any time for us to meet up today."

"I work until five." Sarah strode across the living room, heading for the kitchen. "We could get dinner at the festival again."

"Let's do that. Any chance I could meet Blue?"

Sarah coughed. "I don't think so. He may have disappeared."

"Disappeared? Heavens."

"Not like that. I mean, he may have left town."

"Ah. I see." After a pause, Sue Anne said, "Callie says we're attending a sketching lesson at the gallery this morning. But I'm not one speck artistic!"

"Just come and enjoy the final demo." Sarah's phone vibrated. Was it Blue? "I'm sorry. I have to go. We'll talk later, all right?" She ended the call and opened the text.

I can't make it to the demo. I'm sick. Sorry. Lexi

Lexi Ferris wasn't going to attend her own demo? Oh, no! Why was she only now informing Sarah? Had Blue's negative critiques scared her off? Or was the artist really too sick to attend? Sarah moaned. Why did this happen today? Who could she get as a substitute on such short notice? Should she cancel? That would be a terrible way to end the festival!

She grabbed a banana and a small yogurt from the fridge and tucked both into her tote bag as a thought came to mind. Blue had asked Paul and James to talk on his podcast and they refused. Would they discuss their woodworking journey at the gallery? Maybe if she enlisted Callie's help? "We have an emergency!" she said as soon as Callie answered her phone.

"Are you hurt?"

"No. Lexi can't make it today because she's ill."

"I was looking forward to learning more about sketching."

"I'm sorry. But would you ask James and Paul if they'd come and chat about their woodworking projects?" Sarah cringed. "I know it's a big ask."

"Me?"

"You're James's wife and Paul's sister. Who better to influence them than you? Please?"

Callie huffed. "You know Pauly doesn't like me butting into his business."

"Yes. But I'm desperate." Sarah had to devise a solution that didn't involve her being a one-person band. How could she host the gathering, serve coffee and rolls, and present an informed demonstration, and about what? They'd already had a mosaics session, the only art she could discuss on the fly.

"Why don't you call Pauly, and I'll talk to James?"

Sarah almost debated Callie's suggestion, but resigning herself to it, agreed. "That's fair. Thanks, Callie." Paul might be more understanding toward her than he would be to his sister, anyway. Ending the call, she thumbed through her contacts for his number.

"Yeah?" Paul answered, making chewing sounds like she'd caught him eating.

"This is Sarah."

"Hey. I heard about the debacle at the festival. Sounds like Blue got himself into some hot water with a lady." Paul guffawed like it was a romantic situation that had gone wrong.

"It wasn't like that. She accused him of—" She sighed. "Never mind. I have a favor to ask."

"What's that?"

"Would you and James be willing to come to the gallery this morning and discuss how your dreams of building things out of wood have come true?"

"Who would want to hear anything about that? Did Paxton put you up to this?"

"No! This has nothing to do with him. Lexi Ferris can't do her sketching demo." Sarah spoke quickly, not giving him time to disagree. "She's sick, so I'm asking, no, I'm begging you to share something inspiring about woodworking at the gallery. Please?" A loud clatter in the background made her jerk. "What was that?"

"I'd better check on Piper. I'm watching her today."

"Oh. I didn't know." Her heart sank.

"That's why I can't yack at the gallery, even if I was interested in doing so, which I'm not!" He ended the call abruptly.

Ugh. What now? She didn't have a Plan C for her Plan B.

However, Callie's efforts paid off better than hers. An hour later, James was setting up wooden items around the demonstration table at the gallery. *Thank you, Callie!* Only, the way he alternated between tugging on his tie and stealing glances at the group, mainly consisting of ladies, he was nervous about being dragged into this.

"You can have as many cinnamon rolls and coffees as you'd like," Sarah told him.

"I don't get many sweets since I married Cal." He stroked his chin, eyeing the cinnamon roll on the plate she held.

"Do you still like your coffee black?" She set the snack on the table beside some wooden slats.

"Yes."

"I'll get you some." She pivoted toward the kitchenette, then paused. "I really appreciate what you're doing, James."

"You're welcome. Callie wouldn't hear of me not helping." His face darkened like he was embarrassed to admit that. "You couldn't get Paul to come over?"

"No. Sorry."

"He has his reasons." He leaned forward, muffling his voice behind his hand. "Between you and me, I think he's sort of hiding."

"He said he's watching Piper."

"Oh, he is. But with Sue Anne staying at our place, things are a mite testy between him and Callie."

"I get it." Sarah glanced over to where Callie and Sue Anne were chatting. She'd wondered how Paul might feel about Sue Anne staying with James and Callie.

"I love Callie to the moon and back, but she and Paul have to work out their stuff. I stuck my oar in before and learned my lesson." He continued unloading wooden objects from a cart he'd hauled in. "I think he's watching Piper as a reason to stay home."

"Sorry if my asking you to do this caused any problems between you guys."

"Not to worry. Sue Anne and Paul haven't seen each other in too long for any sparks to be there, anyway." James shrugged dismissively.

"Are you sure about that?" She nodded toward Sue Anne. "You never know how these things might turn out."

"Come to think of it, I'd be tickled pink to see my buddy as happy as me." Grinning, he held up his hand with his wedding ring on it.

The chairs filled quickly. So did coffee, tea, and cinnamon roll orders, which kept Sarah busily scurrying between the kitchenette and the gallery. She was glad for the good attendance on the last day.

Partway through James's talk, she spotted a familiar black-haired man sitting on the far side of the group, head down, staring at a legal pad. So Blue hadn't left town! Their gazes met, and zings of lightning raced through her middle, creating longings for them to reconnect and kiss as they had beneath the mistletoe.

A shadowed look crossed his face. He shook his head and lowered his gaze. Was this goodbye, after all?

Chapter Twenty-six

When Blue's gaze met Sarah's across the crowded gallery, hope churned in him for about twenty seconds before burning out like a flame in the wind. Had she read yearnings in his gaze he couldn't act on? Did she imagine a forever with him that included marriage, parenting, and growing old together? Those ideals sounded more appealing to him by the hour, but he wouldn't make promises he couldn't keep. That would be unfair to her—and him.

He broke their locked gaze, trusting she understood what he was trying to convey. The next time he looked her way, the sparkle in her eyes had faded, affirming she'd received his message. A painful ache in his chest felt like a foreboding of how deeply he was going to miss her, how connected to her he already felt.

But how could their two worlds coexist? Sarah found help and redemption in a small town, while his family experienced tragedy in such a place. His mom had been the brunt of cruel gossip and a lack of support in the small church and tiny community where they lived thirty years ago. If it hadn't been for Gram, they wouldn't have survived after Dad's abandonment and pursuit of his only true love—chasing and photographing sunsets.

Dad's mistress hadn't been a woman wearing skimpy clothes and red lipstick—but the art he couldn't live without. Why did that bug Blue so much after all these years? Why did angst churn inside him every time he drove into a small town, passed a church, or saw a photograph or painting of a sunset? Would he forever feel trapped by remembering the bad decisions of one man and a few grumpy church guys?

Would he make better decisions, given the chance? He knew one thing. He wouldn't put a wife and family through the same neglect his father had, which was reason enough not to get involved with Sarah or make promises to her that he couldn't keep.

But did he want to live his whole life without a woman's companionship or a family to call his own? Was his podcast and lifestyle worth that sacrifice? He stared at his blank legal pad. He should be listening to James.

His thoughts drifted to Ingrid Glasser, the woman who had shouted accusations at him. Thanks to Alfie, Blue knew her name and connection to Evelyn Glasser now. While "coward" and "deceiver" played in his brain like a country song he despised, he also heard himself blaming his father for the same things over the years. Like father, like son? *Man.* He hoped not.

Sarah, *beautiful Sarah*, had expressed compassion for Ingrid last night, while he had been annoyed, resentful, and wanted to flee from Ingrid's critique of him. What did that say about his character, his integrity? He groaned inwardly. Sarah's words replayed in his thoughts. *"What about allowing kindness and compassion to guide you as you highlight artists whose hearts bleed into their work?"* He'd judged his dad and the men who hadn't helped his mother as lacking any compassion or kindness. What about him? When was the last time he showed those qualities to anyone? He ran to Sarah's aid last night. Did that count?

He let out a long sigh and tuned back into James.

The older man's fingers tugging at the knot of his tie and the occasionally stuttered word revealed his discomfort in public speaking. However, the more he shared about making objects out of wood, the more confident he sounded. James picked up a few rough-hewn boards—cedar, pine, hemlock, and birch—and explained about what each one was best suited for. He talked about the patience it took to sand boards to a satin finish, the complex staining process, and how much he enjoyed it all.

Besides the interruption of someone ordering coffee from the café, the audience appeared engaged. Blue was tempted to order something, mainly to talk with Sarah. But then he'd wind up saying something flirtatious to get her eyes to sparkle at him again.

He jotted a couple of notes. *James and Paul didn't start their business until their senior years. Friends their whole lives. Live across the street from each other. Work in a shed in one of their yards. Store furniture in a bedroom, utilizing the space they have. First-time vendors.*

A cup of steaming coffee materialized in front of him. He glanced up, meeting chocolaty dark eyes that made him feel like he was drowning in them. "Thanks," he mouthed. Sarah nodded once and returned to the other side of the room. The space between them felt like an ocean.

Is this how he wanted their relationship to end? What could he do or say to make things right and still be able to hop into his Stang and drive to the next gallery? Alfie had arranged a northern tour, and Blue needed to stick to his plan. But everything within him urged him to take Sarah in his arms and promise to stay as long as she wanted him to.

He sipped the hot drink, grateful she brought it to him.

"Who hasn't picked up a piece of wood and run their fingers over it? Maybe even got a sliver?" James chuckled like he was thinking of a memory. "My love of woodworking started when I was a kid, helping my dad. Throughout my adult years, I worked on other people's projects. But now I have the time to devote to the craft I love." A wide smile crossed his face, making him look younger. "Between marrying the woman I adore"—he winked toward Callie—"and making wood products, my dreams are being fulfilled.

"If you ever get the chance to build something out of pine or oak, I hope you'll make it into a lovely item for your home, like this frame." James lifted the edge of a distressed wood picture frame, which reminded Blue of the one he'd seen on Sarah's mosaic at the silent auction. "Or maybe you'll be more ambitious and try an end table." He motioned toward a glistening square wooden table. "Whatever you decide to create, with some work and determination, you can do it and be happy with the outcome. Thank you for listening to my chat about wood and life and how they fit together." He dipped his head, and the audience clapped.

Blue stuffed his legal pad in his computer bag and joined in the applause. He stood, planning to leave promptly without any emotional farewells.

"Leaving so soon?" Sarah's voice stopped him before he reached the exit.

He swallowed hard and met her gaze with effort. "My time here is up."

"So it seems." She pressed her lips together like she was keeping herself from speaking or crying. Picturing her being sad as he drove away tugged at his heart, and the desire to kiss her increased. They'd known each other for such a brief time, yet in the hours they'd spent hanging out, he felt so drawn to her. He longed to get to know more about her and give them a chance to form a relationship. Yet the road and his podcasting career called to him like a melody he couldn't ignore. "I wish things were—"

"What?" she whispered.

"Different. I hate leaving like this."

"Then don't."

"I can't stay." *Someday, maybe. Not now.* "I'm sorry." He clasped her hand even though he didn't have the right. He gazed into her eyes more fully, wishing they were alone for a romantic goodbye, if that were possible now. "I'm glad to have met you."

"I'm glad to have met you, too." Her lips wobbled around the smile she was bravely attempting.

Saying goodbye was a part of his life and job, so he should have been good at it, but he wasn't. He hated saying goodbye to Sarah and what might have been if he were willing to park his convertible in Basalt Bay indefinitely.

"Goodbye." He released her hand.

"Goodbye, Blue."

Walking out the door was one of the hardest things he'd ever done. He didn't trust what he'd do if he looked back and saw her crying or gazing at him yearningly. So he remained resolute and jogged out to his Stang.

Chapter Twenty-seven

At the eager expressions of friends and neighbors gathered around the silent auction tables, Sarah felt pride in her work and all the effort the ladies had done to pull off the festival. A little sadness filled her, too. The event was over, and Blue was gone.

"Place your final bids!" Sue Taylor called. "Ten minutes until the auction ends and winners will be announced!"

"Then our festival is in the books." Callie shifted in her chair. "I wasn't keen on it happening at first. Now, I'm sad to see it end."

"Me too." Sarah glanced at Callie and Kathleen, seated to her left, and Sue Anne, on her right. "It's been a fun and challenging week."

"On to the next exciting thing, right?" Kathleen asked optimistically.

"Sure." What did Sarah have to look forward to? The holidays and being with family were special times, but she had hoped Blue would be part of that, too. She'd begun wishing for more to happen between them, even dreaming of spending Christmas and New Year's Day together. Even if she shouldn't be wishing for a long relationship with a man who would always be chasing his dreams elsewhere, she was. How would she continue as usual when she ached from missing him, and he'd only been gone half the day?

"What's wrong?" Kathleen asked.

"I'm feeling some melancholy. I'll never forget everything that took place this week."

"And the man you were swooning over?" Callie grimaced like she found the idea distasteful.

"Let's not tease her," Kathleen said. "We're glad Sarah found happiness with a handsome man like Blue Paxton."

"Aren't there handsome men in Basalt Bay she could fall for instead of him?" Callie asked.

Sarah glanced away, uncomfortable with how they were talking about her as if she wasn't even there.

"You mean someone of your choosing?" Sue Anne leaned forward, peering around Sarah.

"Don't think I haven't been looking!"

"Callie!" Sarah exclaimed. "You'd better not be matchmaking for me."

"Nor me." Sue Anne wagged her finger at her.

"Fine." Callie harrumphed. "I won't. I have been trying to do better about minding my own business and focusing on the Lord's grace. But sometimes I can't help myself."

Sarah exchanged a glance with Sue Anne, and they both chuckled.

"Have you been trying to steer people together, Callie?" Kathleen's eyes twinkled like she was getting some enjoyment out of this conversation.

"I haven't been meddling like I used to, but I've been tempted to intervene a smidge. It's a bad habit." Callie's face flushed. "Did you notice my brother isn't here tonight?"

"I did." Kathleen nodded. "Does that have anything to do with you?"

"It might." Had Callie pressured Paul about talking with Sue Anne?

A baby cried somewhere in the room, and Sarah felt a twinge in her chest, a longing. Distracted from the conversation, she imagined herself holding a baby who would cry like that, and she'd comfort it and soothe its fears or needs with her mother's touch. In her thoughts, the baby with Blue's beautiful eyes gazed up at her, and a magical moment passed between them—mother and child. She sighed.

With Blue's leaving, the hope of a relationship or a family with him was ebbing away. They hadn't discussed marriage or a future together, yet she'd foolishly allowed thoughts of them as a married couple to live in her mind and heart. She inhaled deeply, then exhaled a slow breath.

"Are you okay?" Sue Anne asked.

"I will be." She met her birth mom's gaze, thankful for her sensitivity. "I've been wishing for something I might never enjoy, that's all."

"Such as? If it's too private, I apologize for asking."

Despite the congestion and chatter in the room, Sarah clasped Sue Anne's hand. "When I hear a baby cry, I—" She couldn't finish. A bond of friendship had been forming between them, but was she ready to share her deepest thoughts?

"When you hear a baby cry, what happens?" The older woman's gaze held warmth, compassion, and a little prompting.

Sarah really did want to be vulnerable and honest with her. "The deepest wish of my heart is to carry a baby in my body, birth it, and be a mom for its whole life." Once she started, the words came easier. "I've desired motherhood for such a long time, and even though I'm nearing forty, I don't want to give up on that dream." She dropped Sue Anne's hand, covered her face, and fighting a sob, shuddered. "I don't want to lose my hope about it. I don't want to give up on having a family."

"Then don't." Sue Anne slid her arm over Sarah's shoulder, tugging her closer until their heads rested against each other. "I used to experience similar yearnings."

"You did?" Sarah sniffed a couple of times.

"Yes. I wanted you and what I'd lost. I grieved terribly." Sue Anne lowered her arm but kept it loosely across Sarah's back. "My husband and I couldn't have children. I thought my body might be grieving, too."

"I'm sorry."

"It's in the past. Still." Sue Anne stroked some hair back from Sarah's cheek like she might have if she were ten. "The desire to hold my child, and my grandchild, hasn't disappeared."

Tears welled in Sarah's eyes, and she was comforted by their mutual empathy and caring. "The Lord has healed so much in my heart. I'm sure He will hold me through whatever comes my way, even if I never get to experience being a mom." She touched her palm to her chest. "I'll keep trusting and believing that God is good, no matter what, but heartache hits me right here sometimes."

"I know, honey. Don't give up. Your dreams of having a child may yet come true." Sue Anne clasped her hand and squeezed it gently. "I'll be praying with you about it."

"Thank you. I have a lot to look forward to. I've found a new life in Basalt Bay, have close family and friends, and a job I love."

"And Blue?"

Hearing his name softly spoken, more tender emotions rose up in her. "I don't know if I'll get to see him again, but I like him a lot."

"Did you tell him how you feel?"

"Not really. Well, a little." After the way they kissed, he had to know something about how she felt. "I started to hope he—" She shrugged. She'd said enough.

"Any chance he'll come back?"

"There's always a chance." But she wouldn't live as if she expected his return, holding her breath at every jangle of the gallery door.

The baby she'd heard before cried again in a cute infant wail. Sarah listened closely, and then she saw who was jostling a baby near the back of the crowd—Paige! *Aww.* Paige was here with Baby Addie. And right beside her, Paisley was holding Tanner.

Sarah stood quickly, tugging Sue Anne's arm. "Please come with me and meet Paisley and Paige and their babies! Paisley is Judah's wife. Her sister, Paige, is my boss."

"I'd love to meet them." Sue Anne stood but looked concerned. "Don't we need to stay close to hear the auction winners?"

"We'll be able to hear from over there, too." Sarah waved toward Paige, and she returned the gesture.

"Okay. If you're sure."

Sarah drew Sue Anne to the far side of the room. "Hi, you guys," she said as soon as they were close enough to the other ladies. She hugged Paisley and Paige and then introduced them to Sue Anne.

"I'm so glad for the chance to meet you." Paisley smiled warmly.

"Me too. Oh, my. Look at these sweet babies," Sue Anne cooed. "They look like twins!"

"Almost," Paisley said. "They are only six weeks apart."

"Miss Adelaide is being fussy tonight!" Paige said, but her pride in her baby was evident in her tone and adoring smile.

"May I?" Sarah held out her arms to her nephew.

"Absolutely." Paisley handed her Tanner. "He needs some Auntie Sarah time."

And I need him. She held the baby close, enjoying the comforting feelings of carrying a little one she was related to. Maybe someday, her child and this guy would run on the beach, cousins playing together. She met her birth mom's gaze, and a look passed between them. Sue

Anne understood her emotionally, and that was a powerful feeling for her to experience with another person.

Thank You, Lord, for sending Sue Anne into my life. And thank You for this baby who I dearly love.

"The winner for item number three is"—Sarah listened to Sue Taylor's voice, since number three was her mosaic—"Blue Paxton!"

What? Blue bid on her artwork and won? A squeal bubbled in her throat, and she met Sue Anne's gaze, grinning. Only Sue Anne wasn't smiling. "What is it?"

"I was hoping I'd win!" she said mournfully.

"You bid on my mosaic also?"

"Of course. I wanted my daughter's mosaic for myself."

"Aww. Thank you."

"For what?"

"For being here and wanting to buy my mosaic. That was very nice of you."

"Oh, sweetie." Sue Anne lightly touched her cheek. "I want to take a part of you back to North Carolina with me."

Did Blue want to take a part of her with him, too? Would he keep her artwork tucked in his suitcase?

Maybe then, he'd never forget her.

Chapter Twenty-eight

After Blue shut off the light in his Seattle motel room and tried to get comfortable, his phone vibrated on the bedside table. He'd been on the phone with Alfie for an hour, rehashing all that happened in Basalt Bay, and listening to Alfie lecture him on never going to another small-town gallery again. He was exhausted, ready to sleep, and didn't want to communicate with anyone else. But what if Sarah was texting him? He sat up, grabbed his phone, put on his glasses, and read the screen.

Blue Paxton, congratulations! You have won Item 3 in the Basalt Bay silent auction.

He won Sarah's mosaic? *Yes!* The tightness he'd been feeling eased from his shoulders. A smile spread across his mouth.

But now that he won Sarah's art, what was he going to do with it? If he hauled it around in his suitcase and displayed it in every motel room where he went, her work might get lost or damaged. He could have the mosaic shipped to Gram. She would love it, and he'd occasionally get to see it. If the time came for him to explain his feelings about Sarah, Gram would appreciate it even more. Decision made, he tapped in his credit card information and her address.

With the details completed, his euphoria faded. He ached with the loneliness of missing Sarah and wanting to talk with her. He'd never questioned his nomadic lifestyle nor felt so lonely before now. After four days in Basalt Bay, would he ever have the same fulfillment in his work and traveling again? *Sarah, Sarah. What have you done to me?*

His first stop on his northern tour was Seattle, followed by Spokane, where he'd critique several galleries before heading to Montana. Alfie had a lineup of events planned, keeping him hopping between galleries, museums, and art shows for the rest of December. Hopefully, the busy schedule would keep negative publicity concerning Ingrid and the Glasser Gallery at bay. Even so, the woman's name conjured up negative feelings in him.

During his brief time in Bend, Oregon, three months ago, he critiqued Evelyn Glasser's work and other artists' pieces in the Glasser Gallery. On his podcast, he'd expounded on how he wasn't impressed with the art he'd seen there and the pitfalls of family-run galleries. His typically blunt critique had obviously gone over poorly with the Glassers, namely Ingrid.

Sighing, he rested against the pillows and closed his eyes, but his mind churned. What happened after his podcast that caused Evelyn's health problems? Did it have anything to do with something he said? For her to have been hospitalized and the business to have plummeted because of his podcast seemed highly irregular and suspicious. In his experience, the opposite usually happened. Listeners were more inclined to be interested in the artist's work. He hadn't set out to sabotage anyone's livelihood or health, especially not someone's grandmother. He wasn't that heartless, despite what the online gossip said.

When he thought about Gram and how he wanted her to be safe and healthy, he understood Ingrid's protectiveness toward her grandmother. But he didn't condone her ferocious rage. She'd gone too far in chasing him down along the coastal highway—he was confident she was the one who followed him that day. What if she had crashed into him and caused a tragic accident? He shivered, imagining his Stang sliding off the road into the sea with him inside.

His phone buzzed and he glanced at the screen. Gram? He sat up quickly and turned on the light. "Gram? Are you okay?"

"I'm all right. It's you I'm worried about. Where are you? And what's this nonsense about a scandal?" So she'd heard about Ingrid venting against him?

"It's nothing." He pinched the bridge of his nose. "I'm sorry you were worried. I'm in Seattle, Washington."

"I'm glad you're all right. When are you coming home for a visit?"

"Home" sounded inviting. Gram's warm tone and appealing offer soothed some of his loneliness. "It's good to hear your voice, Gram."

"And yours. You should call your grandmother more often!"

"You're right. I should."

"Are you seeing someone?"

Why was she asking that? But then, wasn't Gram always asking him such questions? He decided to indulge her. "There is a woman in Basalt Bay who I like."

"Really?" Gram swallowed noisily. "Can you tell me about her?"

"I'm not sure if anything more will happen between us."

"Grandson—"

"You must have heard about the woman from Bend who's causing me some grief. Which one do you want to hear about?"

"The woman you like sounds more interesting than the one my neighbor, Barb, said attacked your good name with expletives." Gram huffed. "I received three prank calls tonight."

"What?" Blue jumped to his feet. "You received prank calls? From whom?" Who had his grandmother's phone number?

"Some woman called, pretending to be your girlfriend."

"You've got to be kidding me!"

"Now you say there's someone up the coast you like?"

"Yes. But Sarah would never call and say such things."

"Sarah, hmm?" Gram's tone softened.

"Yes. Explain about the calls, please. What did the woman say?"

"Other than being your girlfriend?" Gram made a disgruntled sound. "She asked where you were and where you were going next. She wanted personal details about your life, but I could tell she was digging for dirt."

"What did you say?" Blue clutched the phone and strode to the window. He wouldn't put it past Ingrid to try to trick his grandmother into talking about his past. He didn't want any news stories spreading on the internet about his mom and sister's fatal accident. Or about his father's demise while attempting to photograph a sunset off a cliff over the Pacific.

"I didn't give her any family history or anything personal about you. Don't worry. Your grandmother is smarter than that woman thought!"

"Yes, you are." Blue took a long look at the parking lot through a narrow slit between the paisley curtains, searching for a black SUV. Some green Christmas lights flashing around the office window cast an eerie glow over his Stang. "Thanks, Gram."

"Now, can you tell me about Sarah?"

"All right." He sat down on the bed and leaned against the headboard. He thought he'd talk only about Sarah's work in the gallery. But soon, he was telling Gram all about their first meeting when he hugged her accidentally, a few of their humorous interactions, the podcast episode he invited her to, and about their unexpected kiss beneath the mistletoe. Gram was so easy to talk with that it all came rolling out.

"Is she the same one from the podcast?"

"Yes." He grinned.

"I knew it!" Gram said. "Even when you sounded annoyed, you were polite with her. I thought you must have feelings for her.

Bartholomew, why did you leave Basalt Bay without settling things with her?"

"I'm on the road all the time. What do I have to offer her?" *I don't want to be like Dad.*

"You! That's what you have to offer!"

"You have to say that. You're my grandmother. But thanks." He shuffled his shoulders. "My career takes me all over the western side of the country. I don't have the time or devotion it takes for a relationship. And not for a family."

"Stop making excuses!"

"Gram—"

"I know you, grandson. You love them and leave them so nothing deeper ever comes of your acquaintances." Her voice took on the parenting tone she'd used when he was an adolescent and made foolish mistakes. "When are you going to stop doing that? You're forty years old! I'd like to hold my great-grandchild before I die."

He wished she wouldn't mention his lack of kids and her eventual death in the same sentence. Besides, he'd given up on the hope of experiencing everyday family life and wasn't ready to give up his career. "It would never work."

"Never is a long, lonely time."

"Don't I know it?" The hollowness of spending his life alone, living in sparse motel rooms, and being without Sarah for the rest of his life weighed heavily on him.

"Go back to her. Your happiness is worth whatever it takes to win her heart."

Whatever it takes? What if he checked out and hightailed it back to Basalt Bay at first light? He gritted his teeth. What good would that do if he couldn't figure out how to make a relationship work? Besides, he had commitments he couldn't cancel. "I have a full December schedule."

"Schedule be drowned in the sea!" Gram said dramatically. "You're always on the run."

"I chose this lifestyle. I happen to like it!" At least, he used to before he met Sarah.

Five years ago, he and Alfie had plotted out a phenomenal career, which included crazy roleplaying, on-the-go traveling, and delving into the art world in a way Blue loved. But he had never considered the toll it might take on his personal life or what would happen if he became seriously involved with someone. Now, he was questioning everything. Remembering everything.

"The woman who called implied she was more than a girlfriend and very close to you."

"Not true!" Blue raked his fingers through his hair.

"In fact"—Gram paused—"she says you are her baby's daddy."

"That's not possible!"

"And she wants compensation."

"Unbelievable! It's all lies!" He grabbed a pillow off the bed, hurled it against the headboard, and the whole structure shook.

"Blue?"

"Sorry. I feel awful that you got dragged into this. Hang up if she calls again."

"I will. But why is she claiming to be my great-grandchild's mother?"

"It's nonsense. A ridiculous prank call. Um, just pray about it, and me, will you?" It was the first time he'd asked her to pray for him in ages. He didn't know why the request fell from his lips so easily this time.

"My dear boy, I will continue praying for you, and I'm going to pray for Sarah."

"Thank you. If you get any more calls like those, let me know. Okay?"

"All right. But when do I get to meet your lady friend?"

"I don't know if that will ever happen." Although, his heart beat fast at the idea of introducing Gram to his "lady friend."

"I want to meet her. Will you please introduce us?" she asked coaxingly.

He sighed. "Someday, perhaps."

"I'll take that as a yes. Love you forever, grandson. Stay safe."

"You, too." He thought of something else. "Hey, Gram? I'm sending you a gift I got in a silent auction in Basalt Bay." Sarah's name would be marked on the packaging, so there wasn't any reason for him to try to disguise it. "The artist's name is Sarah Blackstone."

"As in your Sarah?"

If only. "We'll talk again soon." Blue ended the call knowing his grandmother had questions he wasn't prepared to answer.

But her promise to pray for him and Sarah gave him a sliver of hope.

Chapter Twenty-nine

In the days following the winter festival and Blue's departure, Sarah spent as much time as she could with Sue Anne. Despite chilly winds, they took long beach walks, talking about their lives and learning more about each other. They ate their evening meals together. And at Sue Anne's request, Sarah showed her the basics of mosaic art. Sue Anne said she wasn't artistic, but she seemed to enjoy the experience as much as Sarah did. With each passing day, she felt closer to the woman who'd birthed her and sensed a deeper connection between them.

Blue hadn't called or texted, and she didn't reach out to him, either. She longed to talk with him and find out how he was feeling during their absence from one another. Did he miss her like she missed him? She'd had a couple of dreams about him—one where they were kissing and one where they argued about a painting. Even in her sleep, she seemed conflicted about whether to love him or disagree with him.

Had he received her mosaic? If so, what did he think of it? She pictured him holding her work in his hands, critiquing it. *Garish colors.*

Unrealistic shadows. Amateurish work. How would he judge her, given the chance? *Fascinating? Alluring? Good kisser?* She almost laughed. Then she thought of a few other assessments he might make of her and groaned. *Unremarkable. Stubbornly choosing a small town. Too honest.*

She lifted her cup of hot coffee to her lips and savored the flavor of Bert's coffee. Bert's Fish Shack had great coffee, almost as good as hers. *Almost.* She smiled.

Sue Anne sat quietly across from her as if sensing her introspection. Sarah was thankful for the chance to share one more meal with Sue Anne before she trekked back across the country. What would it be like without her or Blue to help fill her days? With the holidays approaching, the gallery would be busy. Still, she'd miss Sue Anne and their unhurried conversations.

They had attended church on Sunday, and Sue Anne and Pastor Sagle seemed to hit it off. Sue Anne said they were discussing becoming pen pals. How weird would that be if Sarah's pastor and her birth mom fell in love? If Sue Anne spoke with Paul during the week, Sarah didn't know about it. Maybe that part of the past was better off left in the cobwebs of yesteryear. However, if Sue Anne were to move here, would she be interested in Pastor Sagle, or would her old flame with Paul be rekindled? What were the chances of a senior-citizen love triangle happening in Basalt Bay? Sarah stifled a snicker.

She had continued listening to Blue's podcasts, mostly to satisfy her curiosity about where he was going next. She heard rumors that Ingrid spent only one night in the Basalt Bay jail before being released. Some fans reported seeing her in Seattle. Would she follow Blue to Spokane? A video recording from the night Ingrid ranted about him in front of City Hall had gone viral, causing his podcast ratings to shoot up. But why would a drunken woman's whining be popular with viewers? And why should Blue get positive press about it?

Sarah exhaled a long sigh.

"Are you okay?" Sue Anne smiled sympathetically.

"Yeah. I wonder if I should stop listening to *Blue's Art Clash*. Hearing Blue's voice and not knowing if I'll see him again is hard." Tension tightened her neck and shoulder muscles. "I don't know why I waste my time thinking about him."

"Yet you do?"

"Yet I do." She sighed again, annoyed with herself for not emotionally letting him go.

"Are you in love with him?"

Was she? Sarah glanced around the noisy diner and found Maggie Thomas and Miss Patty, some of Basalt Bay's notorious gossips, staring back at her with matching expressions of curiosity. She shrugged. *I thought I might be in love with him. Was it only infatuation?*

"Never mind. You don't have to answer that," Sue Anne said. "What would you think about a getaway?"

"A getaway? Where to?"

"North Carolina. Why don't you visit me there?"

"You know that Paige is counting on me to keep the gallery running during her parental leave, right?" Sarah wasn't ready to take a trip away from Basalt Bay yet, either.

"Sure. But how about when it's over?"

"Possibly. Does this mean Callie failed at convincing you to move here?"

"Believe me, she tried." Sue Anne stirred her broccoli-cheese soup, a whimsical expression on her face. "Basalt Bay holds a sea of memories for me. Your being here makes it enticing to pack my bags and move west." She clasped Sarah's hand for a moment. "I'm so grateful for the chance we've had to spend time together. I'd like to extend that longer if I could."

"If you moved here, it would be okay with me." Sarah meant that. "Not to pressure you, but would you consider moving here and being a part of my life in Basalt Bay?"

"Oh, Sarah." Sue Anne's eyes filled with tears. "I have considered it and am open to pondering it some more. I'm glad to hear my visit has been okay with you."

"It's been more than okay." Sarah dipped a sweet potato fry into ketchup and thought of one more thing she'd like to say. "You could stay at the project house if you wanted to."

"Bess mentioned that also." Sue Anne had shared how well their chat went and how thankful she was for clearing the air about the past with Bess. "I have another question for you."

"All right." Sarah wiped her lips with her napkin.

"Let's say I moved to Basalt Bay, and then you married Blue—"

"Sue Anne—"

"Seriously, if you two got together, what then? I wouldn't want to sell my house and move all the way back here only to lose you again."

"Blue lives on the road." He wouldn't move to Basalt Bay even if he fell in love with her, which he probably wasn't going to do. "I enjoy my life here and plan to stay."

"But what if your love for each other made it impossible to live apart?"

"I don't think that's going to happen." *No matter how much I'd like it to.* "Basalt Bay is my forever home. Callie, Kathleen, Bess, Lola, Teal, and whoever God sends to the project house are my family. I will stay close to them for the rest of my life. It's a decision I've already prayed about and made."

"I respect that, but what if you get married?"

Sarah leaned closer to Sue Anne, keeping her voice low. "If I'm blessed to fall in love again, it will be with someone who loves small-town life like I do and wants to be with me more than he wants to be anywhere else." As she said the words, she knew they disqualified Blue from being that someone.

Chapter Thirty

"There are rumors," Alfie spoke nasally during a phone conversation following Blue's last podcast from Seattle.

"Rumors?" It was the second week of December, and Blue hoped to convince Alfie to alter his schedule so he could drive south of Oregon to find warmer weather and avoid the snowfall in Spokane. Then he'd also have the chance to stop in Basalt Bay and find out how things stood between him and Sarah. He hadn't gotten her out of his mind, and he didn't want to. Unfortunately, his business partner was evading every request he'd made to cancel his tour. "What are the rumors about now?"

"Her." *Ingrid?* "She's back."

"In Seattle?" Blue's heart rate shot up even though he'd imagined Ingrid at every location in his tour. Would she follow him east as some subscribers had suggested? The news outlets were reporting hazardous driving conditions along I-90 East. An intentional collision wouldn't be too tricky along an isolated stretch of road in Idaho or Montana. Would Ingrid take advantage of such an opportunity? "Do you have proof she's here?"

"Not in Seattle," Alfie said slowly as if speaking to a child. "In Basalt Bay."

"Why didn't you say that right off? Why is Ingrid Glasser there?"

"You tell me." Alfie cleared his throat. "She's either trying to hurt you or cause our enterprise trouble."

What if Ingrid tried to do something against Sarah to get back at him? Was she in danger? "You have to cancel the rest of my trip! If there's a chance Ingrid is planning to hurt or intimidate people I care about, I won't go any farther east."

"I'll call the police in Basalt Bay, but I'm not rescheduling."

"Alfie, you have to! I am going back there today. I'm the one she's after. Let her do her worst to me—not Sarah!"

"Why the sudden concern about that gallery worker?" Alfie asked in a scoffing tone. "Is she the same one you argued with on the podcast?"

"Yes."

"Are you two dating?" Alfie's voice reeked of derision.

"Sort of." He couldn't say no. But would Sarah consider them dating when he'd left without promising to see her again and hadn't called or texted?

"Does Ingrid know about your attachment to Sarah?" Alfie snorted. "According to my well-paid sources, she's already there, so your heroic rescue attempt would be too late."

A knot formed in Blue's stomach. Was Alfie paying someone to follow Ingrid as a protective measure or to fuel social media chatter and get more publicity? What if Alfie was using Ingrid to stir up trouble and increase the podcast's ratings? What if he was behind the phone call Gram received? Would he go that far? If so, he was crossing an ethical line! And if Ingrid was bent on ruining him by doing something to Sarah, Blue had to warn her and do everything he could to keep her safe. She didn't deserve any of this! "Cancel my shows. I mean it, Alfie. I am going to Basalt Bay!"

"Blue, buddy. Don't do anything foolish." Even the sleazy way he spoke sounded like he hoped Blue would do something irrational or stupid, and then he'd leak the news about it. "Keep in touch." Alfie ended the call abruptly.

Blue groaned. How far was his business partner willing to go to make money and boost ratings? The way Alfie pushed him to be edgier and blunter in his critiques had, at times, chafed. But he had learned to stuff down his concerns and accept that he had to do some disagreeable things on the podcast to maintain their success. In the Glasser case, would he have spoken as arrogantly and have been as pushy if Alfie hadn't badgered him to dig deeper for something dramatic to discuss?

Sighing, Blue threw the few items he'd removed from his suitcase back in. He couldn't blame Alfie entirely for his online conduct. He was responsible for what came out of his mouth—and his heart, according to Gram. He wanted to make *Blue's Art Clash* successful, too. However, he would never purposefully inflict pain or personal harm on anyone, including Ingrid's grandmother!

How many times had Gram warned him about being too prideful? How many conversations had she encouraged him to be kinder, much like Sarah tried to do? Yet repeatedly, he brushed it off and savored the exhilarating feeling of his rise in popularity and monetary rewards.

He groaned, and a desperate prayer burst from him that felt startling yet soothing. "God, protect Sarah. Don't let Ingrid do something that would hurt her or break the tender ties that have begun to form between us." He needed to express his feelings about the life he'd been leading and how his heart had turned cold and bitter. But right now, only one thing prodded him to pray.

Lord Jesus, please protect Sarah! I care for her so much. I haven't spent much time talking to You lately, but I'm asking You to keep her safe and help us determine if we have something lasting and worth fighting for. He gnawed on his inner cheek, pondering the cost of such a prayer.

Then he packed his bags and equipment into the Stang, checked out of the motel, and let the car warm up for a few minutes before hitting the road. While he waited, he tapped Sarah's name on his phone screen. Her voicemail came up, and he hated not getting to speak to her. "This is Blue. Sorry to miss you. I want to warn you that Ingrid might be in Basalt Bay. She could be dangerous. Please, be careful." He didn't tell her he was coming back. "Stay safe."

Hopefully, she'd heed his warning, and God would be watching over her.

Chapter Thirty-one

"Do you have any Gracie Parker paintings?" A woman with short, curly black hair, darkly tinted sunglasses, and a twangy voice asked before closing time. Why was she wearing such dark glasses on a cloudy afternoon in December? Something about her seemed familiar and made Sarah uneasy.

"We have a few of her watercolors. Come this way." She led the woman to a corner of the gallery where Gracie's paintings were.

"Ever since I heard Blue Paxton's atrocious critique, I've wanted to purchase some of Gracie's art to show my support and sympathy for her." Her twangy voice didn't sound like the woman who had shouted about Blue near City Hall, but her angry tone sure did. Was this Ingrid in disguise? She was the same height and build. "Don't you think he was out of line?"

"I'd rather not comment about that." Sarah gestured toward the paintings, trying to subdue her concern. "Here they are. They've been going quickly."

"Only three? What a shame!" The woman tugged on her hair, revealing a thin line of red above her forehead. *She's wearing a wig! She has red hair like Ingrid!* Heart pounding, Sarah backed up.

"These are magnificent! Why did Blue Paxton talk so disparagingly about them? Other than throwing mud at another artist, what was his point?" The woman cleared her throat harshly. "The man is a menace to the art world! If I were wealthier, I'd buy all three. That would show Blue Paxton what I think of his churlish review!" No doubt about it, this had to be Ingrid!

"You could do that over time." Sarah tried to sound professional despite her rising anxiety. Why was Ingrid here? "Gracie is a prolific artist who makes new pieces regularly. If you want—"

"What I want is to sully Blue Paxton's name like he sullied hers! Gracie deserves vindication. Anyone on the receiving end of his criticism does." Was she talking about her grandmother or her? Sarah opened her mouth to say something in Blue's defense and then thought better of it. "Are you so hoodwinked by Blue that you can't defend the artists who have entrusted their art into your care?" Ingrid's twang was gone now, but her agitation came through clearly.

"We all have a right to our opinions, whether publicly expressed or not." Sarah took a few steps toward the café, trying to put distance between her and the other woman.

"Are you defending that wolf in sheep's clothing?" Ingrid followed her, her shoes clomping against the floor. "He's a dirty liar!"

Sarah faced Blue's accuser. "He has a right to voice his opinion, like you have a right to yours."

"He doesn't have the right to be cruel and antagonistic, does he?"

"You mean like you've been doing?" Sarah dared to ask.

"I am nothing like him!" Ingrid thrust out her arms. "I don't profit from people who are trying to reach patrons with their artwork. He benefits from spouting ugly remarks and listeners applaud him. His coffers are full while galleries languish. It's revolting!"

"Are you talking about your family's gallery?"

"I don't know what you're implying. You must not want to make a sale."

Sarah doubted she'd come here to buy anything. Her phone vibrated, but she couldn't risk checking it. "Are you interested in purchasing one of Gracie's paintings? It's closing time."

Ingrid gazed longingly toward the trio of watercolors. "I can't decide which one to choose."

Sarah's phone vibrated again. "Excuse me." She dodged into the kitchenette, saw a voicemail message had been missed, and scanned a text from Blue. *If Ingrid comes by, don't engage with her.* Too late! *I'm worried about you.* It was nice to hear he was worried, but now she was more nervous about Ingrid being here. With Blue's warning in mind, she stepped into the café seating area and gripped a rung of the first chair she came to. "Have you decided yet?"

"Do you know who I am?" Ingrid marched over to the table and stood opposite Sarah, her lips curling.

"Ingrid Glasser." Sarah scanned the path to the door. If Ingrid tried anything, she'd make a run for it.

"You're smarter than I thought. Where is Blue?"

"I have no idea."

"I don't believe you! I saw you two kissing at the festival!" Ingrid slapped her hands on the table. "Why would you make out with a man who has artistic blood on his hands? A man who's ruined artists' lives?"

Sarah clutched the chair tighter, imagining herself swinging it if she had to.

"You are as guilty as he is! You deserve—"

"That's enough!" James entered the gallery, setting off the door chime. "Are you all right, Sarah?"

"Yes." She ran over to him. How had he known she needed help?

"I was just leaving." Ingrid lifted her chin high.

"Perfect timing, then." James slid his arm over Sarah's shoulder. "Otherwise, you'd be here when the gallery manager gives her statement to Deputy Brian."

"You are going to regret this." Ingrid squinted harshly at Sarah and marched toward the door. She paused before exiting. "If you continue seeing Blue, he'll make your life miserable. Ask his previous girlfriends. Ask my sister!" She slammed the door on her way out, causing a few things to rattle on the walls.

"Thank you." Sarah hugged James. "How did you know I needed a friend?"

James doffed his derby hat. "I followed up on a call."

"From whom?"

"Who else?" His eyes twinkled.

"Blue?" Had he reached out to James about her?

"He was beside himself with worry. Said you weren't picking up or answering his texts."

"Because she was here." Sarah shuddered.

"I figured." James strolled around the gallery like he had all the time in the world. "Blue seems to care about you a great deal."

"Did he say that?" Hope sprang up in her.

"Not exactly."

"Oh." She sighed. "He's probably concerned with how Ingrid will harm his business." That sounded a bit harsh, so she asked in a softer tone, "How did he know your number?"

"I gave him one of my business cards at the festival."

"I see. Hey, would you like some coffee while I finish cleaning up?" And maybe he'd stick around in case Ingrid returned.

"Some tea would be nice. Callie has me sold on the stuff."

"You've got it." While she prepared a cup of Earl Gray and wiped down the counters, she thought about Ingrid's accusations. What had she meant about asking her sister about Blue? Was she implying her sister was one of his past girlfriends?

James took another lap around the gallery and peered into the bathroom. Afterward, he stood at the counter, sipping his tea and sighing like it was the best drink he'd ever tasted. "Would you consider displaying some locally-made wood products here?" His wide smile gave him a boyish look. "A few small items?"

She smiled back at him. "I'd have to run it by Paige, but considering your partner in this woodworking operation is her dad, I think she'll agree."

"That's what I was thinking, too." He raised his cup in a faux toast. "Paul and I could check on you and our products from time to time and make sure everything is okay."

"Like my personal protectors?"

"Something along those lines."

"That's nice of you, James. Thank you."

"Thank Callie. It was her idea." He winked. "I happen to agree with her."

Sarah loved Callie and James and so many others who'd embraced her as part of the Basalt Bay family. How could she ever leave this place she called home?

Chapter Thirty-two

Blue drove through Basalt Bay at eight p.m., fighting the urge to speed through the sleepy town. The place looked dark and lonely without all the festival lights. The gallery was closed, as he knew it would be. Had Sarah got home safely?

What was Ingrid up to? He peered toward the dark storefronts. A lone figure shuffled along the sidewalk. Was that her? No. A different build. A female jogged across the street ahead. He slowed down, peering into the shadows, but the woman was already out of sight. He exhaled a long sigh.

He was tired and weary after driving, stopping only for gas and food. He'd be relieved for a place to crash for the night, even if it meant heading to the archaic Beachside Inn with its cold shower and barely flushing toilet.

Are you okay? He texted Sarah as soon as he settled into a room like the previous one he'd stayed in.

I'm okay. Your friend was at the gallery today.

Ingrid? Tension raced through him. He should have driven faster to get here sooner.

Yes. She disguised herself in a black wig and dark glasses. But it was her.
He gritted his teeth. *Are you all right?*

I'm fine. Thankfully James checked on me.

Good. His shoulders loosened from their knots. *I'm glad you're okay.*

Me too. Thanks for sending him.

A warm feeling spread through him. *When I heard Ingrid was here, I didn't know who else to call. I came as quickly as I could.*

You're in town?

Yes. Hadn't James told her he was coming?

Aren't you supposed to be heading to Spokane? So she had been listening to his podcasts! Had hearing his voice made her think fondly of him? Miss him?

I was until I heard about Ingrid. We'll talk tomorrow, okay? I want to see you. Holding his breath, he waited for her reply.

I'd like to see you also.

He sighed. *Good night then.*

Night.

He held the phone to his chest as if holding Sarah's hand and felt an urgency to pray like he had several times on his drive back today. *Please keep Sarah safe. If there's any hope for a relationship between us, help us figure out how to make it happen.*

Throughout the afternoon, he'd pondered what he hoped would occur between them—not that it made any sense, considering nothing had changed about their jobs. He only knew he had deep feelings for Sarah, and he didn't want to live the rest of his life without finding out if they had what it took to be a couple. If they were to get together, he'd have to figure out how to prioritize her and their relationship. Could he do that better than his father had done?

His thoughts shifted to the circumstances which led Ingrid to search for him in the first place. Were any of her grandmother's problems his fault? He'd debated that on his drive back to Oregon, too. He wasn't the cause of Evelyn Glasser's health difficulties, whatever they were, but had he pushed her too hard mentally or emotionally? Was he morally at fault, even if he wasn't fiscally to blame?

Alfie fervently denied Blue's guilt, saying he hadn't expressed anything about Evelyn that he wouldn't have said about other artists, which seemed accurate. But what would Sarah say about it? Hadn't she questioned why he couldn't be more compassionate and caring in his critiques? Hadn't Gram spoken with him about being kinder and more loving multiple times?

He yanked the thin blankets over his shoulders and stretched out, hoping sleep would come swiftly and troublesome thoughts would vanish. They didn't. He prayed again, asking God to stop Ingrid's search for revenge and for her to find peace.

He also prayed that something good would happen in Evelyn Glasser's life and gallery. He thought of Gram and prayed for her. Once he started, praying became more natural. He hadn't turned his thoughts inward enough to expose his need for personal prayer yet, but by the stirring ache in his chest, that day was approaching. His last thought before drifting off was of Sarah and how he hoped their next meeting would go well.

He awoke to his cell phone buzzing. "Yeah?" he answered groggily.

"Know where I am?" Ingrid asked in a surly voice.

He sat up. "Where?"

"Your grandmother has the cutest cottage. I love her garden art!"

"Stay away from her! You hear me?" Blue propelled himself off the bed. "Get away from my grandmother's house now!"

"Or what? You'll publicly criticize my family? Oops. Too late."

Blue wanted to punch a hole in the wall. "What do you want?" He hated feeling like Ingrid was holding him emotionally hostage. If she did anything to Gram or told her any more lies—

"To watch you suffer, what else?"

"Come after me, then. Leave my grandmother out of this. Leave Sarah alone, too! Let's meet in Medford or Coos Bay." Anywhere other than Redding or Basalt Bay.

"You didn't leave my grandmother alone. Why should I leave yours alone?"

"Look." He gritted his teeth. "I'm sorry for whatever happened to your grandmother."

"But you aren't sorry for your obnoxious words and ridicule that sent her to death's door?"

"That wasn't my fault!"

"Not your fault?" she shrieked. "How can you say that?"

"Let's talk face to face," he attempted to speak calmly as he strode across the orangish 70's carpet. "I'm in Oregon. Let's meet in Medford."

"No!"

"Then where?" He toe-kicked a shoe out of his way.

"I know where you are. Look how fast you ran to your small-town girlfriend!"

"Ingrid—" Silence. "Ingrid?" Nothing. He groaned and tapped Gram's name, hoping she was awake.

"Bartholomew?" She was the only one who called him by his legal name anymore.

"Hey, Gram. Peek out your window and see if there's a black SUV parked outside, will you?"

"What's this about?" she asked sleepily.

"Just do it for me, all right? Don't wiggle the curtains when you peer out."

"I've watched enough detective shows to know how to be sneaky." Her shuffling sounds reached him. "No SUV, black or otherwise. Feel better?"

"Yes. But don't answer your door to any strangers today, okay? Better yet, can you stay at Barb's house for a few days?"

"Why would I do that? Bartholomew, I am too independent to run from a problem. Now tell me what's going on."

He didn't want to cause her more worry, but she had a right to know the truth. "Remember those prank calls you received?"

"Mmhmm."

"I think the person who made them just contacted me from outside your house."

"What?" More shuffling sounds followed. Gram cleared her throat. "I took a second look. There's a strange green car in the driveway next door."

"Anyone inside?"

"Not that I can see."

"Okay. But please go to Barb's house?"

"If I ran to her house every time you spoke gruffly about someone on your podcast, I'd never get to stay in my own home." Gram moaned softly. "Sorry, grandson. I love you more than life. God loves you, too. You know I'm praying for you, don't you?"

"I know, Gram." What should he do if she wouldn't leave? Was Ingrid planning to stay in Redding? Or was she on her way to Basalt Bay? Gram was safe if he'd successfully discouraged Ingrid from hanging around her house.

He checked his watch. Six a.m. He'd take a quick shower, and then see Sarah.

Chapter Thirty-three

An hour later, Blue stood in front of the project house door, his hand poised to knock, but Kathleen opened it first. "Well, if it isn't Blue Paxton gracing our front porch. Come in. Welcome." The white-haired woman backed up and waved toward a dining room with a long table and expansive windows overlooking the bay. A beautiful acrylic painting of this house, centered on the far wall, drew his eye like a beacon. Who was the artist? Someone local?

"Thank you. Is Sarah here?"

"It's early, but I'll get her. Would you like some coffee or tea while you wait?"

He wanted to see Sarah, but he could also use some caffeine. "Black coffee would be great."

"Certainly. Have a seat or take in our amazing view." She gestured toward the windows. "This panorama inspires me daily."

"I can imagine." Stuffing his hands into his coat pocket, he watched an eagle swoop around a tree, hunting for prey. A bushy tailed squirrel ambled up a trunk. Something splashed in the water in the distance—a salmon?

"Here you go." He hadn't heard Kathleen's approach.

"Thank you." He accepted the steaming cup she extended.

"You're welcome. I'll be right back." She shuffled from the room, and her footsteps faded as she went up some stairs.

He sipped the hot coffee, gazing toward the bay and watching for a salmon to emerge again. When it didn't, he took a closer look at the painting and saw "Paige" scrawled along the bottom right corner. This painting was done by the same artist as the lighthouse painting in the gallery. *Nice work.*

Sarah strode into the room dressed in jeans and a soft turquoise sweater that looked gorgeous on her. "Blue. What are you doing here this early?"

"I had to see you." He set his cup down and met her at the head of the dining table. Relief swept through him that she was fine and seemed okay with his being here, followed by an intense desire to take her in his arms and kiss her as if no time had passed between the last time they kissed and now. What would she say if he did?

"What about your podcast?"

"I'm doing a rerun."

"Blue Paxton doing reruns?" She gave him a skeptical look. "What's happening to you?"

"Life." He drew in a ragged breath. "Ingrid."

"Oh. You didn't have to come all this way because of her. I can call the deputy if she shows up at the gallery again."

"I had to see for myself that you're okay." He clasped her warm hand, and she didn't pull away. "I've missed you, Sarah."

"Blue—" She drew back this time. "We were only work acquaintances. Let's not fool ourselves into thinking otherwise."

He groaned. He had no one other than himself to blame for her lukewarm response. Had she given up on them? That possibility cut through him like a sculptor chiseling through clay. However, he couldn't fault her for not believing they had anything going after some of the things he'd said to her. But he was far from thinking of their relationship as only a work-related friendship now.

"Do you have a few minutes to talk?"

"Sure. But I have to work today."

"That's okay." Her schedule was partly the reason he came straight here. "I drove like crazy to get to you and make sure Ingrid didn't cause trouble, but I didn't get here soon enough."

"You sent James, which was sweet." She drew in a slow breath. "Ingrid asked for your whereabouts. But anyone listening to your podcast knows you've been in Seattle and plan to go to Spokane." Her statement was another confirmation that she'd listened to his podcast recently.

"She was at my grandmother's house this morning."

"What? Is your grandmother all right?" The concern in Sarah's tone warmed his heart.

"She's okay. Gram's brave and fiercely independent. I don't know whether to drive to Redding and check on her or stay here with you." He felt a sinking feeling in his gut. "Even when I asked her to go to a friend's house as a precautionary measure, she refused. I'm worried about her, but I don't want to leave you alone, either."

"Hey, now." Sarah gently placed her palms on his wrists, initiating contact between them. "I'm not alone, Blue. I have good friends and family who will run to my rescue if I need help. Didn't James prove that? If you need to take care of your grandmother, do that. She's your family."

"Thank you." Sarah was such an amazing woman—kind, thoughtful, and beautiful. He wanted to kiss her. "Sarah?" Should he ask permission or kiss her and apologize later? "Not a day has passed that I haven't wished we could spend more time together." He stroked a strand of hair from her warm cheek and tucked it behind her ear. A startled look crossed her face. "Would it be okay if I kissed you?" Heart pounding against his ribcage, he leaned forward, hoping her answer would be yes. "If it's too soon, tell me."

"Is that a good idea? I mean, us kissing? Acting as if we're—"

"Together? On a journey toward something meaningful?"

"Blue—"

"Didn't you miss me a little?" He smoothed his palms up and down her arms slowly. "I've missed you like crazy."

"I may have missed sparring with you." She smiled softly, and his gaze was drawn to her lips like a moth to a light. *Sweet Sarah.*

"See," he said, keeping his tone light. "I'm useful for something."

"I can think of a few things you might be useful for," she said in a flirty tone, then sighed. "But I've had doubts while you've been away. I didn't know if I'd see you again. You didn't call or text."

"I'm sorry. I should have. But I've thought about you a lot." He touched her hands, teasing at holding them but not doing so. "Does this mean no kissing?" He wouldn't push her into doing anything she didn't want to do, even if everything within him ached to kiss her and hold her.

"I didn't say no kissing."

"I'm glad to hear it." He shuffled closer to her.

She met his gaze tenderly, and his heart leaped into his throat. Her warm breath brushed his cheek. Did she feel the heat of his breath on her face?

"Sarah—"

"Blue—"

Then they were in each other's arms, kissing softly like butterfly wings were brushing against each other's mouths. Gentle first kisses became more intense, filled with a hungrier passion for more kisses. He'd never felt such an attraction and emotional connection with anyone before. In those moments, he knew beyond any doubt that he wanted a real, lifelong relationship with her. He wanted to know her heart, personality, and emotions like he needed to understand the depths of his soul. And he wanted more and more of her kisses.

Someone cleared her throat. Blue and Sarah stumbled backward, exchanging embarrassed smiles. Sarah's face turned rosy. He clasped her hand and tugged her closer to his side.

"Sorry for intruding." A Latino woman stood at the entryway holding a toddler, gazing uncertainly from Sarah to Blue. "May I pass through to the kitchen?"

"Lola." Sarah chuckled weakly. "Yes, of course. This is Blue Paxton. Blue, this is my good friend and housemate, Lola Presley. Her son, Micah, is the cutest toddler in the world."

"So I see! Nice to meet you," Blue said, glad to meet another friend of Sarah's, although a tad disappointed by the interruption.

"Nice to meet you, also." Lola pressed her lips together like she was stifling a grin.

"Blue is here to update me about what's going on with Ingrid Glasser." Sarah shot him an imploring look. He nodded and shrugged.

"Uh-huh. I'm going to get Micah some breakfast." The woman hurried through the dining area and into the kitchen, snickering.

As soon as she was out of sight, Blue whispered, "Can we talk privately?"

"Only to talk?" Sarah's smile held a hint of lingering flirtation.

"Maybe more than talking. I like kissing you, Sarah."

"I like it, too. But I have questions you might not like when we talk." He appreciated her honesty and vulnerability, but her forthrightness also surprised him.

"Okay. I reserve the right to—" Her wide-eyed expression stopped him. "What did I say?"

"I thought you were going to say you reserve the right not to tell me something."

"No. I was going to say I reserve the right to ask you some questions, too." He dropped a quick kiss on her soft-looking lips.

"Sorry for jumping to conclusions." She shook her head. "You can't keep kissing me like that here."

"Why not?"

She huffed. "Lola, Kathleen, Bess, or Teal might walk through and see us."

"Are you embarrassed for them to find us kissing?"

"Not embarrassed, exactly."

"Then what?" He set his palms lightly on her shoulders, gazing into her lovely brown eyes. "If we are a couple, I'll want to steal kisses with you in the future."

"I'm not a giddy teenager who has to steal kisses." She lifted her chin, her eyes gleaming. "If we decide to be in a relationship, I'll kiss you whenever I want."

"Okay. I'm all for that!" He moved in for a kiss right then, but her palm at his chest stopped him.

"But not here. This house is a place of refuge for women. I don't want anyone walking in, finding us wrapped in each other's arms and feeling uncomfortable."

"So where can we talk privately and kiss each other?

"We could drive to one of the overlooks. I can grab some of Kathleen's pumpkin spice muffins and coffee for breakfast. Would you mind dropping me off at work afterward?" She took a few steps away and glanced back.

"I'll take you anywhere you want to go."

She smiled tenderly. "What about your grandmother?"

"I'll call and check on her. I hope Ingrid is heading this way."

"Okay. I'll be right back." She looked back at him one more time. "Don't leave without talking to me, okay?"

"I won't." He never wanted to drive away from her again—if only he could promise her that!

Chapter Thirty-four

When Blue arrived in town last night, he hadn't imagined his time with Sarah turning out so romantic today. Their kisses and how warm and responsive she felt in his arms made him wish they could discuss how to make a long-term relationship work immediately. Was it too soon to bring that up? Despite some doubts, his feelings about dating a gallery worker had changed tremendously since meeting her.

"Pull over here." Sarah pointed to an overlook with waves tumbling along the rocky beach below. While this wasn't like the wintry weather he'd anticipated in the north, the gusty winds and churning waves didn't invite a stroll, which was too bad. He would have enjoyed walking hand in hand with Sarah and telling her how he felt about her. Of course, he wanted to hear how she felt about him, too.

She handed him a delicious-smelling muffin and steaming coffee from a thermos. Their fingers touched, and a zing of electrical current flashed through him. He was so attracted to her. She set a muffin in her lap and poured herself a cup of coffee, sending brief glances in his direction. "Can't get much more private than this."

"I guess not." He kissed her softly. "This is nice."

"Mmhmm." Her smile invited another kiss, which he was more than happy to do. Each time his lips brushed hers, and she eagerly reciprocated, he was reminded of how much he valued their unexpected romance. But how could theirs be a happy-ever-after? That is what Sarah wanted, right? *It's what I want, too.* But how to accomplish that was a mystery he hadn't solved.

They ate their breakfasts watching the surf, and Blue loved spending time alone with Sarah. He wished every morning could begin like this.

"What do you picture happening between us?" she asked.

He worked to swallow his bite of muffin without choking. "Happening?"

"You drove a long way to come to my rescue and kissed me like you're crazy about me." She winked at him. "I don't want a fling, Blue. I'm looking for something more with a man who has similar values about life and faith."

He sighed, a mix of sadness and hope stirring within him. Were his values similar enough to hers to help them through a long relationship? Was he the man she needed when their philosophies about art and small towns were vastly different? Their belief in trusting Jesus as their savior was comparable, at least like how he'd been raised. But there were so many things they hadn't discussed yet.

"I know where I'd like it to go." He touched her cheek softly with the back of his finger. "It has nothing to do with having a fling. But given our professions and diversity of living situations, I am baffled as to how to make it work well, probably as much as you are." She nodded. "However, I am enjoying being with you. Our kissing is a nice benefit of being together."

"True. But there's more to a relationship than that."

"I know. Every time we talk and share our hearts, I feel like we're getting closer. Don't you?"

"Yes," she whispered. "I still want to know how you feel about us beyond this short time you'll be in Basalt Bay."

"I have strong feelings for you. I am very attracted to you." He felt a little heady confessing that, like he was stepping onto a tall diving board and about to leap off. "Since I've been gone, I've thought about you daily. I'm sorry for leaving without properly saying goodbye or staying in contact."

"I appreciate that." Sighing, she leaned back against her seat. "This thing with Ingrid has stirred up some concerns for me."

"For me, too. I'm sorry for the trouble she's caused. I don't want anything about my business to make you worry."

She held his gaze for several moments. "How is Evelyn doing?"

"I haven't heard anything about her recently."

"You or Alfie haven't checked into her condition?" She tipped her head, eyeing him with a troubled look.

"Not me." Had Alfie mentioned checking into Ingrid's grandmother's health? "Alfie says they can't blame health issues on me because of opinions I've stated. My First Amendment Rights protect my speech." He didn't mean to sound uncaring and softened his tone. "You understand I'm not to blame for anyone's reaction to my viewpoint, right?"

"I wasn't implying you are legally responsible. But what about mercy and kindness? Aren't we all responsible for that?" Her questions sounded like what she'd asked him on his podcast. "I get that you feel justified in expressing your views. But what about caring for others in and out of the art community? I think honesty should be coupled with grace in every area of our lives."

Tension rippled across his neck and jaw muscles. He didn't like where this conversation was going, yet he asked, "How do you propose I do that in my podcast?"

"Maybe by showing more thoughtfulness to the artists you're critiquing?" She gazed out the window. "What if you gave the detailed stuff, then shared about the artist's journey and what brought him or her to that place in life?" She glanced at him with a hopeful expression.

"You mean give fluff instead of facts?" His heart clamored. Did she assume that since they were developing a closer bond, she had a right to change how he did his job? "I'm surprised you would suggest such a thing. It would never work!"

"How do you know unless you try?"

"Why don't we leave our careers out of the discussion about where we want our relationship to go?"

"How can we separate the two? You are Blue Paxton!" Her voice rose like being Blue Paxton was a bad thing. "You want us to avoid a topic that is so explosive a woman is seeking revenge against you?"

"Yes." He swallowed hard. While their careers were a part of the equation between them, couldn't they focus on their relationship for now? Even though she'd told him about her expectations of honesty, he wasn't prepared to let her tear his podcast to shreds. But was she doing that? Or was he overreacting?

"Isn't your online persona what has put me and your grandmother in jeopardy?" Her words branded him with an iron of remorse. And fresh concern for Gram rose up in him. "I have a right to express my thoughts after the way Ingrid behaved toward me because of my association with you, don't I?"

"You're right." He expelled a breath. "I thought you were saying you wanted me to change my podcast to meet your ideals. I was being overly sensitive. I'm sorry."

"I'm not trying to push you into doing anything, other than considering talking about artists more thoughtfully." She met his gaze, her eyes moist. "Don't I have a right to question the philosophies of a man I'm kissing?"

"It was difficult to hear, that's all." Although, he'd been questioning a lot of things about the business lately, too.

"Look at the trouble your blunt opinions have caused me." Her voice broke. "If James hadn't intervened yesterday, I'm afraid to think what might have happened with Ingrid."

"Me too." He pictured that woman trying to force him off the road and shuddered. What extreme thing might she do to get his attention next? "I'm sorry for what you went through because of me." He drew Sarah's hand to his lips and pressed a light kiss there. "Of course, you have the right to question me about these things—and about anything you want."

"I told you I was kidnapped." She tugged her hand back and folded her arms over her middle.

"I couldn't let anything like that happen to you again. Yet we don't know how far Ingrid might go to try to bring either of us harm."

"She wouldn't come after Lola or Micah, would she?" Sarah's eyes widened. "You came to the project house. What if she followed you?"

"She was outside my grandmother's house in Redding, so it would take a few hours for her to get here."

"What if she wasn't?" Sarah bit her lower lip between her teeth. "What if she used an app to view your grandmother's house and never left Basalt Bay? She could be watching us now!"

They both swiveled toward the rear window. Blue scanned sand piles where someone might be hiding. "I don't see anyone. I never considered she might be lying about where she was." He'd be relieved if she wasn't near Gram's house this morning.

"Isn't it time you talked to Deputy Brian?"

"Maybe. Alfie wants the gossip to run its course and die down. But will this problem disappear as long as Ingrid wants revenge?"

"How well do you know Alfie?"

"We were friends in college. Business partners for five years." His thoughts flitted between loyalty and concern. Had he trusted

Alfie too much? "I'm annoyed by the way he pushes me to go for trigger reactions that bring higher ratings."

"Sensationalism sells, right?"

"I guess. I admit to allowing some things I shouldn't have." He exhaled a sharp breath. "I wonder where I should have drawn the line, such as with Evelyn Glasser. Was there something I could have said or done differently?"

Sarah smoothed her palm over his hand on the steering wheel. "You aren't responsible for her medical situation. Who's to say how long her condition has been coming on?"

"Thank you." He adjusted his hand to clasp hers. "But you've probably heard the rumors about some other artists I've talked about."

"Like the guy hiding out in Alaska?"

"Yeah." More regret twisted inside him.

"Even though you were tough with Gracie, her sales have tripled."

"It often works that way, but not always."

"What are you going to do about Ingrid?" She let go of his hand and clasped hers in her lap.

"I don't know other than to keep you and Gram safe." He'd call Gram as soon as he dropped Sarah off at the gallery.

"And us? What are you planning to do about us, Blue?" Before he could answer, she continued in a quiet voice, "Before my husband passed away, we fought a lot. Not yelling. We were good at keeping our hurts and anger bottled up. I resented that I didn't get to share my heart with him before we parted ways for the last time."

"I'm sorry."

"That's why I'm determined to say what I need to say to you." She gave him a cautious look. "If this is going to work between us, we have to be able to talk about everything, even if it's uncomfortable, and even if it's about the difficult parts of your job."

"I understand and agree." If his dad had been more forthright about his need to spend time with his art, things might not have ended as badly as they did between his parents. "Thank you for sharing and trusting me with your thoughts."

She nodded, her eyes glistening.

"You asked what I plan to do about us. For now, I'd like to do this, if it's okay." He kissed her gently. When she responded with a soft kiss back, he brushed his lips over hers more fully. He leaned back and smoothed his fingers over her warm cheek. "Can we figure out the rest as we go? Having a real relationship with someone is new to me."

Her tender kiss gave him the answer he hoped for.

Chapter Thirty-five

If ever there was a day Sarah wanted to keep the gallery closed, it was today. But she had work-related tasks to do that didn't include hanging on Blue's every word, gazing into his stunning eyes, and kissing the sweetest lips she'd ever tasted. Without disrespect for her late husband or past boyfriends, Blue was the most tender, passionate kisser she'd ever experienced. She couldn't wait to be in his arms again and enjoy more of his kisses.

Two hours after she opened the gallery, he strolled in, set his laptop on the table like that was part of his regular life now, and gave her a lazy smile. Her heart pounded a wild beat, and imagining forever with him teased her thoughts. What would it be like if they were married, kissing whenever they wanted and doing things married couples did? She longed for him to kiss her like he couldn't wait for another second to do so and hear him say he wanted to spend his whole life with her.

Over the next hour, as she helped customers with purchases and answered questions, her gaze kept snagging with Blue's. Her heart palpitated whenever he smiled warmly back at her. Once, he wet his lips, his gaze locked on hers, and she was so mesmerized, she could hardly answer a patron's query. Without a doubt, she was falling head over heels for him.

But should she feel this strongly about him so soon? She'd talked with him about the way she and Jeremy had argued, but what about other discussions they should be having, like about faith, kids, and how they wanted to live their lives? Should she put on the brakes until they shared more conversations about important things? Hold on! She wanted more of Blue's kisses, affection, and being with him—not less! She wasn't putting on any brakes unless God told her to, and so far, that hadn't happened.

After she said goodbye to the last of three customers who'd been oohing and aahing over Kathleen's mosaics, Blue stepped behind her and wrapped his arms around her, snuggling his face into her hair. "Mmm. This is better."

"Much better." Turning slowly in his embrace, she leaned her cheek against the chest of his brown sweater and inhaled the scent of his musky deodorant and bodily warmth that was becoming familiar. She had never been able to imagine what kind of man she would want to be with after her years with Jeremy. But being in Blue's arms felt perfectly right, like she was where she belonged, and where she wanted to stay.

Even though they hadn't discussed marriage or made promises, her thoughts were leaping ahead toward a wedding, babies, and spending their time together as a married couple. However, when she thought of him driving out of town before any of that could be discussed, she inwardly groaned, maybe stiffened. He tilted up her chin. "Is something bothering you, sweetheart?"

Her heart danced at the endearment. "Other than a client or artist walking in and finding us kissing and embracing?"

"Let them." He lowered his lips to hers, kissing her gently, and the delectable sensations of his lips brushing hers sent a kaleidoscope of happy thoughts and feelings spiraling through her.

The door opened, and Sarah jumped back, heat racing up her face. Callie entered, eyeing her and Blue. Of all the people who might have caught them kissing, why did it have to be Callie?

"Well, well. Look who the tide washed in. What have we here?"

"You remember Blue?" Did Callie hear the thready tone of her voice when she said his name? Did she notice Blue wiping the back of his hand over his mouth, his cheeks ruddy?

"Sure do. But I didn't realize he was still your kissing friend." Sarah coughed hard. Callie nodded toward Blue. "When did you get back in town?"

"Last night." He fiddled with the top button of his dark green shirt beneath his sweater.

"Now you're chasing after Sarah again?"

"Callie—" Sarah protested.

"Right. Not my business." Callie wagged her finger at Blue. "Listen, young man. You can't go dragging her off to Timbuktu without her friends telling you what we think about that!"

"I wouldn't dream of it, ma'am."

"Since we're clear on that"—Callie cast a brief smile at Sarah— "I'd like a cup of peppermint tea, please."

"Right away." Sarah rushed into the kitchenette, stealing glances at Blue and Callie. Did she dare leave them alone? Callie's gesticulating and Blue's ashen face showed that whatever they were discussing wasn't pleasant or friendly. Hopefully Callie wouldn't run him off.

As soon as the water was hot, Sarah dropped in a tea bag and carried the beverage to Callie, trying to catch a bit of their conversation. However, the front door opened, and Paisley entered with baby Tanner in his stroller, diverting her attention. Sarah exchanged greetings with her sister-in-law, and then spent some quality time baby-talking with Tanner. She was overjoyed by the tender feelings of interacting with her three-month-old nephew and forgot all about Blue and what Callie might be saying to him.

Chapter Thirty-six

"Why are you back?" Callie leaned toward Blue and gave him a dark look.

"I was concerned for Sarah's safety."

"So you're dragging her through your messes now?"

He took a breath, trying to calm his irritation "I'm here to do my best to keep her safe."

"As well you should!" Callie's vehemence caused more tension to creep up his neckline. "What are your intentions, young man?" *Intentions, really?*

"We like each other." Did that sound too juvenile? He wasn't going to elaborate. How Sarah chose to explain their relationship to her friends was up to her. "You can trust me when I say I have strong feelings for her."

"Trust is a word loaded with meaning. I noticed you didn't say love."

He wasn't going to discuss that either. A reprieve from Callie's interrogation came when a younger woman entered the gallery pushing a stroller and greeted Sarah and the older woman, whom she called "Aunt Callie." Thankfully, Callie gave her attention to the woman she addressed as "Paisley Rose."

Blue's phone vibrated and he swiped the screen. Gram's text read, *Safe. Everything is fine!*

Good, he responded. *Have a nice afternoon.* When he called to check on Gram earlier, he asked her to text him every hour to let him know she was okay. She reluctantly agreed.

Despite the chatter going on at the next table, Blue focused on his online research. Recently, he'd been curious to learn more about artists who painted on mediums other than canvas. His listeners might also enjoy a change in subject matter. Discussing a different technique or unique surface would probably stir up extra comments in the art community, which Alfie would approve of.

Ever since Gram acquired a couple of painted rocks for her garden, Blue had been planning to do more research about artists who painted rocks and made a living at it. He found the website of an Oregonian artist, Lindsay Smart, who owned a rock shop along the northern shore. After reading about her story and perusing photos of the rocks she'd painted, he was intrigued enough to consider driving up to see the shop and talk to her.

He hated leaving Sarah alone for even a few hours, but she wouldn't want him hanging around the gallery constantly. Besides, he had to keep working.

Sarah looked cute cooing over the baby in the stroller. Warmth filled him as he imagined her as a mom, holding a newborn baby, their baby, and he swallowed down some tender emotions. Hadn't he given up on having a family, despite Gram's reminders about wanting to see her great-grandchild? He certainly didn't want to be like his father, who'd put his dreams selfishly above his wife and kids.

But then, wasn't he, too, pursuing his dreams at any cost? Was he more like Dad than he wanted to admit? He silenced a groan. He needed to stay focused on his research. He visually inspected and critiqued every photo of all the painted rocks on Linsay Smart's website and read most of the data.

When Sarah sat down in the chair opposite him, he glanced around the empty room. "We're alone?" He hadn't heard the others leave.

"Finally." She reached across the table and linked their fingers. "What did Callie say earlier that made you look so uneasy?"

"Nothing important." Nothing worth talking about, anyway.

"You didn't acknowledge me for the last hour, so I figured it must have been serious."

"Sorry. I got caught up in my work." And his thoughts. "However, Callie is terrifying."

Sarah chuckled. "She's trying to do better at not being so intimidating."

"You're kidding!"

"You should have met her a year ago. Did she tell you to stay away from me?"

"Not in so many words." He shrugged. "But sort of."

"Don't let her get to you. She's protective of those she loves, which includes me." She played with his fingers, and he was distracted by her gentle touch. "She should know I wouldn't kiss a man if I didn't have strong feelings for him."

"Do you have strong feelings for me, Sarah?"

"I do. How do you feel about me, Blue?"

He arranged their hands so he could caress her palms with his thumbs. "I came back to Basalt Bay to ensure your safety but also because I didn't want to spend another day regretting not getting to know you when I had the chance. I like you a lot, Sarah." Her beautiful smile made him long to make promises and maybe rush to the courthouse and apply for a marriage license. *Slow down, Blue. Don't get carried away. You need to resolve some things in your life first.* "I want to explain my feelings for you better, but I'm still uncertain about how we can make something permanent work between us. Do you understand what I'm trying to say?"

"I think so. But it's nice to hear your thoughts and feelings."

"I am falling for you fast. But I'm not ready to propose or—" Sarah jerked, and his words died. What she'd said after their first kiss replayed in his mind. *It's not like I expect a proposal.* "I didn't mean—"

"You don't want to stir up false hope in me about a future together?" Her tone said he'd hurt her again, which he didn't want to do. "You like kissing me but don't want to make any promises?"

"Wait. I do want a future with you. And I have thought of promises I'd like to make." He reached out tentatively but didn't touch her. "I don't know how to proceed without giving up my job, which I can't bear the thought of doing right now."

"Nor would I ask you to!"

"You wouldn't?"

"No. I don't want you to give up doing what you love. It's part of who you are. What matters is if we work as a couple. Do we?" Her voice lowered. "Do you think we work as a couple, Blue?"

"There's incredible chemistry between us." She eyed him like she was warning him to tread carefully, so he hastened to add, "I like being with you. We talk and laugh like we've known each other forever. I value everything you've told me about honesty, God's grace, and how you want to live. I treasure the times when we've shared our hearts."

"I've enjoyed those things about us, too." Sarah smoothed her palm over the table, her fingertips brushing the tips of his. "But like you said, you aren't ready to propose. That must mean you aren't ready for our relationship to go deeper." She lowered her hands to her lap. "So why are we kissing and acting like we are moving toward something more if we aren't?"

"I apologize for being abrupt." Yet he felt conflicted between what he wished would happen and what he feared might happen.

"When I'm with you, I have hope that we will figure everything out, despite my traveling schedule and your desire to stay in Basalt Bay. However, those are hurdles we'll have to cross." And he had to figure out how to be a family man, committing to a wife, *and* maintaining his dream job better than his father had done or ever tried to do.

"I believe if we keep talking about it, and with God's help, we can work everything out. But if you take off without us getting to—"

"I won't. I promise to be open and vulnerable about us."

"Do you picture an 'us?'" Her lips wobbled, and he nearly pulled her to himself.

"I've thought of little else since I dropped my plans to do my podcast from Spokane and drove here." He stood, drawing her to her feet. "If wishes come true, we will be together always."

"Really?" Her voice held wonder, and he couldn't believe he'd been given the chance to spend time with a woman like her who was so beautiful, inside and out. She was like the most delicious dessert, and he was becoming more addicted to her by the hour.

"Really and truly." He kissed her softly. When her arms slipped around his neck, pulling them closer, and their kiss intensified, his heart pounded a powerful beat.

He set her back, catching his breath and putting a little distance between them. She didn't want a fling, and he didn't want that either. He held her hand and led her to the window overlooking the waves rolling onto the rocks below.

As the pinkish sky painted rose and orange hues across the water's surface, he was reminded of Sarah's mosaic he'd sent to Gram. With Sarah beside him, their sides touching, he felt like they could be a part of a mosaic, blending all the parts of their lives together. He slid his arm over her shoulders and touched the side of his head to hers. Sighing, he ignored any thought of creating distance or being like his dad.

He wanted Sarah in his life. No matter how much he enjoyed traveling and podcasting, nothing compared to how he felt with her by his side. But how were they going to make a relationship succeed and last?

Chapter Thirty-seven

Callie sat at the kitchen island in the project house across from Sarah the next day, wearing a troubled-looking frown. "Are you certain about Blue?"

"Can anyone be certain about someone else?" Sarah's answer was elusive, but was there any way to be one hundred percent positive about a relationship? "I like Blue a lot. I want to fall in love with him." Why not go for broke? "I'd like to have his children!"

"Sarah!" Callie's mouth dropped two inches.

"Sorry. Thought I'd bring some levity to the discussion."

"You made my heart pound twice as hard." Callie shook her head as if trying to get the picture of Sarah and Blue as a couple out of her mind.

I may already be in love with him. She wouldn't mention that to Callie today. Blue had sounded so sincere when he explained his reluctance to commit to her due to their conflicting jobs and living situations, and she appreciated his honesty and willingness to talk about complex subjects. But she was praying he'd see things differently soon, and with God's help and love, they would find their way to having a future together—children and all!

"If you're falling for a man who's causing trouble at galleries, that concerns me." Callie's gruff tone brought Sarah back to their conversation.

"What do you mean? Causing trouble?"

"I read about his shenanigans online," Callie said indignantly. "Patty sent me some links."

"About what?" Sarah hadn't listened to Blue's podcast for a few days since he wasn't posting any new material from Basalt Bay. Did she miss something? Did she even want to know about these so-called shenanigans?

"A disgruntled gallery worker is accusing him of sexual harassment!"

"What? I don't believe it! What's this person's name?" It had to be Ingrid. Who else would make such an accusation against Blue and cause another public stink?

"I don't recall. But it's out there for all to see. People are commenting like mad! Is it hot in here?" Callie fanned her hand in front of her face. "The thing is, you'd think he was a movie star, or something. Do you want to be with a man like him?"

"Yes, in fact, I do!" Sarah wasn't going to believe and accept whatever the news outlets said about Blue, particularly if their source was Ingrid, and even if it sounded terrible. "I admit I don't know everything there is to know about Blue, but we have gotten close. We're friends—and more." Her throat thickened with emotion.

"Sarah." Callie moaned.

"What? Can't I be happy with a man again?"

"Of course you can. But why him?"

"I believe God brought Blue into my life for a reason. I'm not saying we're going to elope, or anything."

"I should say not!"

"But you saw us kissing." Sarah lifted her chin, not giving in to embarrassment about Callie having seen her in Blue's embrace. "I wouldn't do that with someone I didn't care for and feel connected to. I have strong feelings for him, so please, don't think too harshly of him. What you read about is probably gossip. Or worse, slander!"

"I would never purposefully spread lies." Callie patted her chest like her heart was beating fast again.

"No, you wouldn't." Gratefulness for Callie's friendship filled her. "But I'm asking you to believe in me that I'll make the right decisions concerning Blue. I supported you when you told me you planned to marry James, right?"

"Yes, you did." Callie heaved a sigh.

"I stood by Lola's decision to return to her husband and now, to get a divorce, if that's what she feels she should do." She kept her voice soft, not accusatory, but she needed to say this. "Shouldn't friends and family stand by each other, no matter what?"

"Yes. You're right. I want what's best for you, Sarah. But selfishly, I prefer that you stay in Basalt Bay."

"So do I!"

"You do?" Callie sounded astonished.

"Yes!" Sarah stood and wrapped her arms around Callie's shoulders. "I plan to stay here with you and my Basalt Bay family."

"That's wonderful! But I don't understand." Callie wiped her palms across her cheeks. "What if you marry a man who travels for a living?" Meaning Blue, of course.

"Then I'd expect him to accept my decision to remain here, the same way I'd accept his choice to travel for work." A feeling of hope and new possibilities spread through her, causing goosebumps to skitter up her skin. God was working everything out for good in her life and Blue's life—she had to believe that. "I won't shut down the chance to find out if a relationship might work because I'm afraid it might not."

Callie's eyes shimmered with moisture. "You are a wise woman, Sarah. From now on, I will trust you to make the best decision for you without sticking my nose into your business."

"Thank you."

"However, I don't like this stuff I read about online." Callie crossed her arms over her chest, showing she wasn't backing down on that point.

"I don't like it either. But I'm going to trust that Blue is more honorable than to be at fault for sexual harassment." She prayed she would stay resolute in the days ahead.

Chapter Thirty-eight

Blue's phone kept vibrating. It was probably Alfie again. His business partner wouldn't stop texting him until he responded—he knew that from experience. However, he was preoccupied with his visit to the Rock Shop in Lincoln City and wasn't in the mood to read Alfie's disparaging comments about him ditching the tour. No matter what he said, Blue wasn't heading back to the northern regions until spring!

"Have you entered your painted rocks in any art shows?" he asked the thirty-year-old female artist, wearing a colorful paint-splattered smock and a sunny yellow bandana. Lindsay Smart's disposition seemed as cheerful and bright as her apparel.

"Yes. But I prefer this venue for highlighting my work." She waved her hands toward multiple counters and shelves displaying painted rocks of varying shapes and sizes. Blue had already perused the nautical-themed rocks, which included realistic portrayals of orcas, sea lions, crabs, and fish, among other sea creatures. He also enjoyed the sections with paintings grouped by colors and the children's section with age-appropriate cartoonish paintings. "I feel at home in this setting," Lindsay said with a smile. "Guests stop in from all over the country and the world, and I get to chat with them. Locals shop here regularly, too. I also teach a class for anyone who wants to learn how to paint garden stones. It's great fun!"

"Sounds impressive. How much is the fee to attend the class?" Blue had been typing Lindsay's answers into a page on his phone, and he was ready for her next response.

"Nothing. It's my way of saying thanks to those who frequent my shop." The woman's wide smile showed her pleasure in her art and getting to share that with others. With her upbeat, friendly attitude, he imagined Lindsay and Kathleen Baker would get along fabulously. He pictured them chatting about the benefits of their given art mediums and having a grand time doing it. For a second, he envisioned that conversation taking place on his podcast. Would Alfie go for such a thing?

"How long have you been running this shop?"

"Five years."

"Are you the sole proprietor?"

"No. My grandfather is my business partner." She chuckled softly. "We've been working on our rock shop plans since I was three!"

"A true family business, then. Good for you." Even though he'd previously viewed family businesses negatively and mistrustingly, it was working here. "Is your grandfather an artist, too?"

"No. He's in charge of the business side. Oh, and the encouragement department, meaning he brings me pastries and coffee." Lindsay grinned and nodded hello to an older gentleman, who held up a rock with a painting of a calico cat sniffing a shell on the sand. "The cat is supposed to look like mine," she told him. "He's always sniffing around my flowerbed, making messes."

"Mine does the same thing!" The customer affectionately cradled the palm-sized rock. "I'm bringing this one home."

"Great!" Lindsay swayed her hand toward the checkout counter. "I have to—"

"Go ahead," Blue said. "I'll meander around." Maybe he'd find a painted rock to buy Sarah for a Christmas gift. Now, that was a novel idea. In his five years of traveling, he'd only purchased unique gifts for Gram. Thinking of choosing something special for Sarah, the woman he was daring to hope would one day be his wife, made him feel lighthearted. Her comments about not expecting him to give up traveling to be in a relationship with her had been such a relief that his mind had been spinning with the possibilities of a family life with her. Could their two worlds blend? Could they live in harmony even if he continued with his current job and she stayed in Basalt Bay?

He took a deep breath and reminded himself to stay focused on what he came to do—observe and critique Lindsay's paintings and shop. So far, he liked everything about the artwork and the location. From the expansive windows letting in tons of natural light to the paintings themselves, he hadn't spotted anything to critique adversely, so maybe he would give another artist a positive review. Alfie would be livid! Sarah, on the other hand, would be pleased. He smiled.

While Lindsay helped her customer with his purchase, Blue perused a seasonal display, a Christmas section, and a nook of family-themed paintings of moms and dads doing activities with their kids, all painted on rocks. He picked up one stone with a painting of a dad lifting a boy high in the air and waves rolling up a beach, and the emotional scene made his heart race. Someday, that could be him and his and Sarah's child. Gulping, he set it back on the display table and moved on. If he stood there much longer, he'd buy all those rocks!

Lindsay's products were a splendid example of someone taking their art to the next level and making a full-time business from it. And she'd done all this with her grandfather? Impressive. Her paintings were worth taking a second look at, and her personable manner had to be a win-win for their success.

At a counter along the back wall, a series of flat rocks with ocean scenes caught his attention. One was about ten by seven inches and had a naturally jagged edge on top, which the artist had used to paint a monolith with frothy waves splashing up. This one looked like a monolith he'd seen near Basalt Bay. Sarah would love it!

After getting a few more quotes from Lindsay for his podcast, he purchased the rock and put it in his car. Then he strode down the street, hunting for a food joint before he headed back to Basalt Bay. He wasn't ready to refer to Sarah's hometown as his own, but the tiny berg was growing on him because she lived there. And wherever she was, that's where he wanted to be. *I'm falling for her fast.* He shook his head in happy disbelief.

He purchased a cheeseburger and a cup of hot coffee from a food truck decorated with Christmas lights, then sat down on a driftwood log facing the sea. He took a few sips of coffee with the wind blowing hard against him and forced himself to open the texts from Alfie.

Where are you?

Have you seen the latest from your friend?

Call me. This is urgent!

What friend was he talking about? What was so urgent? With Alfie, everything had to be so dramatic. Blue ate a couple of bites of his burger. *Mmm. Delicious.* He opened the next message and coughed so hard he nearly choked.

Ingrid is claiming sexual harassment! What did you do?

Do? He didn't do anything! How could she claim sexual harassment against him when he couldn't remember meeting her at her family's gallery in Bend? How could he have given her unwanted attention when he didn't spend time with or talk with her? He pressed his fingers against the space between his eyebrows where a headache was forming. The timing couldn't be worse. Things were just coming together between him and Sarah. What would she think of the accusation? What if she believed the outrageous claim against him?

His phone vibrated. *Don't worry. I'll take care of everything like I always do.* Alfie's text didn't make Blue feel any better.

No longer hungry, he threw the rest of his meal in the trash, then glanced over his other texts and calls. None were from Sarah. Had she heard about Ingrid's allegations? Why was that woman gunning for him? First, she tried running him off the road. Then, she verbally attacked him in Basalt Bay. Now, publicly lambasting him with false claims? If anyone was harassing anyone, it was her!

His critique of the Glasser Gallery hadn't been excessively mean or rude to cause such a backlash. While he was in Seattle, he'd listened to the podcasts he made from Bend, searching for any grossly insulting or misrepresentative criticism of Evelyn's art without finding anything reprehensible. He'd expressed how he genuinely felt about the woman's art, including his thoughts on how her composition of a bloody-looking human heart made him feel sick to his stomach. But what had she been trying to say with the garish painting other than to get a disapproving reaction from observers?

And what was behind Ingrid's hateful angst toward him? Was it all retaliation because of his critique? Or did it have anything to do with her younger sister, Elly? He pictured the petite gallery attendant who had chatted with him and, admittedly, he'd flirted with her a little. Nothing came of it. They shared a meal as friends, and he adhered to his rule about not dating gallery workers. Even if he had been slightly interested in Elly, that shouldn't have caused Ingrid to become extremely angry, make insinuations, or try to run him off the road!

Too irritated to drive, Blue strode down to the beach and crossed the rocky shore to the water's edge. Gusty wind billowed against him, but he didn't care. The cool sea air brushing his face and hair reminded him of driving with the top down on his convertible. Would Sarah enjoy a long ride along the coast with her hair blowing in the wind when the weather improved? He imagined them taking relaxing day trips in the spring, exploring galleries and visiting artists, like he'd done with Lindsay today. He bet Sarah would like to do that, too.

If they were married, would she travel with him on longer trips? Thinking about a future with her made him feel more optimistic. But what if she heard about the harassment complaint and thought the worst of him before he had the chance to talk with her? He bent over, picked up a few smooth stones, and threw them one by one into the surf. Sarah valued truth and honesty too much to accept bizarre gossip as gospel. Still, Ingrid's claim rattled him. What if it rattled Sarah, too?

He trudged farther down the beach, the wet sand seeping into his shoes. He hadn't dressed for beach walking. But with each step, his shoulders and neck relaxed a little more, although his thoughts continued swirling with questions and concerns. Would Alife make the false claims go away? Or would he pursue more shock tactics, even profiting because of them? Blue gritted his teeth. Would Alfie go that far? What if he already had?

Over the last five years, Blue had talked negatively about some artists' work—that was the nature of his job. But he would never take part in sexual harassment against anyone. He had more integrity than that! He had to find a way to clear his name.

"I'm praying for you," Gram always told him when they talked. Today, he was thankful for her prayers and how she reminded him of her love during every phone call. The thought of her supporting him no matter what was comforting, especially when he felt he needed every ounce of support he could get. If his mom and sister had lived, he could have counted on their love, too. A burning ache of sadness and loss, that he usually did better at subduing, came over him, pulling him inward into thoughts of the past.

Why had God allowed that horrible accident to happen when Blue was just a kid? Couldn't He have stopped it if He wanted to? *Why did You let Mom and Desi die?* It was an age-old question, one he'd asked God many times.

Blue stopped walking across the empty beach, the front of his body taking the full assault of the wind and beginning drops of rain. He lifted his face toward the darkening sky and shouted, "Why did You let them die in that wreck? Why couldn't You have saved them?" Like the first time he'd asked the question thirty-two years ago, he didn't get an answer. However, a crack in his emotional armor widened. Salty tears trickled down his cheeks mixing with raindrops. A loud groan came from his chest that equaled the roaring of the waves.

"Why couldn't You have done something?" *Anything.* He bent over, breathing raggedly, unable to believe the strong feelings hitting him after three decades, and grabbed a handful of rocks. Hoping to spend some of his rage, he hurled them one at a time as far as he could. "If You can do anything, why didn't You stop the accident and let them live?" Grief pummeled through him like the waves hitting the boulders nearby. *Why did they have to leave me? Why didn't Dad want me even after Mom and Desi died?*

Blue stared out to sea, inhaling and exhaling the salty, tangy air, letting all the emotional upheaval churn to the surface of his heart. Although he was alone on the beach, he didn't feel entirely alone. It was like this stretch of sand between the rocks and the sea had become something other than the seashore. It was like a holy place, and God was standing beside him and hearing him. If that were the case, what would Blue say to Him, especially after all his yelling and questioning?

A feeling of humbleness squeezed into his spirit, along with a sense of being loved and accepted. An unusual peace came over him, followed by an intense need for some gut-honesty and repentance.

Words that had been a long time coming wrestled free, and he brokenly said, "I'm sorry for all my anger and how enraged I've been with You these years. I've missed Mom and Desi so much it nearly kills me to think of them. So many times, I've longed for them to see the man I've become and for me to have my family again." He bit back another emotional tsunami. "Could You … give them my love? Maybe tell them about Sarah? They'd get a kick out of how she makes me laugh." He took a stuttering breath, then exhaled slowly, letting out some more of his internal pain.

"I've made a million mistakes." If anyone knew that, God did. There wasn't any use in trying to hide the fact. "I've been hardnosed and held onto grudges like a kid clinging to a security blanket. I pursued fame and financial gain to the point of being rude and obnoxious to get it." Admitting his faults was like pulling teeth one by one. He picked up another rock and hurled it into the waves. "Jesus, I'm sorry for neglecting what I've known was right since I was a boy. I wish I had remained sensitive to You like Gram tried to get me to do." He gazed up at the sky, and with the rain falling harder over his face, it felt like he stood beneath a healing spigot, and he was drawing closer to faith and the One he once knew.

"I promise to be a better man." *A better man than my dad was.* He gulped. He was going to have to let the bitterness of his father's desertion go, too. But how? *Help me forgive him.* It was a beginning. "I want to follow Your path, Lord, wherever that leads." A cloud spread apart, allowing filtered sunlight through. The warm rays caressed him like a gentle hug.

Feeling more renewed and alive than he had in decades, he sang the lyrics to "Amazing Grace," a song that had played in his mind many times throughout his adult life, even when he hadn't wanted it to. At first, the words came haltingly. Then he sang with heartfelt gusto, reminiscent of his days in high school theater.

He spent a few more minutes praying, and then he jogged to his car, suddenly eager to get back to Basalt Bay and Sarah.

Chapter Thirty-nine

Sarah had been busy all morning greeting patrons, answering questions about local artists highlighted in Blue's podcasts, finalizing sales, and fixing coffee and cinnamon rolls for guests. She loved it when the gallery was busy, and with the Christmas season in full swing, things were hopping!

There was even a run on Gracie's paintings, and she had to call and plead for more watercolor paintings to be delivered. Gracie sounded excited about all the sales. But when she said she didn't believe the news about Blue in a way that sounded like she not only agreed with it but endorsed it, Sarah was tempted to tell her what she thought of her opinion. She didn't, but it was all she could do to end the call politely without expressing her honest feelings. Throughout the day, she also had to endure several comments from patrons who made begrudging statements about Blue, which put her in a grumpier mood.

At four p.m., Blue strode through the door, looking weary. He walked straight to her and hugged her, and since the gallery was empty and she could use a hug, Sarah returned his embrace. His arms around her were comforting, and she sighed, glad he was back from his day trip. "How did it go?"

"Okay." He tipped up her chin, his eyes moist. "It never happened."

"Ingrid's claims?"

"Yeah. I never—"

"I believe you."

"Thank you." He kissed her softly, and a few of his tears mingled with hers on her cheek. Hearing about the allegations must have been rough on him, too. He leaned his forehead against hers, his eyes closed. "I'm so sorry this happened. I don't know how you heard—"

"From Callie." His eyelids shot open. She shrugged. "It wasn't too bad." She rested her palms against his chest, gazing into his deep blue eyes, and something about him seemed different. His irises were as gorgeous as ever, but they looked clearer and more focused on her. That personal attention was so appealing she wanted to spend the rest of the day kissing him and forget all about discussing problems or anything related to Ingrid. But there were things she needed to know. "What happened to make Ingrid lash out with a sexual harassment accusation against you?"

"I have no idea." He stepped back, raking his fingers through his dark hair. "I've wracked my brain trying to picture her at her grandmother's gallery, but I don't recall meeting her."

"Yet she's accusing you of—"

"Uh-huh." He rubbed his temples like he had a headache.

"What are you going to do about it?"

"I'll talk with Deputy Brian as I should have done when I first arrived. Other than that, I'm not sure." Sighing, he walked over to the window. With each step he took, it felt like the emotional space between them widened, too. "Alfie says he'll take care of everything. No doubt, he plans to glean more publicity, which is frustrating. But he's in charge of the business side of our partnership, including public relations, and I hate challenging him."

"His methods seem untrustworthy." Blue glanced at her sharply, and she shrugged. "I'm sorry. I didn't mean to badmouth your friend." She followed him to the window where they stood yesterday with so much harmony between them. Where were those good feelings now? "But the things you've said make me leery of him."

"Yeah, me too. But he's still my partner." He gazed at her like he was weighing his next words. "I have been rethinking a lot of things and spent some time praying about it today."

"That's great to hear." She loved that he was sharing part of his spiritual journey with her. Her thoughts flitted through some of the hurdles that had brought them to this point, even if everything hadn't been ironed out yet. "We can bring all our worries and cares to the Lord and trust that He hears and is working in us. I'm living proof of Him changing a life."

"That's how I felt on the beach today, like He was right there, hearing me."

"Oh, Blue." They reached for each other's hands at the same time.

"You get that, don't you?" He smiled affectionately at her.

"I do. I also have experienced the tenderness and closeness of the Lord. Thank you for sharing your experience with me. I'm here if you want to talk about it some more."

"Just as friends?" An uncertain look crossed his face. Why? After hearing the news today and what people said about Blue, she probably was acting less emotionally vulnerable to him. Did he sense that?

"I hope we'll always be friends." She squeezed his hands gently. "And more."

"Okay. Good." Sighing, he leaned in like he was about to kiss her, but she put up her hand.

"I wonder if we should hold off on romantic things until you've had time to work out all the stuff with Ingrid and Alfie. It's a lot for you to be dealing with right now." His crushed look made her want to take back the words.

"I don't want to lose you, Sarah."

"You won't lose me as long as we continue being open and sharing our hearts like we've been doing." She held onto his wrists, gazing into his eyes.

"Do you doubt that I'm being honest with you?"

"No. However, I don't know everything I'd like to know about you."

"What do you want to know?" He moved their hands until their fingers were linked together. "Today, I felt like my heart got ripped apart and put back together piece by piece. My one certainty was knowing you would stand by me and that we can talk about everything."

"I am standing by you." Tears flooded her eyes, and she didn't know why other than it had been a challenging day. "I want to feel like we can tell each other whatever is troubling us or what makes us happy. I want to know your heart, Blue."

"Thank you." He swallowed like it was difficult. "I couldn't wait to get back and share with you about my trip. I loved the Rock Shop. I almost threw up over Ingrid's claims. I stood at the edge of the sea and shouted at God. Then wept before Him." He shrugged. Sighed. Shrugged again. "It's been a day."

"Oh, Blue. I'm so sorry." She hadn't pondered how deeply he might take the news of Ingrid's latest vendetta when she should have thought about it and prayed for him.

"But you're right about this thing with Ingrid hanging over my head, our heads. I have to deal with it. Also, I need to tell you about a situation in Bend that might be—"

The door opened, and a white-haired woman entered the gallery.

"Sorry," Sarah whispered to Blue, and then said, "Welcome to Paige's Gallery," to the visitor. She clasped his hand briefly. "We'll talk later?"

"Sure."

What had he been about to tell her? Did it have anything to do with Ingrid's sister?

"How may I help you?" she asked the woman as Blue exited.

"I'm looking for one of Gracie Parker's paintings to give my grandniece for Christmas."

"I'm sorry, but we don't have any in stock."

"None?" The woman put her hands over her chest in dismay. "You mean I've wasted a trip driving here?"

"I apologize for any inconvenience." Sarah's conversation with Gracie came to mind. "Actually, the artist sent me photos of two new paintings that will be arriving soon. You can have first dibs on them if you're interested."

"Thank you! That makes my day." The woman beamed. "Please, tell me about those paintings."

"I'll do even better." Sarah accessed the photo gallery on her phone and held up a snapshot of a watercolor painting of a sailboat moving through calm water. In the second photo, a seagull rode blissfully on a piece of driftwood while a storm raged around it. The woman expressed her delight over the second photo, promptly paid for it, and left with Sarah's promise to ship the watercolor upon arrival.

With the rest of the afternoon to herself, she spent some time mulling over what Blue said about praying by the sea and his situation with Ingrid and the Glasser family. Would he stop by later and talk with her? Or did he agree that they should put their relationship on hold?

Chapter Forty

With his jaw clenched and foot tapping, Blue sat in front of Deputy Brian's messy desk, awaiting his next question. Between slurping coffee and checking his computer screen, the officer had been taking his statement, but none of it was going fast enough for Blue. He wanted to get back to the gallery and talk with Sarah some more.

"Tell me again, when did this accusation occur?" Deputy Brian poised a pen over a form on which he'd been entering information.

"I heard about the harassment complaint today while I was in Lincoln City."

"Why were you there?" The deputy peered at him, eyebrows drawn together.

"Just doing my job."

"Which is?"

How many times did he have to explain the same thing? "I was researching a rock artist."

"Rock artist?" Deputy Brian shook his head. "Seriously?"

"Lindsay Smart is a professional painter who paints rocks and sells them." Painting rocks wasn't that unusual.

"And this job of yours brought you to Basalt Bay, where you've been belittling our local talent?"

"That's not what I've been doing!"

"I thought you said a woman nearly caused an accident because of your profession."

Blue clenched his jaw. "I think the driver was Ingrid Glasser, the same person you detained during the winter festival."

"Do you have any proof?" The deputy tapped his pen on the desk.

"No."

"Then it's your word against hers?"

"I guess." Blue tossed up his hands.

"She didn't confess to driving erratically." Deputy Brian fiddled with a medal on his shirt. "I only charged her with disorderly conduct." So Ingrid got away with what she did? *Unbelievable.* "Now, about this sexual misconduct accusation." Deputy Brian scribbled more words on the form. "Are you sure it's fabricated?"

"Positive."

"You didn't make any romantic advances or suggestive comments to Ingrid Glasser?"

"Absolutely not!"

"Did you say or do anything to her that could be perceived as unwelcome interest or coercion concerning your business?"

"No! If she says I did, she's making it up." Blue closed his eyes briefly and took a calming breath. "If it helps, she called me honey during an art demo last week."

"Why would she call you that if you aren't dating?"

"Who knows? She also phoned and acted like she was standing outside my grandmother's house in Redding. I took what she said as a threat."

"Any proof she was on her property?"

"No." He released a weary sigh. He didn't have proof she made the prank calls to Gram, either.

"And you have no idea why Ingrid might retaliate or speak harshly against you?" The deputy had already asked him about that, too.

"All I know is I gave her grandmother a negative review on my podcast three months ago. I'm an art critic. I say what I think about art. It isn't personal."

"To you, maybe." Deputy Brian clucked his tongue.

"I mean, my review wasn't meant as an insult. I have a right to state my opinion!" Blue tried to deflect his emotions with a cough. "I regularly tell my audience I'm expressing my view and mine alone."

"Some folks might not take kindly to your view." The deputy set the form on his messy desk. "Where can I find this review that you deem not personal?"

Blue bit his tongue to stop himself from saying something rude. "There's a backlog of shows listed on *Blue's Art Clash*."

"*Blue's Art Clash*, hmm?" Deputy Brian stroked his shadowed chin. "Says a lot, doesn't it?"

"Have you ever listened to my show?"

"Why would I?"

"You'd understand my situation better if you had." Blue shuffled his shoulders, trying to release some stress. "There's hype and drama associated with it. Some people listen to my podcast for its artistic content, while others jump on board for the more extreme things I say in character."

"Otherwise, known as insulting?"

"It's part of the biz." He rubbed his palm across the back of his neck.

"I bet you're thinking twice about 'the biz' now."

"You have no idea." His thoughts returned to the time he'd spent on the beach earlier, and he longed for the peace he felt then. *Lord, help me.*

Deputy Brian clicked the end of his pen with his thumb and gazed around the room. "I'll put out an APB on Ingrid's vehicle and try to find out about her connection to the gallery in Bend. Your number is here if I need to reach you."

"Right. I'm staying at the Beachside Inn." Blue stood. "Thanks for your time."

"Are you planning to contact a lawyer?"

"My business partner is taking care of that. But I thought I should talk with you also."

"You should have filed a complaint here when you first came to town and thought someone tried to cause an accident."

"You're probably right." Blue left the small station feeling doubtful that anything would come of his complaint now. If the officer had issued a restraining order against Ingrid or volunteered to watch the gallery for a few days, he'd feel better.

Should he go over and talk with Sarah or head back to the inn and lay low as Alfie expected him to do? Maybe Ingrid had returned to Bend. But what if she hadn't? What if she was watching him? A chill skittered up his neck. He glanced over his shoulder at the empty sidewalk. Was that a woman's shadow in an alcove? Probably shadows of dusk settling in. *I'm too jumpy.*

Back in his Stang, he started the engine and withdrew his phone from his pocket. Would Sarah meet him for dinner if he asked? After what she said about them backing off from their relationship, he doubted it. Still, he shot her a text. *Want to meet at Bert's and talk?*

I'm tired. I think I'll head home after work.

Okay. See you tomorrow? He tapped the steering wheel, waiting for her reply.

As I said—

Two minutes later, she still hadn't resumed their conversation.

Chapter Forty-one

Sarah stared pensively at the phone screen, contemplating Blue's dinner invitation and how she answered that she was tired, which was true. However, she'd like to sit across from him at Bert's, gazing into his sapphire eyes and hearing every detail about his trip, including more about his spiritual experience. Why did she tell him they should put their relationship on hold? That sounded terrible now.

A jangle and a door click signaled someone's entry into the gallery. She tapped send without finishing the text message and strode around the counter. "Welcome to Paige's Gallery!"

A well-dressed man with teal-rimmed glasses and copper streaks in his balayage-styled hair stood stiffly with his arms crossed, peering around the gallery and scowling, almost sneering. Sarah's sensors leaped to high alert. It was late, and this guy looked agitated or volatile.

"May I help you? It's nearly closing time." She clutched her phone tightly.

"No wonder he painted such a dreary picture of this place." *Dreary?* "Where's Blue?"

He was here to see Blue? "Who are you?"

"His business partner."

"Oh. You're Alfie?" She released her death grip on the phone.

"So he's mentioned me?" He smoothed his hand over his glistening hair. "How well do you know Blue Paxton?" He looked her over with a lazy gleam that made her uncomfortable.

Sarah's feelings from another day when she was gagged and kidnapped caused her heart to race. Her ears rang with an eerie foreboding. "It's closing time. I'll have to ask you to leave."

"You must be the prim and proper gallery attendant who's got Blue tied up in knots," he said in a belittling tone.

"I'm not prim or proper." She lifted her chin, trying not to let an ounce of fear show. "I doubt I'm tying him in knots, either. Now, I asked you to leave, so please go." She pointed toward the door. "If you're interested in a painting or sculpture, return tomorrow during business hours. We open at ten."

"Why would I want any of these amateur works of so-called art?" He grimaced toward Paige's lighthouse painting. "I live in a mansion. My walls boast the works of great artists."

"I consider these works great," Sarah said, feeling a surge of loyalty to Paige and her other artist friends. She would be proud to have *The Storm* hanging on her bedroom wall. "It's all a matter of perspective, isn't it?"

"With that attitude, why do you even work in an art gallery?" He shook his head like he thought she was an idiot. "You have no idea how important I am in Blue's world, do you?"

"I guess I don't." She clutched her phone again. "As I said, it's closing time."

"I'll leave when I'm ready!" he said insistently. "You might have Blue hoodwinked with your small-town charm, but not me. I know what you're after."

He knew nothing about her! "I said it's time for you to leave, and I meant it!"

"And I said—"

"If the lady says it's time to go, then go!" Blue marched through the front door. Sarah didn't even hear the jingle. "How dare you shout at her!"

She wanted to run to him and kiss him in relief, but she stayed rooted to the spot.

Alfie's lips curled in an innocent-looking smile. "Blue, buddy, it's good to see you. I came straight here when I got into town, looking for you."

"Is that so?" Blue mouthed "Sorry" to her as he grabbed Alfie by the arm and propelled him toward the door. "Like the lady said, it's time for the gallery to close. Never try strong-arming Sarah again, or you'll answer to me and a lawyer!"

"Hey, now." Alfie twisted back and smiled artificially in her direction, reminding her of an actor in a play. "If I offended you, fair lady, I apologize." He strode the rest of the way on his own and peered back at Blue from the doorway. "Coming?"

"I'll be out in a minute."

"See that you do." Alfie glanced between Blue and Sarah, smirked again, and exited.

"I'm sorry about that." Blue's compassionate expression chased some of her anxiety away, and she hurried to him.

"How did you know to come here?"

"When you didn't finish your text, I got worried."

"Thank you for coming so quickly."

"Of course." He clasped her hands gently. "Are you okay? Do you have a ride home? Or should I stay for a while?"

"I'm okay. I have an Uber ride scheduled." She wished he'd hug her or say something meaningful, but why would he do those things when she was the one who said they should put their romance on pause? "Alfie made me feel uneasy."

"I'm sorry. I apologize for his bad behavior. Can we talk tomorrow? There's something I have to do tonight, but I want to see you."

"Sure. Tomorrow is fine."

They said goodbye, and Sarah locked the door. Her introduction to Alfie had been awkward and a little creepy. She'd felt afraid of him. And she sensed a rift between Alfie and Blue. Was that because of Alfie's lack of integrity in their business?

Or because he despised her?

Chapter Forty-two

Blue had been peering out the motel window for the last half hour, awaiting Alfie's arrival. The Beachside Inn was the only overnight accommodation in Basalt Bay, so he'd have to show up eventually or else drive to another city. As frustrated as he was with Alfie, Blue wanted to pound on every door in the three parallel buildings until he found him. Then he'd tell his business partner what he thought of his obnoxious behavior toward Sarah. Who did he think he was, acting like that? She said he made her feel uneasy, but Blue witnessed the look of fear in her eyes, which made him feel protective of her and astronomically irate with Alfie. But since he didn't want to bring down the innkeeper's wrath, he refrained from hammering on every door.

Finally, Alfie strolled up the path, fingering some french fries like he didn't have a care in the world. When he entered the room across the way, Blue followed and knocked hard on his door.

"Who is it?" Alfie asked in a muffled tone.

"Open up. It's me."

"Hold your horses."

As soon as the door opened, Blue charged inside the room that almost matched his. "Why did you go to the gallery and speak so rudely to Sarah? Why are you in Basalt Bay at all?" He stood in front of the door, arms crossed, glaring at the man he was tempted to punch in the nose.

"Can't a guy visit the seashore? Check up on his old pal, Blue?"

"What I heard didn't sound like you were checking up on me, but rather, my girlfriend!"

"Girlfriend?" Alfie pulsed his finger. "You have let personal stuff get in the way of your work—and with a gallery manager, no less! What about not forming attachments with personnel? Where are your work ethics? Where's your commitment to our enterprise?"

"Don't lecture me. You don't own my life!"

Alfie cackled like he found the statement hilarious. "Reread our contract, Blue, buddy. I run most of your life and brand right down to that fancy car you drive."

Blue ground his teeth. "My friendship with Sarah has nothing to do with you! Stay away from her and the gallery where she works."

"Everything you say and do as Blue Paxton has to do with me. Every success and dollar earned have my name written all over them."

"Are you nuts?" Blue's fists clenched and unclenched. "You aren't in charge of my thoughts and ideas. You have never been nor ever will be in control of what I say."

"Open your eyes! That's what I've been doing for the last five years." Alfie marched across the small space, flinging out his arms. "Before I made you into something, you were a nobody! I invented Blue Paxton. You are successful because of me!"

"So my degree means nothing? All the hundreds of art shows and galleries I've attended don't matter?" Fists tight, Blue's fingernails dug into his palms. "I'm the one who came to you with the original idea for my podcast. Yes, you convoluted my ideas and created the ratings-lure it is today. But from the show's inception, I disagreed with your trying to train me like a dog."

Alfie laughed. "Blue, buddy, you love seeing your name in lights as much as I do! You love the money and fame."

What could Blue say to that? Alfie wasn't all wrong. For the last five years, he had tried to succeed in every area of being a contemporary art critic and an engaging podcaster. He'd given himself wholly to being the best in the business, stirring up interest in art and getting people to listen to his show anyway he could. But he drew the line when it came to protecting the people he cared about, and that included Sarah!

"I'm the one who came up with a plan to take the art world by storm and give them what they craved—the gritty, dirty truth about artists and art." Alfie gesticulated like he was on a stage, not in a tiny vintage-styled room with sea noises rumbling in the background. "The podcast has your name, but I've been the wind keeping your sails going. I'm the one who's supported you and made your voice heard. So it might as well be *Alfie's Art Clash*." He fanned out his fingers as if he were visualizing a neon sign with his name written in bold letters.

"That's ridiculous!" Blue had assumed Alfie's decisions and direction for the podcast were for the good of their partnership, not for him to become dictatorial and greedy. Sarah was right. Alfie's methods were untrustworthy. Why hadn't Blue seen that clearly before?

"Every place you go, every gallery you visit, I've been directing your path."

"Give me a break! You aren't God. Only He gets to direct my path." Alfie cackled like he thought Blue was joking. Blue bit his lip to stop himself from saying something so contentious they'd end things now. "You didn't have anything to do with me driving into Basalt Bay!"

"Think again. You should leave and cool off before either of us says something we'll regret." Too late. Alfie had already said things Blue regretted and wouldn't forget. "If I said anything offensive, I apologize." Alfie's sentiment sounded as fake as his apology to Sarah earlier. "As a friend and colleague, I'm warning you to break all ties with Sarah Blackstone."

"I won't." Where did he get off telling Blue what to do?

"She's cute for her age." Alfie coughed. "But she's small-town nothing. You can't afford to hole up in a pointless berg like this. Break free of her stranglehold while you can."

"How dare you intrude on my personal life!" Blue pulled his glasses down and glared at Alfie over the top. "How dare you try to control who I date or who I marry, for that matter!"

"Marry?" The word exploded from Alfie. "I'm trying to salvage what's left of your career and what we've built together." He sounded almost sincere. "Do you honestly see yourself giving up being a traveling podcaster and prominent commentator to spend your life in a Nowheresville like this with someone like her?"

"Don't say one more word about her! I mean it!" Blue pointed at Alfie, glaring darts of rage at him. He'd quit their partnership if he said anything else against Sarah.

Alfie made a dismissive gesture. "Shut the door on your way out."

Blue stood there fuming, glaring at Alfie for several long seconds before stomping outside. Despite the late hour and the fussy owner's rules about not slamming doors, he shut the door hard and headed for the beach. Only when he reached the sandy shore did he wonder why Alfie hadn't mentioned Ingrid's false claims. Did that have anything to do with why he was in Basalt Bay?

Chapter Forty-three

Sarah awoke to knocking and Lola's hushed whispers. "Sarah! Wake up. Hurry! Come downstairs. There's something you must see. There's talk!"

What now? She moaned. "I'll be there in a second." She checked her cell phone and found five texts from Blue, one from Callie, and another from Sue Anne. What was going on? She glanced at Blue's first message. *I need to talk with you right away.* Why? What was the urgency about? She threw on her robe and ran downstairs.

When she reached the dining room, Lola was pacing in front of the window. "There you are! Some bad stuff is going on."

"What is it? I have a bunch of texts, but I wanted to talk to you first."

"Look at this!" Lola thrust her electronic tablet toward her. A bold headline read, "Gold Digger in Basalt Bay Contends for Blue Paxton's Positive Reviews!"

"Gold digger?" Sarah sucked in a breath. "Is that article referring to me?"

"Keep reading. You'll see."

Sagging into a chair at the table, she fixed her gaze on the fine print. "Blue Paxton is caught in a love triangle between Sarah Blackstone, Basalt Bay gallery manager, and Ingrid Glasser, granddaughter of Evelyn Glasser, a Bend, Oregon artist, recuperating after suffering from work-related health issues." Love triangle? Her name smeared across the internet? How did this happen so soon after the allegations against Blue yesterday? Sarah pressed her hands over her eyes. *Lord, help.* What else could go wrong?

"Are you okay?" Lola patted her shoulder. "I'm sorry, but I had to tell you."

"I'm glad you did" Sighing, she lowered her hands. "I had to know." She skimmed the rest of the article, which mostly consisted of exaggerated gossip about Blue seeing two women simultaneously. Her phone vibrated several times. Blue's and Callie's names came up, but she didn't answer either. "Ingrid must be trying to cause Blue more embarrassment. But why involve me?"

"Because you befriended him?"

"I had nothing to do with his critique of her family's gallery. And there's no love triangle!" How could she even defend herself? Vent on social media? Post on Blue's website and argue with whoever was spreading this garbage? She groaned. Commenting online wasn't her style or how she knew God wanted her to act. But Ingrid Glasser had to be stopped!

"Are you going to confront Blue?" Lola asked softly.

"About what?" Sarah was thinking only about confronting Ingrid.

"About the other woman?"

"He said he never dated her. Ingrid must have concocted this story to make him and me look bad." First the harassment tale and now this? But what if Ingrid's version wasn't entirely fabricated? Blue said he needed to tell Sarah something. Did that have anything to do with Ingrid?

She closed her eyes for a few moments. Getting all worked up about this wasn't helping her have peace, and it wasn't how she wanted to live. If there were questions to be asked, she would ask them. If uncomfortable topics needed to be addressed between her and Blue, she would do that. But in every situation, she wanted the love of Jesus and His grace and mercy to fill her heart and mind. And she wanted to trust Blue completely. How else could she hope for a future with him?

She thought about how sweet he had been with her lately—kind, tender, protective, and seemingly trying to be as honest with her as she was with him. He rushed to her aid last night, concerned about her safety. He stood up to Alfie, didn't he? Why would she deem him untrustworthy based on anything Ingrid Glasser said? She valued honesty too much to get caught in that web. *I trust you, Blue.*

Lola dropped into the chair beside her and clasped her hand. "Are you all right? What are you going to do?"

"I'm okay. I plan to talk with Blue and stand by him." She hugged Lola. "Thank you for caring and talking with me. Now, I need to prepare for the day and spend some time praying before I leave."

"If I can help in the smallest way, just ask."

"If anyone comes looking for me"—she thought of Ingrid and Alfie—"don't let them in."

"I won't. I'll tell the others also."

"Thank you." Sarah hurried up the stairs and ladder, entered her room, and dropped onto her knees by the bed. *Lord, Blue and I need Your wisdom and grace. Thank You for bringing him into my life. I don't know if we'll end up getting married, but I care deeply about him already. Please guide us and help us to know what to do about all this stuff.*

Were any of the problems they were facing part of God's plan to draw them together? Or were they foreshadowing that a relationship with a public figure like Blue Paxton might be especially difficult?

"Doesn't God have a plan in this?" she imagined Judah asking her. She pictured her brother's serene features as he quoted a passage of scripture like he had many times over the last year. *"'And we know that in all things God works for the good of those who love him.' Sarah, God is working out good for us in everything. We can trust Him with our whole lives."*

"Lord Jesus, I trust You."

She continued praying for a few more minutes. Afterward, she sensed a greater peace about Blue and her, yet one question nibbled at her thoughts. While she believed the Lord had brought Blue into her life, was he the man she was supposed to spend the rest of her life with?

Chapter Forty-four

Blue waited, hunkered down in his car seat a block from the gallery. When he arrived, press members were already congregating outside the building, cameras and microphones ready. This had to be Alfie's doing! Who else would spin a contemptible tale about him being involved with two women and getting this much press to show up in Basalt Bay? But why would his business partner go to such lengths? Was he retaliating against Blue for having a relationship with Sarah? How bizarre!

Alfie hadn't responded to any of his texts or voicemails this morning. Sarah hadn't answered any, either. Hopefully, that wasn't because she believed any of the nonsense about him and Ingrid having a romantic relationship.

As soon as he spotted Sarah leaving the City Hall parking lot and heading toward the gallery, he hopped out of his vehicle and ran straight for her. "Sarah!"

"What's going on?" She peered toward the crowd, her mouth dropping open.

"Come on! Let's get out of here!" He clutched her hand and ran with her to the passenger side of his car.

Some press members ran toward them. "That's her!"

"Get a picture of them together!"

"Is that Sarah Blackstone?"

"Can I get a quote?"

Blue helped Sarah get inside, sprinted around the Stang, dropped into his seat, started the engine, and accelerated before the reporters could block their exit. Through the rearview mirror, he watched them standing in the street, frowning and looking puzzled.

"What are they doing here?" Sarah asked bewilderedly. "I have to get to work."

"I know. I'm sorry about all of this."

"It's not your fault." She met his gaze without any blame in her expression, which was a relief after this morning's headlines.

"I didn't approve of anyone writing that trash about us. However, because of the podcast's popularity, people may talk about me and spread untrue rumors, like what happened yesterday." He glanced in the rearview mirror as he drove and didn't see another car. "I hate that you're getting dragged into this because of me."

"The article was shocking." Her voice trembled. "Where are you taking me? I have to get back to the gallery."

"I'll pull over at an overlook and give Deputy Brian a few minutes to talk some sense into the reporters."

"You called the deputy?"

"I did."

"That's good. How about here?" She pointed to a narrow overlook on the right side, and he brought the car to a controlled stop.

"Are you okay?" He smoothed his palm over the backs of her hands, clutched in her lap.

"This is all so strange. I'd better text Paige and tell her what's happening and that I'll be late." She pulled her phone out of her pocket, tapped the screen, and typed with her thumbs. A few moments later, her phone buzzed. "Paige says her husband, Forest, will check on the gallery and talk to Deputy Brian. He's a part-time PI and travels for work sometimes, too."

Too? Was she implying that if Paige and Forest could make their marriage work despite his travels, the two of them ought to be able to make a relationship succeed, too? He smiled at the thought. "Maybe I should talk to him."

"Why?"

"I usually try not to react to gossip." He glanced back, checking the road for other cars. "But this fabricated tale about you, me, and Ingrid is driving me crazy! Forest might be able to find out where it originated."

"Why not go to the source? Isn't this Ingrid's brainchild?"

"I thought so. Now, I'm not so certain she acted alone."

"Alfie?" She grimaced.

"Yeah. After last night—"

"Is he still your business partner?"

"He is, but if he's behind this—" Blue raked his fingers through his hair. "Ingrid has a grudge against me. But why would she go public with misinformation? What does she gain?"

"Notoriety. Public support." Sarah shrugged. "Sympathy for her grandmother and their family gallery?"

"Possibly." Blue sighed, feeling tired and stressed. He removed his glasses and pressed his fingers against his eyelids. He could use a good night's sleep after two rough ones.

"What would Alfie gain?" Sarah asked like she was still engaged in the discussion and needed answers.

"Beyond publicity? I don't know. The love triangle stuff doesn't even make sense."

"Did you ever date Ingrid?" He'd already told her he didn't, so she must be worried about it to ask. "Was it a fling and she wants you back?"

"No! Nothing like that happened."

"Then why did someone report it did?"

"It's made-up media hype that seems to point to Alfie. At times, his methods are questionable." He put his glasses back on and clutched the steering wheel, remembering his verbal altercation with him last night. "I'm afraid he's attempting to profit from people getting stirred up and talking about us. We're finished working together if I find out he's behind these lies!"

"Why would he concoct an outlandish tale that might hurt both of you?"

"He's always pushing for more drama in the podcast. I don't like all his ideas." Blue felt his blood pressure rising and shot another look over his shoulder. "But I never realized how far he'd go for more money and fame."

"Is your business having financial problems?" she asked in a softer tone.

"Not that I'm aware of. Alfie may sense a different kind of loss, though."

"Such as?"

"My loyalty." He clasped her hand gently, gazing at her and hoping to convey his feelings. "He's worried I'll settle down in a hamlet like Basalt Bay and lose focus on my work."

"Is he right?"

"That I've been tempted to stay here with you?" He leaned forward, glancing from her beautiful, deep brown eyes to her sweet, kissable lips, and then back to her eyes.

"Are you?"

He brushed his lips softly over hers. "Am I tempted to spend my life with you, kissing and holding you, wherever that may lead and whatever it might cost me?" He kissed her again, lingering over the gentleness and beauty of their mouths caressing. "Yes. Sweet Sarah, I am tempted to do that."

"Oh, Blue."

"I care for you. It's like I—" He didn't know how much he should say when they hadn't discussed the possibilities of a long-term relationship and how to make it work. But how could he hold back when he was experiencing such a strong emotional connection with her? He stroked her cheek. "While I was away from Basalt Bay, I hated how far I'd driven from you. Each mile created more angst and longing for you." She smiled like she understood, and he wanted to express everything in his heart. "When I'm with you, it feels like I'm home. Is that sentimental nonsense when we haven't known each other long?"

"No." She shook her head. "It makes perfect sense. I feel at home when I'm with you, too."

"I'm glad. Don't get me wrong, I still don't want to stop doing the job I love."

"And you shouldn't have to." She placed her hand on his chest and gazed into his eyes. "I told you I would never ask you to quit being a traveling podcaster. That's who you are and what you are meant to do. It's important for both of us to follow our hearts."

Her supportive attitude amazed him. "But how can I spend all my waking hours with you and continue doing my current job? Doesn't the hero in the story always leave everything else behind to be with the person he loves?"

Sarah chuckled softly and played with a button on his shirt. "In fictional tales, yes. But this is real life, yours and mine. It's about what we want and how we let God use our gifts and talents for His glory. When you and I met, we were podcaster and temp gallery manager. You shouldn't have to give up what you enjoy doing. I shouldn't have to, either."

"Even if that means we won't be together as much as we'd like to be?" She wet her lower lip as if anticipating another kiss, but he didn't close the gap, awaiting her answer. "Sarah?"

"I plan to continue living in Basalt Bay and working in the gallery. This place and the people here have become my world." Knowing that about her, he nodded. "But I want you in my world, too. I want us to explore where these feelings we have for each other will go. I want to give *us* a chance." Her eyes sparkled with warmth and hope, it seemed.

"I'd like that, too, more than anything." Although he was in a quandary about how to divide time and distance, he loved her and— He loved her? *I love Sarah!* He wanted to jump out of the vehicle and shout the words at the ocean and the sky.

"We'll have obstacles to face," she continued, unaware of his epiphany. "What you and I do for a living complicates our relationship." She stroked her finger over her mouth, bringing his attention to her ruby lips, and he wanted to kiss her for the next hour and tell her he loved her repeatedly. "As much as I hate to bring it up, what someone wrote about us and the press showing up at my workplace proves that."

"But you believe me, right?" Did she hear the desperation in his voice?

"Yes. I believe you. I want to see only the best in you."

"Thank you. Now, please, may I kiss you?"

"Why would you want to do that?" she asked teasingly.

"Because I love you, Sarah." His heart pounded a rapid cadence.

She gasped softly. "Love? Really?"

"And truly."

"Oh, Blue. I love you, too."

Their lips met in an unhurried kiss that morphed into something tenderly passionate and consuming. Blue could have continued their affectionate kissing for a long time, but he drew back and whispered near her ear, "I love you. I want only you."

"I think I've loved you since we kissed under the mistletoe."

He smiled and gazed into her moist chocolaty eyes. She loved him! They loved each other! Sweet, wonderful, powerful feelings rushed over him like gentle waves rolling on the shore. They kissed again. He couldn't imagine spending the rest of his life with anyone but this beautiful, precious woman. His Sarah.

"What now?" She leaned back, stroking his cheeks with her fingertips and gazing at him adoringly. "I can hardly go back to acting like my heart isn't linked with yours."

"Nor would I want you to." He smoothed his palm over her soft hair. "Will you face this problem about Ingrid with me? Will you help me get to the truth and stick with me, no matter what?"

"Absolutely. If there's any way I can help, I will."

"Thank you." He leaned forward until his forehead rested against hers. "I promise to protect you from any future problems like this."

"That sounds great to me." She danced her fingertips around the edges of his mouth, creating ticklish sensations. "I have to go to work. But what I said about you continuing to do what you love and me doing the same, I mean that."

He loved her for believing in their future, as unorthodox as it might be. His phone vibrated with an incoming text he'd rather ignore. "It's from Deputy Brian." He scanned the message. "He says the coast is clear. He'll keep watch at the gallery for a few hours."

"I should get back then."

Blue didn't want this time alone with her to end, especially after they confessed their love for each other. And he still needed to explain about Elly. "There's something else we should talk about later."

"I can't wait to hear what's in your heart." She pressed her lips softly against his, making him wish they could stay right here and not go back to the gallery.

As he drove toward town, he thought he saw a black vehicle in the rearview mirror. Was it his imagination? Or was Ingrid back?

Chapter Forty-five

Two hours after arriving at the gallery, Sarah wondered if her lips might still be tingling from Blue's kisses. That he'd declared his love for her was surreal. When did they go from liking each other to falling wholeheartedly in love? And what did it all mean? She'd been in love before, so she knew what she felt was real—so much that she wanted to dance and sing their names together. *Blue and Sarah. Blue and Sarah Paxton?* Chills raced over her skin.

Wasn't it just this morning she'd prayed about God's will and pondered all the good things He was doing in her life? Falling for Blue and him falling for her was one of those amazingly good things! But was Blue considering marriage like she was? Did he want them to experience a forever kind of love together?

She glanced out the door window as she'd been doing off and on over the last couple of hours and appreciated Deputy Brian for standing guard. She'd taken him hot coffee twice and thanked him both times.

Blue stayed for a while after they arrived but said he was too distracted to write or do research, as if she was the cause of his distraction, and left to get some work done. She grinned at the thought of being even a slight disruption to his concentration. *Watch out, Blue! I hope to be more of a distraction to you in the coming days!*

Hardly anyone came into the gallery, probably due to the officer's presence outside. Since things were so quiet, Sarah called Callie, hoping to reassure her that everything was okay despite the tales spreading around. Callie expounded on how outraged she'd been over hearing Ingrid's claims, and Sarah did her best to calm her down. Afterward, she wrote texts to the others who'd sent concerned messages—Sue Anne, Judah, Craig, Paige, and even Ruby in Alaska.

She was thinking about texting Blue regarding dinner plans when the door opened. A redhead with a scarf wrapped around the lower portion of her face marched inside the gallery. *Ingrid!* Sarah bolted upright. How did she get past Deputy Brian? "What are you doing here?"

"I'm a paying customer. I haven't gotten my Gracie Parker painting yet."

"We're sold out. But there's one arriving tomorrow. If you want it, I can finalize the sale and ship it to you," she spoke professionally despite her heart pounding in her throat. After Ingrid's previous visit and all the online garbage, every self-protective sensor in Sarah's body was preparing to flee or fight.

"Too bad you don't have one available now." Ingrid peered around the room like one of Gracie's paintings might be hiding somewhere.

Ingrid is here! Sarah discreetly texted Blue.

Where's the deputy?

Good question!

I'll be right there.

Sarah stepped behind the chair she'd been sitting in, searching for any useful item to grab if her encounter with Ingrid became a physical struggle. She prayed it wouldn't.

"Where's lover boy?" Ingrid demanded.

"Who?"

"Don't play the innocent." Ingrid clenched her hands, squinting at Sarah. Was she a violent person? If she was the one who tried running Blue off the road, she was. By her previous threat to Sarah, she was. "I saw you two making out by the sea. It was disgusting!"

"You were spying on us?" They had only been kissing, but the thought of Ingrid sneaking around watching them made her shudder.

"I warned you he'd hurt you." Ingrid strode toward her with a menacing look on her face.

"Meaning?" Sarah clutched the top rung of the chair.

"He isn't free to chase after you. He's taken."

"I doubt that."

"Are you calling me a liar?" Ingrid glowered.

"No, but—" Since Blue was on his way and Sarah needed to stall, she asked, "How did you get past the deputy?"

"That attention-seeking buffoon?" Ingrid laughed disdainfully. "I told him a sob story. He raced off to capture the villain who assaulted me."

"You lied to get your way?"

"You are so naïve."

"I value honesty. Maybe you should give it a try." She regretted her comment when Ingrid stepped directly before her, glaring ominously.

"How dare you mock me!"

"How dare I challenge you to be honest?" Sarah's heart pounded like a drumbeat, but she didn't cower before the other woman.

"You want honesty?" Ingrid's green eyes gleamed gold like a fire raged inside them. "Blue Paxton needs to pay for his crimes, and you're caught in the crossfire."

"Why risk everything for revenge?" Sarah lifted her chin, despite the threat.

"Because he ruined everything! We lost our gallery's respect. My grandmother's health deteriorated. His pathetic lies destroyed my sister's happiness!"

"Your sister?"

"He promised her—" Ingrid clenched her teeth.

"What?"

"He told Elly he'd come back and marry her." Was that what Blue had been about to tell her? "Instead, he's here kissy-lipping with you. So it's your fault, too!"

Sarah swallowed the dryness in her throat. "When did this supposedly happen?"

"Three months ago." Ingrid's scarf slipped, revealing more of her face. "But he flirted with Elly. He took advantage of her kind-hearted nature and coerced information from her about our grandmother. He did the most despicable thing!"

What had Blue done that Ingrid found so contemptible? Had he really— As if a neon light flashed above her, Sarah realized what Ingrid was doing. She was trying to sabotage Blue by lying about him, as she lied to the deputy about a villain hurting her, about the online harassment complaint, and the love triangle tale. "Blue Paxton would never do that!" Sarah said boldly.

"You're wrong! You don't know everything about him!"

"I know enough to trust him."

Her face contorting, Ingrid grabbed Sarah's chair and yanked strongly. Sarah shouted at her to let go and tugged, but Ingrid pulled more forcefully, and she lost her grip. She covered her face, expecting the worst. But instead of striking her, Ingrid roared and hurled the chair.

"Nooooo!" Sarah cried as it crashed into Kathleen's mosaic display. Pictures careened to the floor, breaking into hundreds of pieces. "What have you done? The mosaics!" *Kathleen's prized work ruined!* Was this Ingrid's plan all along? To destroy the gallery? What else did she plan to wreck? *I have to get out of here!* Sarah scrambled for the door with Ingrid clawing at her, attempting to stop her. "Let me go!"

"Stay here!" Ingrid lunged in front of her, hands out. "You aren't getting past me. You are my trump card!"

"No, I'm not!" All the emotions of the nightmares she suffered after the last time she was kidnapped twisted through her. She tried to reach the door again, but Ingrid grabbed her and shoved her against a table. *God, help! Save me.*

"You're not going anywhere!" Nostrils flaring, Ingrid seized another chair. "I'm in charge of this gallery now! When I've destroyed every piece of art and smashed that window and everything else of value here, you'll be ruined and know how my family feels." Ingrid's eyes shone like she was a victor in a battle.

"If you hold me against my will, you will face years in prison for kidnapping." Sarah tried to keep her voice from shaking and revealing her fear.

"Then it will be worth it." Ingrid lifted the chair. "This is all Blue Paxton's fault!"

The door burst open, hitting the wall, and Deputy Brian ran in, shouting, "Put down that chair!"

"Get away from her!" Blue yelled from right behind him.

Blue.

Ingrid froze, chair mid-air, her gaze darting from Sarah to the men. For a second, it looked like she was still going to hurl the chair.

"Ingrid Glasser, you are under arrest." The deputy wrestled the chair from her. "You have the right to remain silent." He read the rest of her Miranda Rights, but the words were muffled by Blue's strong arms enfolding Sarah.

"It's okay," he whispered. "Everything's going to be okay."

She buried her nose in the crease of his sweater, focusing on breathing and the fact that he and Deputy Brian had arrived before Ingrid could do any more damage.

"You two deserve each other!" Ingrid yelled on her way out the door in handcuffs. "You both deserve what's coming!"

"I'll take your statement later," the deputy called over his shoulder.

Dazed, Sarah stared at the floor where Kathleen's artwork lay broken and destroyed. What a senseless loss! Tears flooded her eyes. Even though Blue held her, she trembled. "How could she damage Kathleen's mosaics like that? How could she be so violent toward me?"

"I don't know. I assumed the deputy would stay out front. I never would have left if I thought you'd be alone." He smoothed his hand down the back of her hair. "I'm sorry. So sorry."

"Ingrid lied about an assailant to get Deputy Brian to leave."

"I figured she must have concocted some tale."

"What—" She swallowed hard. "What did she mean about us deserving what's coming? Hasn't she caused enough trouble?"

"Yes, she has." He continued holding her and stroking her hair. "I have no idea what she meant. Idle threats, no doubt."

Sarah stepped out of his embrace, trying to pull herself together and assess the damage. "I need to take photos. Send them to Paige and the insurance company. Call Kathleen. Clean this mess." Yet all she wanted to do was fall back into Blue's comforting arms and forget the harm Ingrid had done.

"I'll help with picking up the pieces."

"Thank you." Her hands shook around the cell phone, but she made herself take a dozen pictures from various angles. "And thanks for being here and holding me. I needed that."

"I'm here for you as long as you need me to be."

What would he say if she asked him to stay forever?

Chapter Forty-six

Blue had been on the phone at the motel for the last hour, calling old contacts and researching any details of him and Ingrid allegedly having a relationship and who might have reported it to news outlets. He called a couple of gallery owners and reporters without getting any reliable information. There was some speculation, but most of his leads were dead ends. Alfie didn't answer his door. Had he left town?

Blue's phone buzzed. *Gram.* "Gram? Are you okay?"

"I'm fine." Her nervous chuckle said otherwise.

"What's going on?"

"Barb said she heard some news about you dating two women at the same time." Gram took a small intake of breath. "That doesn't sound like my grandson. Is there any truth to it?"

"Not a speck."

"Just like I figured." Gram sighed. "I want you to find someone nice, settle down, and give me a great-grandbaby."

"Gram—"

"Would you rob an old woman of her hope?"

"No. You can hope." And things were changing. He had recommitted his life to the Lord and told Sarah he loved her. "Remember what I shared with you about Sarah? We're serious about each other now."

"That's great news! Tell me her age, hair color, favorite food, everything!"

Blue smiled, picturing Sarah when they were sitting in the car, kissing and talking, earlier. "She's nearly my age, has beautiful dark hair, and wants only the truth between us."

"As it should be!"

"You'll be glad to hear she believes in Jesus and has a strong faith."

"That makes me so happy!"

"She's a widow, but she doesn't have any kids." He tried saying the next part without a hint of negativity. "She wants to stay in Basalt Bay for the rest of her life."

"And that's a problem because—?"

"You know about me and small towns." Gram groaned but he kept talking. "However, she's sweet and supportive. She wants us to continue doing what we love without either of us having to sacrifice our careers."

"Sounds like you've worked out a business plan."

"It's not like that. She'll continue living in the small town she loves. I'll keep traveling and doing my podcast." Why didn't the arrangement sound as appealing as before?

"B-b-but"—Gram sputtered—"how will that work after you're married and have children? You can't keep wandering the planet when you have a family back home!"

"You're jumping ahead of things."

"Am I? I want a great-grandbaby. And I want assurance that you're happily married before I die—not living separately from your wife."

"This is a new relationship. We haven't discussed marriage. And will you please stop talking about dying and me being married in the same conversation?"

"Fine. Hurry up and discuss marriage with her. What are you waiting for? You're forty-two!" Did she have to keep reminding him of his age? An awkward silence followed. Then Gram said, "I'm sorry. I don't mean to intrude into your personal affairs. But you know God is working everything out for your good, right?"

"I believe that now more than I used to."

"I'm glad to hear it."

"He's already used some unusual circumstances to lead me to Sarah and back to Him." A lump formed in his throat. "Her belief that God is doing good in our lives has made me reconsider some of the things you taught me, too."

"You're getting me all choked up." Gram's voice broke. "Hearing you talk about God and faith is a balm to this grandma's heart and an answer to my prayers. If your Sarah is responsible, I'll be eternally grateful to her."

"You're going to like her."

"I already do! Oh. Wait. Someone is at the door."

"Don't open it without looking out the window first." He heard her shuffling footsteps. "Gram, I'm serious. Don't answer the door!"

"It's your friend. What's his name? Albert?"

"Alfie? Don't open the door for him! Don't let him into your house! Gram!"

"Hello. What can I do for you?" Her softened voice reached Blue, and he groaned.

"I thought we could have a chat," Alfie said.

"Tell him to leave!" Blue yelled, his frustration rising. "Tell him to call me. I'm the one he should be talking with—not you!"

"Come in. Come in," Gram said cordially. Blue ground his teeth together. "I was just talking on the phone with my grandson." At least she'd kept the line open so he could hear them.

"You're talking with Blue?" Alfie's voice rose an octave.

"Yeah, she is! Leave her house now. I mean it!" Why was Alfie even there?

"He has some great news for me," Gram said proudly.

"What news might that be?"

"He has a girlfriend! Isn't that wonderful? I can't wait to meet her. She sounds amazing."

Oh, Gram.

"Well, that beats all." Alfie's chuckle sounded mechanical. "Maybe we should just, uh—"

Silence.

"Gram? Gram?" Nothing. Blue frantically pressed redial, but it went straight to voicemail. He tapped Gram's name on the screen. No answer. He dialed 911 and quickly explained that his grandmother had a possible intruder in Redding, California. After giving the dispatcher her address and answering a few questions, he contacted Gram's neighbor, Barb, and asked her to check on Gram. She said she would.

While the call might have been inadvertently disconnected, he doubted it. Was Alfie at Gram's house to cause trouble or to twist Blue's arm about not seeing Sarah?

Blue grabbed his jacket and keys and sprinted out to his Stang. He sent Sarah a quick text. *I have to go to Redding. Alfie is at my grandmother's house!*

He hated leaving so soon after they'd expressed their love for each other and following Ingrid's aggressive actions at the gallery, but it couldn't be helped. Ingrid was in jail. Sarah was safe, for now. He had to check on Gram!

He prayed Sarah would understand.

Chapter Forty-seven

After Blue left the gallery, Sarah called Kathleen and told her about what Ingrid had done to her mosaics. Kathleen accepted the disparaging news about her ruined artwork gracefully. "I'm glad you are all right, dear—that's what matters." But Sarah felt awful about it and wished she could have stopped the damage from happening.

She spent some time talking with Paige, filled out the insurance forms, and then rearranged other art pieces to fill in the empty spaces on Kathleen's table. Deputy Brian came by to take her statement, and she had to mentally relive the anxious moments she experienced with Ingrid.

Feeling emotionally exhausted and wishing the work day were over, Blue's text came as a surprise. Alfie was at his grandmother's house? What was he doing there? Whatever the reason, Sarah was glad Blue was rushing to be with his grandmother. That showed how much he cared for her and valued his family. Sarah loved that about him, even though she'd miss being with him.

She fixed herself a cup of chamomile tea and imagined soaking in a hot bubble bath when she got home. That and working for an hour on her ocean mosaic should calm her enough to fall asleep—if only her mind would stop churning with thoughts of Ingrid's ruthless actions and Alfie's weird behavior.

Had Ingrid acted alone? Was the timing of Alfie's arrival at Blue's grandmother's house and Ingrid's altercation with Sarah planned or coincidental? What about what Ingrid said concerning Blue falling for her sister and then leaving suddenly? His departure now didn't have anything to do with that. Yet why hadn't he mentioned Elly Glasser? Shouldn't he have said something if he was dating someone a few months ago?

She'd taken only a few sips of tea when the gallery door opened, and every muscle in her neck and shoulders tensed. Was she going to react like that every time the door opened or the chime jingled? She set down her teacup and stood. When Callie, James, and Paul walked toward her, she heaved a shaky sigh. "Hey, guys! What's going on?"

"That's what we want to know. We heard about a woman causing you some trouble today." Callie hugged Sarah. "Are you all right? Why didn't you call me? I would have been here in minutes."

"Us, too." James rocked his thumb between him and Paul.

"Thank you, but I'm okay. I was scared when Ingrid barged in acting combative, but Deputy Brian took her to jail. Sorry for making you worry." She waved her hand toward her teacup. "This is the first chance I've had to sit down and decompress."

"If she's locked up, that's a mercy," Callie said.

Judah, Craig, and Forest rushed in next, peering at her and then eyeing the gallery as if expecting bad guys to jump out at them.

"Everything okay here?" Judah looked around the corner of the kitchenette. "What's going on, sis?"

Craig gave her a bear hug. "We're not letting anything bad happen to you. If someone is looking for a fight, Judah and I will give them one."

Sarah chuckled at his ferocious declaration. She appreciated her brothers, who she'd met only a year ago, hearing about a problem and rushing to her defense, even if they were too late to do anything about it.

"He's right. We've got this covered." Forest strode to the storage closet and peered inside. Craig jogged over to the bathroom and checked behind the door.

"You guys are sweet. But I'm fine." By their troubled expressions, she hadn't convinced them. "Some things happened that I wish wouldn't have, but it's over. Things are back to normal, other than the damage Ingrid caused to Kathleen's mosaics. That was the real tragedy."

"You weren't injured?" Callie stroked her arm.

"It brought back some bad memories. But that's to be expected after such an ordeal."

"Is there anything we can do?" James asked. "We're here for you one hundred percent!"

"That's right." Paul nodded, squinting around the room. "That Blue isn't here, is he?"

"No." *But I wish he was.* "Thank you all for coming to check on me." She leaned against Callie's shoulder. "Deputy Brian and Blue charged in here like valiant rescuers."

"I wish I'd been here," Craig muttered.

"You and me, both." She smiled at him.

"That woman didn't steal anything?" Callie asked.

"No. The deputy arrested Ingrid before she had a chance to assault me or do any more damage to the gallery."

"Assault you?" Callie put her hand to her throat. "I was terrified when Patty texted me that she had seen the deputy run over here like there was an emergency."

"Paige was anxious, too," Forest said. "Especially considering what you went through earlier this year."

"We were all worried." Judah nodded.

"Your concern is heartwarming." Sarah waved toward the mosaic section. "Kathleen hopes to fix her artwork, but some of it is beyond repair." Her throat tightened as the emotional impact hit her again. "But you know Kathleen. She said it's like when hardships come our way, we take a big breath, work on the things we can, and then rise again."

"That sounds just like her," Callie said.

"I wish I had done something differently."

"Like what?" Forest frowned.

"Like stopping Ingrid from hurling that chair. It's my job to protect the artwork."

"No." He shook his head. "You are standing here, uninjured, because you did the right thing. No work of art is worth getting hurt, as much as we value the items in this gallery."

"I agree," Judah said. Followed by Craig saying, "Yeah. Same here."

"Is there a panic button?" Callie peered into the kitchenette.

"No. But I wouldn't have had time to reach for one."

"It's not a bad idea, though." Forest stroked his chin. "You and Paige work here by yourselves. It's worth looking into improving the security."

"Then that's settled!" Callie nodded as if her decision resolved the matter.

"Why don't I fix everyone coffee and tea before you head home?" Sarah looked around the group wanting to do something for them.

"Tea makes everything better," Callie said.

The others nodded, and Sarah asked about their drink preferences even though she knew most of them by heart.

"Do you know how long your intruder will be in jail?" Judah followed her to the serving counter, leaning his elbows against the surface while the others perused the mosaic section.

"No." She prepped the to-go cups. "I hope Ingrid heads back to Bend as soon as she's released. The deputy mentioned a restraining order to keep her away from here."

"That should help. Say, why haven't I met Blue?" Judah gave Sarah a big brotherly look, even though she was older than him.

"You've heard about him, right?"

"Sure. Callie keeps Paisley informed. But we were hoping you'd tell us about him." Sarah continued working on the hot drinks until Judah cleared his throat. "Are you going to fess up?"

"Here's the coffee and tea!" She passed out the cups, and everyone thanked her.

"About Blue?" Judah tipped his head, eyeing her.

There didn't seem to be any way of avoiding this discussion. "All right. Blue Paxton is a great guy who I happen to be falling in love with."

"In love with?" Callie gasped.

"More aptly put, I am completely besotted, bewildered, amazed, and falling head-over-heels in love with someone I never thought I could love. But I do! Oh, how I do!" She grinned. "Satisfied?"

"Not in the least!" Judah exclaimed.

"Not even!" Craig said.

"Are you thinking of marrying him now, too?" Callie frowned.

"Maybe she doesn't wish to talk about such sensitive topics with all of us here, Callie." James grimaced apologetically at Sarah.

"Nonsense," Callie said. "She says she's in love with the man!"

"I am. But our conversations haven't evolved to discussing marriage yet." Sarah reveled in their surprised expressions. "We'll see what happens, okay?"

"Yes, we will." Callie waved her hand like she was waving away an outcome she didn't like.

"If I were the one besotted and completely in love," Judah said, "I'd be chasing the woman—in my case, Paisley—and pursuing her with all my heart. And there would be plenty of discussions about marriage."

"Not all men are like you, Judah." Sarah took a sip of her latte.

"More's the pity." Callie shook her head sadly.

"I didn't mean to put you on the spot." Judah gave her a sheepish look. "Just watching out for you."

"Thanks for that." She felt comfortable sharing most things with this family of hers. However, what she and Blue chose to do in the future was a private matter, at least something they should talk about first. Even so, she felt a need to explain a little bit. "Blue's and my jobs are like warring entities. There are things we have to figure out, so that's why I don't have all the answers you want to hear. I'm praying and trusting God to work everything out for good in our lives. Isn't that what you always tell me to do, Judah?"

"That I do. If you ever want to talk about it, come by the beach house and visit with Paisley and me."

"I appreciate the invitation." But the person she needed to spend more time talking with was Blue.

"We love and care for you," Craig said from beyond Judah. "We won't let anything happen to you like what happened today, right, guys?"

"Absolutely!" Judah said.

"You've got that right." Paul nodded firmly.

"You can count on us," James said.

"We'll guard this place day and night if need be!" Forest lifted his chin toward the door.

"What is family for if not to help each other?" Callie embraced Sarah in a warm hug. "You are precious to us."

"Thank you! All of you are amazing." She met their gazes individually. "You are the best support group I could wish for. You make me appreciate living in Basalt Bay even more." And it reinforced her desire to stay here with the people she loved.

Chapter Forty-eight

Blue pulled into Gram's driveway after driving from Basalt Bay to Redding with only one stop for gas. He'd heard from the police department that Alfie had left her house before their arrival, and since Gram willingly let him inside, there wasn't any cause for them to put out an APB on his vehicle. Even with that report, Blue wanted to make sure his grandmother was safe. He knocked quietly on her door. "It's me, Gram!"

The deadbolt clinked, and her smiling face made the drive even more worthwhile. "Gram." He stepped inside her warm home that smelled of delicious cooking, shut the door, and embraced her. "Are you okay?" He leaned back and saw moisture in her eyes. "What is it? Did Alfie hurt you?"

"No, no. I'm all right. I'm thankful you are here and safe." She reached up and patted his cheek. "Everything is better with you here, grandson. I wish we lived closer."

"Me too," he said, locking the door. "I'm sorry Alfie showed up the way he did and caused you alarm."

"Eh. Nothing I couldn't handle." Yet she sniffled like the ordeal had been trying. "Could have done without the police questioning me like a criminal."

"Sorry about that. They were trying to find out why Alfie came here. What did he want?"

"He seemed lonely. I gave him some of my vegetable soup." Gram waved toward the stove, where a red stewpot rested on the front burner. "Sit. Sit. I have some left."

"Soup sounds great. Thanks." Sighing, Blue dropped into one of the two chairs at the small kitchen table, feeling hungry and beat from the drive and the emotional turmoil. He set his glasses on the tabletop and pressed his fingers against his tired eyes. He could use a week of sleep, but one night would do. "What did Alfie say to you?"

"Not much." Gram's hands shook as she poured the heated soup from a pan into a turquoise pottery cup large enough to be a bowl. "Here you go. Want some bread to go with it?"

"No thanks. This smells amazing." He took a bite of potatoes and broth, the warm liquid soothing his throat. The blend of herbs and spices was familiar and satisfying. "I've always loved your home-made soup."

Sitting across from him, Gram smiled. "If you came back more often, you'd get to enjoy my home-cooked meals, and I'd get to enjoy my grandson's company."

"Sorry I haven't visited much lately." He thought of Sarah and how bad she wanted to stay close to her family in Basalt Bay. Could he do less with his grandmother?

"I understand. You lead a busy life. Besides, I have my senior friends who keep me company." A sad look crossed her features, which she quickly dispelled with another smile.

"What did Alfie want?"

"To find out about you and Sarah. He was agitated and angry with you, too." Gram shook her head, her short gray hair fluttering. "He scared me a little, so I told him he should leave."

"Did he hurt you in any way?" Blue reached across the table and clasped her thin hand.

"No." She patted his knuckles. "But I thought he might be drunk or on drugs with the way he kept mumbling, pacing, and flailing his arms about."

Blue's heart pounded. "Did he leave when you told him to?"

"Not at first. He grumbled about you not doing what he said, and your head being turned by a small-town girl who's ruining his plans." She tapped her fingers against the table. "Then he noticed something and grew very agitated."

"What was it?"

"The mosaic you sent." Gram pointed her wrinkled finger toward the living room. Blue swiveled in his chair until he saw Sarah's wooden-framed mosaic resting against a flower pot in the middle of the coffee table. "He picked it up, said the artist's name harshly, and groaned like he was in agony."

"Then did he leave?" Blue asked with a heavy feeling.

"Not until Barb came over, glared fire bombs at him, and said she wasn't leaving until he did. He hightailed it out of here after that." She chuckled. "I think he was afraid of Barb."

"Good. I'm glad he left without causing you any other trouble."

"Me too. So you drove all this way to check on your ole Gram?"

"I did and would do so in a heartbeat from wherever I am." He met her gaze, appreciating all she'd done for him over the years and what she meant to him. Even his praying and talking to God lately had to be due to her faithful prayers for him. "I love you, Gram."

"Love you too. I can tell you're troubled about something." She picked up his empty cup and carried it to the sink. "Let's sit on the couch and chat before bedtime."

"Okay." He helped clean up the dishes like old times. Then they went into the living room and sat on the worn-out floral couch. He felt relaxed, being home and sitting beside Gram. Soon, she leaned her head against his shoulder and snored softly.

He picked up Sarah's mosaic and fingered the blue and green glass pieces resembling ocean water and the tan ones that looked like a sandy beach. He imagined Sarah bent over this miniature work of art, painstakingly putting her best efforts into it. He caressed the edges of the wooden frame. Who made that part? Paul or James?

How would he feel if someone criticized this lovingly crafted piece like he had done with some other artists and their works? Would he defend Sarah like Ingrid was doing with her grandmother? He set the mosaic back on the coffee table. No, he wouldn't go so far as to harm anyone because of something they said. But he would speak up for her—like he should have spoken up for some of the artists he'd critiqued? He sighed.

What was that rule Gram used to lecture him about? *"You should treat others the way you want to be treated."* If he'd followed that wisdom in his business model instead of listening to Alfie's philosophies, *Blue's Art Clash* would be a different entity than it was today. How he'd talked about Evelyn Glasser and other artists who'd put their heart into their artwork, even if he didn't like their style, medium, or color choices, made him feel unsettled and remorseful now.

But what am I going to do about it?

In the future, how could he improve his podcast so that it portrayed the changes he was experiencing internally? Was there a way to critique artists fervently and passionately without being so antagonistic or rude? Boldly broadcasting his findings as he traveled from gallery to gallery had been his calling card for five years—he couldn't just walk away from that. As Blue Paxton, he had to be brutally honest, or so Alfie had told him a million times. Was he brave enough to stand up for who he wanted to be as a man of integrity and faith? Stand up to Alfie?

Lord, I want to be a better man. I long to be the person You want me to be and someone Gram and Sarah can be proud of. Could You help me figure that out?

Alfie would never hear of altering their format, even for the betterment of artists. He was too focused on profit and notoriety. Hadn't Blue been that way, too, before meeting Sarah? He pinched the bridge of his nose, feeling the pressure of two opposing sides clashing. He didn't want to weaken his podcast but to make it better. How far was he willing to go to make the revisions he was considering? What if he lost everything? He groaned.

"Bartholomew?" Gram asked in a sleepy voice. "What's troubling you?" She leaned back against the couch, gazing sleepily at him. "Are you worried about this Alfie business?"

"I'm pondering who I want to be versus who I have been."

She sat up straighter and met his gaze. "Who do you want to be besides the sweet Bartholomew Paxton I've always known and loved, the one I was blessed to help raise?"

He kissed her cheek. "Thank you for that, Gram. I'm praying about some things in my life. Asking God for wisdom."

"That's great to hear, grandson."

"I'd like you to meet Sarah. I think you're going to love her."

"I'm sure I will. But is something troubling you about her?"

Blue drew in a slow breath. "She wants a transparent, honest relationship with me."

"Isn't that a good thing?" Gram squeezed his arm gently.

"Yes, it is. However, you've heard my podcasts. She disagrees with some of my—"

"Criticisms? Rudeness?" Gram lifted an eyebrow. She would undoubtedly agree with Sarah's viewpoint.

"Let's say it's made me reconsider some things."

"You don't doubt her loyalty, do you?"

"Not at all." Warmth spread through his chest, soothing some of the day's frustrations. "In some ways, it's like I've loved her forever."

"Honey, that's how it should be with the woman you're going to marry."

"Who said anything about marriage?"

"For you to talk to me about loving a woman, you're pondering marriage and a family." She elbow-bumped his arm. "Besides, I've been praying about getting a great-grandbaby. God's listening and nudging you toward Sarah."

"Do you really think so?"

"With my whole heart."

"Then I have a question for you."

"If you need a million bucks, you're out of luck." She cracked a grin. He smiled too.

"What would you say about meeting Sarah in Basalt Bay?"

Gram clapped. "Does this mean you are going to ask her to marry you?"

"No." Despite his denial, a spark of anticipation shot through him. "It means I want my grandmother to meet the woman I love and for you to see Basalt Bay for yourself."

"Are you thinking of moving there?"

"I'm thinking about you moving there." He winked.

"What?" Gram huffed. "Like I'd leave my house after living here for thirty-two years! Leave Barb and my friends?"

"You would consider moving to live closer to me, wouldn't you?" He clasped her hand gently. "I might be spending more time in Basalt Bay. If you were there, I'd also get to see you and eat more of your delicious home-cooked meals."

"Now you're sweet-talking me to get on my good side. I can't say I'd move anywhere." Gram sighed as if he'd asked her to relocate to China instead of the next state. "But I would like to meet your Sarah."

His Sarah. How he hoped that was true!

Chapter Forty-nine

Sarah sat across from Callie at a table in the otherwise vacant gallery, sharing about the winter festival's results. She'd been so busy lately that she hadn't taken the time to draft a report until last night. As the group's secretary, she wanted to make sure they had a written account of the event to reflect on next year. She'd sent an email copy to Callie and Sue Taylor, the president and treasurer, asking them if they wanted to meet and discuss it today. Sue wasn't available, but she sent a spreadsheet of data so Sarah and Callie could look it over. They agreed to discuss the information in detail at their regular meeting in January.

"I'm pleased our efforts turned out so well. Thirty-five booths and forty-two silent auction items are impressive for our first festival." Callie nodded toward the pages Sarah printed out. "Let's do it again next year!"

"I agree! At our next meeting, we should discuss how to make the festival an even bigger event with all the proceeds going to the Caring Society."

"Absolutely!"

Sarah jotted a note about it. "Also, we should talk with the other ladies about how we want to allocate these funds."

"I have an idea." Callie leaned forward, her eyes twinkling.

"You do?" Sarah chuckled. Even though Callie didn't live at the project house anymore, she often came by to visit and help with household chores and baking. Her involvement with the project house ladies, the Caring Society, and her new husband seemed to fill her with so much joy she radiated enthusiasm.

"I think we need office space." Callie grinned like having an office was a prize.

"We do? For what exactly?"

"For the Caring Society." Callie picked up her teacup. "We should have a point of contact here in town where ladies can walk in off the street and ask questions, seek advice, or get the help they need. At the same time, others can drop off donations or sign up to volunteer." She took a sip of her beverage. "We want easy access for anyone in a desperate situation, right?"

"Well, yes. But wouldn't a rental take a lot of money?"

"It might." Callie squinted toward the ceiling as if searching for an answer. "What if we got local businesses to chip in with the costs? If I convinced a few business owners to help with an office, do you think the others would go for it?"

"Uh, Callie." Sarah didn't want to dampen her spirits. "I agree that having a designated place in town for our group would be convenient and beneficial. But we're a small charitable nonprofit. I think we'd have to consider free options, talk with Sue about that, and bring it up at our next meeting."

Callie sighed defeatedly. "I had such high hopes."

"I know. I'm sorry." Sarah hated disappointing Callie, who had been at the heart of getting the women's group going. "There's another matter, something confidential, I want to talk with you about, too."

"Oh?" Callie's eyes brightened.

"It concerns Lola and others like her."

"What's wrong with Lola?" Callie set her cup down firmly. "Is Micah okay? Did Lola's ex show up again? If he did, I'll—"

"Nothing like that. Micah is fine." Thankfully, the gallery was quiet, allowing them privacy to visit. "You know Lola is considering getting a divorce."

"I wish she'd done so already."

"But it takes money for the legal process, and she doesn't have any resources." Sarah thought of herself when she first came to Basalt Bay—homeless, needy, carrying all her possessions in a backpack—and felt more sympathy for Lola or anyone in her situation. "She had an interview at Bert's. But even if she got a job today, she'd need childcare, work clothes, and personal necessities before she could invest in legal help."

"You're right. Why didn't I think of that?" Callie shuffled in her chair. "Should I talk with her?"

"I'm sure she'd welcome a compassionate listener." Sarah patted the table. "But I wanted you to be aware of her situation. I think all the Caring Society proceeds should go toward helping women get the services they need, as we talked about before the festival. It seems more important—"

"Than an office space. I hear you." Callie heaved a sigh. "Sue Taylor spoke with us about that, but I got all wound up, thinking an office was a grand idea. What Lola needs is more important. I'm sorry."

"It's all right. Maybe we can find a way to do both." Sarah squeezed Callie's hand, trying to reassure her that her idea was worthwhile. "What if we used a corner in the community hall or the church for a temporary office?"

"That wouldn't be very private." Callie shrugged. "Let's concentrate on the needs in our community and table my idea."

"If you're sure."

"I am."

They sipped their drinks quietly for a few minutes. The front door opened, and Craig stuck his head in. "Is everything okay here?"

"Yes, thank you!" Sarah waved at him.

"Sure thing." He closed the door.

"That's nice of the guys to stop by like that." Sarah fingered the handle of her cup, feeling grateful to Craig, Judah, Forest, James, and Paul for staying true to their word and checking on her.

"Sure is." Callie turned her cup in a slow circle on the table. "I have something else to share, too. I've had a request for someone to stay in the project house temporarily."

"You have? That's terrific! The old planning room is ready for occupancy. Who is this person?"

Callie groaned. "I shouldn't have said anything until I had confirmation. I'll just, uh—" Standing, she gathered her coat and purse. Why was she leaving so suddenly?

Was this about Sue Anne? Was she coming back to stay in the project house? If so, why didn't she ask Sarah about it since they discussed it already? She followed Callie to the door. "Is Sue Anne the one who's coming?"

Callie paused. "Would that be so bad?"

"Not at all. I just wondered."

Callie gave her a brief hug. "You'll know all the details soon enough. I hope you'll be okay with it. I just wanted to give you a tiny warning." *Warning?*

Who was this mystery person? And why was Callie being secretive about it?

Chapter Fifty

"What an adorable town!" Gram cooed as they passed through Basalt Bay's sparse business section. Blue made a U-turn at Bert's Fish Shack, circled back through Front Street, made another U-turn, and parked in front of the gallery. "Paige's Gallery and Coffee Shop," Gram read the sign. "Looks like a lovely, quaint shop—my kind of place."

"Sarah loves it."

"But not you?" Gram touched his arm resting on the console. "You can be honest with me."

"Honesty gets me into trouble sometimes," he said ruefully.

"We are to speak the truth in love with our whole hearts."

"Okay." Blue visually inspected the weathered building, trying to imagine the double hurricanes that swept through the town over a year ago. "I don't love the gallery or Basalt Bay, but I care a great deal about one person here."

"I recall you talking negatively about some similar towns." Gram's smile softened her words. "But I never understood why."

It had been years since they discussed family history. Was this the time or place to be open about it? He placed his hands on the steering wheel again, gripping it tightly. "Remember what happened with Mom and that small-town church?"

"Yes." Gram nodded slowly.

"I've been skeptical of small towns ever since."

"But that incident was over thirty years ago."

"I know." He breathed deeply, and then exhaled. "But it's a part of the fabric of my life. Wasn't it their judgmental attitude that made others turn against a mom struggling to survive? If they'd looked beyond their rules and reached out to her with love, she might be alive today."

"Oh, honey, we don't know that for certain. Your mama would never have wanted you to grow up despising anyone. Yes, that church had some hypocritical folks." She clicked her lips together. "But there were good ones, too. Your mama had enough love in her heart to forgive and even made some friends there." Gram patted his hands. "For your happiness, try to forgive those men who didn't know what they were doing or how long-lasting the results would be." She grimaced. "Including your father."

"I'm trying. Really, I am."

"I had to forgive them too." She sniffled.

He met Gram's teary gaze. He hadn't thought much about how the pain of losing her daughter and granddaughter had affected her. His focus had been on himself.

"How did you ever let that pain go?"

"My heart was broken. But recalling that I, too, had sinned and needed grace and forgiveness helped. Even when it's hard, we've got to forgive and try to love. Otherwise, the pain eats us alive." Her eyes shone toward him with caring and understanding and lacked any condemnation. "Shall I pray with you about this, too?"

"Yes, Gram," he said hoarsely. "I love Sarah. She wants to stay here, which means I'll keep coming back, but I don't want to begrudge the town she cares about for the rest of my life."

"Is that what you've been doing? Begrudging small towns?"

"I think I've held Mom's experience against every little town I've ever been to." *And every sunset picture against Dad.* The realization and anguish of that admission scoured through him, nicking away more of his emotional hurts and callouses. *God, help. Heal me. Make me a better man.*

"Oh, grandson." Gram leaned her head against his shoulder and thrust her arm over his chest in a semi-hug. "With God's love and mercy, everything is possible. I believe in His power to heal. I believe in accepting all He has for me. And you, too." She mumbled a prayer, but not loud enough for him to hear it well. He caught a few words—"Jesus," and "Help my grandson," and "Bless him"—and those were enough to make tears flood his eyes. Wiping her eyes and sniffing, Gram leaned back and tugged on the door handle. "Now, will you introduce me to Sarah?"

"Let me get that." Blue dashed around to her side of the car. Since he hadn't called ahead, Sarah didn't know he was bringing Gram here. Hopefully, she didn't mind surprises. He opened his grandmother's door and helped her to her feet, still reeling from the emotions of the past few minutes.

"Lead me to your future bride."

"Now, Gram, none of that. Promise me?"

"All right." She sighed melodramatically. "But don't make me wait too long!"

"Okay." Blue linked their arms, directing her toward the gallery entrance. Just then, someone clutched his other arm.

"Here you are, honey!" *Ingrid!*

"Honey?" Gram swiveled toward the woman. "Is this your Sarah?"

"No, it is not." He jerked his arm from Ingrid's grip, all the tender emotions he'd been experiencing evaporating.

"I'm Elly's sister. Remember Ingrid and Elly Glasser, the granddaughters of the woman whose reputation your grandson smeared?" Ingrid's lips curled contemptuously.

"Go on in, Gram." Blue opened the door and propelled her into the gallery. "Sarah," he called without seeing her. "Please assist my grandmother." He shut the door, crossed his arms, and, bracing his legs, faced Ingrid. "What do you want? Why are you here?"

"Alfie told me to meet him here."

"Alfie?"

"Who else?" She rubbed her hands together. "Let's go inside and your new girlfriend can get us some coffee. Are you going to drop her as fast as you dropped Elly? Break her heart, too?" She pressed her lips together. "She's still pining for you. She thinks you're coming back to marry her."

"She does not!" They hadn't even kissed, let alone talked about marriage.

"You'd be surprised what your treachery and lies have caused." She fingered some pearls around her neck. "Alfie came by and tried to talk some sense into her."

"Alfie was in Bend?" When did Alfie and Ingrid get so close?

"He offered to pay off our debts that have piled up since your repugnant podcast aired." She tilted her face one way, then the other, with each point. "*He's* a gentleman. *He* promised to make restitution. *He* apologized for your misconduct."

"Then he's taken care of your complaints, so I'll ask again—why are you here?" After this was over, he needed to have a long discussion with his business partner.

The door cracked open behind him. "Is everything okay, Blue?" Sarah asked.

"Yes. I'll be in as soon as this is resolved. Take care of my grandmother, okay?"

"I will." The door whooshed closed.

"You two sound like an old married couple already." Ingrid squinted at him. "I am glad you dropped Elly. Alfie is a much better fit for her."

Alfie. "If anyone is insincere in all this, it's him and you." He hated the thought of Elly, the nicer of the two sisters, being hoodwinked into a relationship with Alfie because of his and Ingrid's scheming.

"You're the despicable one! Alfie is trying to make things right with my family."

"That's his job. He's covering his bases and hoping to profit because of it." Blue clenched his jaw, tension crawling up his neck. "I left without saying goodbye to Elly. I plan to apologize to her about that." Among other things. "I'm also sorry for what I said about your grandmother's work. But there's no way of knowing if it brought on any health issues."

"You are a coward if you don't own up to your mistakes!" Her voice rose shrilly. "I plan to tell the whole world about your flaws and blunders!"

"You mean like you invented that lie about me harassing you?"

"It wasn't a lie!" Even though she spoke forcefully, she didn't look him in the eye. She clenched and unclenched her fist around the pearls. "It wasn't a lie!"

"It's time for you to leave."

"I'm waiting for Alfie right here!"

"Then I'll wait here, too." Sarah and Gram were safe inside. He would stay in this position all day if necessary.

But where was Alfie? And why had he told Ingrid to meet him here?

Chapter Fifty-one

Sarah set a cup of hot tea on the table in front of Blue's grand-mother. Even though the woman who'd introduced herself as Francis Bell was petite in size, Sarah recognized her resemblance to Blue in her sapphire eyes and broad smile. "Can I get you anything else? I have blueberry muffins and cinnamon rolls."

"I'd love a cinnamon roll." The older woman's eyes lit up. "Will you join me?"

"Certainly." Sarah returned to the kitchenette, set two cinnamon rolls on plates, and warmed them in the microwave, all the while stealing glances at Francis. Why had Blue brought his grandmother here? Did this mean anything? Her brain buzzed with thoughts of a proposal. Too soon, right? He was probably trying to keep his grand-mother safe. Had Alfie caused her emotional distress or threatened her safety? Sarah set the rolls on the table and reclaimed her seat across from Francis.

"It looks delicious. Thank you."

"You're welcome." Sarah brushed the tines of her fork over the frosting on her cinnamon roll. Blue's and Ingrid's voices rose outside.

What was Ingrid doing here? Why had she been released from jail? What about the restraining order? Blue said he was fine, but Ingrid could do physical harm—she proved that already. Sarah closed her eyes and prayed silently for his safety. When she met Francis's gaze, the woman nodded like she agreed with what she was doing. "So Blue brought you up from Redding?" Sarah asked.

"That's right. He took me on a road trip to meet you."

"Really?" So it wasn't just about keeping his grandmother safe?

"He said he wanted to introduce us and show me the town you love."

"That's great! I've wanted to meet his beloved grandmother. And I do love Basalt Bay." Francis's shining gaze seemed like an invitation for Sarah to share more about herself. "While some people call their house a forever home, the individuals in this city who embraced me and loved me when I felt I had nothing to live for are my forever home. When I came here, I met such wonderful friends who shared their faith and home with me. Before long, I was praying again, and my hope in God and life was restored."

"Oh, my dear. I'm glad you met those loving, accepting folks and found the healing you needed." Francis's hand shook as she patted Sarah's. "You are a joy to this grandma's heart. I see why my grandson has fallen in love with you."

Had Blue confessed his love for her to his grandmother? A chuckle bubbled out of Sarah despite the trying circumstances outside. She subdued it with a question. "Do you know where you'll be staying while you're here?" She bit into the pastry, and the cinnamon tickled her taste buds.

"Somewhere called a project house?" Francis's eyebrows drew together. "I have no idea what Blue was talking about."

"Ohhh! You must be the visitor my friend told me about. I live at the project house!"

"You do? I'll be staying at the house you love?" Francis clapped gleefully.

"Yes! I live there with several other ladies—the mayor, a mosaic artist, a young mom, and another lady who is currently out of town—and an adorable toddler." Sarah felt lighter than she had in days. "I'm so glad we'll be staying under the same roof and can get better acquainted." Was that Blue's plan?

"That sounds delightful. I want to know everything about you. I hope that doesn't sound too daunting." Francis grinned. "Aren't you a mosaic artist?"

"I enjoy working on mosaics." She felt uncomfortable being called an artist when she had such high regard for the artists whose works were displayed in the gallery. And her skill level wasn't anywhere near Kathleen's.

"I received one of your pieces as a gift from Blue."

"You did?" That's what Blue had done with her mosaic? *Aww.* How sweet of him!

"It's quite beautiful! The card said it was created by Sarah Blackstone. That's you, right?"

"It is. Blue must have given you the mosaic he bought at our silent auction."

"Isn't he the most thoughtful grandson? I'm so proud of him. And I'm grateful he met someone like you who loves our Lord Jesus." Her words warmed Sarah's heart even more.

"Blue has helped bring some joy back into my life that was missing. I'll always be thankful for that."

"He told me about your being widowed." A compassionate expression crossed Francis's face. "I'm sorry to hear about a young person like you going through that."

"Thank you. It's been two years. But that is why my life took a downward spiral for a while." Sarah clasped her arms in a self-soothing gesture. "It's why I ended up in Basalt Bay, where my grandmother lived when I was a girl."

"Now Blue is here with his grandmother, which seems fitting somehow, doesn't it?" Francis's eyes widened, revealing more of her blue irises.

"I believe it does." Sarah was already beginning to love Blue's grandmother and her sensitive heart.

"Maybe my grandson wants me to move here because he hopes for a similar experience as you have found."

"Move here? Blue wants you to move to Basalt Bay?" Sarah nearly fell off her chair. "Sorry. That's just—"

"I thought you two had discussed my possible move." A panicked look crossed Francis's features. "Perhaps I shouldn't have said anything."

"It's okay. But, no, we haven't discussed it." Sarah's heart pounded fast. "I'm surprised but in a good way. Did he, by any chance, mention moving here, too?"

"Hasn't he talked with you about it?"

"Not at all. We've discussed the incompatibility of our jobs and how difficult a relationship would be considering his traveling schedule and how he dislikes small towns." Why was Blue talking to his grandmother about moving to Basalt Bay? Had his heart warmed to the idea of living closer to her? Was he also thinking about marriage? *Oh, Lord, please.* Her phone vibrated. Callie's name crossed the screen. "Sorry. I should take this."

"Go ahead. I'll finish my delicious snack."

"Hello?"

"Have you heard who will be staying in the old planning room yet?" Callie sounded ready to burst with the news.

"Yes. I've met Blue's grandmother. She's a sweetheart who's sitting here with me now."

"Perfect! Are you okay with the arrangement?"

"Absolutely!" Sarah smiled at Francis.

"Is everything okay there?"

"Ingrid is outside shouting at Blue." She turned away from the sound of their voices. "He's guarding the door, keeping her out."

"Do you want me to send James over? Or Judah?"

"If we need someone, I'll call Deputy Brian."

"Maybe I will send James," Callie said as if she hadn't heard and ended the call.

Sarah returned to her seat with one question swirling in her thoughts. Was Blue thinking of moving to Basalt Bay?

Chapter Fifty-two

Blue held his stance for over forty-five minutes. His toes were cold and his arms stiff, but he wasn't moving an inch unless Ingrid attempted to get past him. Then he'd charge into the gallery and lock her out. He'd already sent two potential customers away with a brief explanation that there was an emergency. He hoped Sarah was okay with that.

A green luxury car with dark tinted glass pulled up and parallel parked in front of them. Alfie exited the vehicle wearing a long black coat, sweeping his hand over his copper hair streaks, and strolling toward Blue like an actor on the red carpet. He'd always preferred a grand entrance. "Hey. I'm glad you two are working things out amicably."

You've got to be kidding. Alfie thought that Blue standing with his legs spread and arms crossed, ready to forcefully stop Ingrid from entering the gallery, was amicable?

"You're finally here," Ingrid said in a whiny tone. "I thought I'd have to tackle this moron to get inside and nab my painting!"

"Now, now. Blue can be reasonable when he wants to be." Alfie smirked.

"What's this about?" Blue demanded. "What painting are you talking about? And why are you two meeting here?"

"Gracie Parker's. Haven't you heard?" Ingrid touched her necklace. "Alfie arranged for Gracie's art to be exclusively available in my family's gallery. Her last painting in this hole-in-the-wall is mine!"

"Is that right?" Blue shot glances between them. "Why would Gracie agree to that kind of deal? Why would she choose your gallery over this one since it's closer to where she lives?"

Ingrid rolled her eyes. "This puny gallery is going down. You're going to be the one to tell the world about Gracie and the Glasser Gallery's new partnership."

"I am not!" Blue stiffened his posture and clenched his fists at his side. "Alfie, why are you scheming and making deals between artists and galleries? Isn't that a conflict of interest?"

"Isn't your current fling a conflict of interest?" Alfie eyed him disdainfully.

"That's telling him." Ingrid cackled.

"Things are changing," Alfie said.

"So I see." What else was Alfie changing that would affect Blue? "Why are you making promises about what I'll say on the podcast when I haven't approved it?"

"Blue, buddy, haven't I been telling you what to say and what galleries you'll visit for the last five years?" He smoothed his hair in place. "It's too windy out here. Let's go inside and sort this out. They are open, aren't they?" Alfie extended his wrist and stared at his gold watch.

Blue didn't budge.

"Finally, I can get my painting!"

"What is she talking about? What have you done, Alfie? And why did you go to my grandmother's house?" He focused his attention on Alfie but remained aware of Ingrid's movements in case she tried anything. "You had no business barging into her house."

"She was fine with it," Alfie said nonchalantly.

"Well, I wasn't!"

"Can't we chat about this over coffee like business partners?" Alfie made a begging pose with his hands. "C'mon, Blue, buddy. Be a little understanding. Let's all work together."

"Ingrid isn't my business partner. Why should I work with her?"

"Well—" Alfie chuckled uneasily. "That may not be entirely the case."

"What's that supposed to mean?"

"Inside?" Alfie pulled his sunglasses down the bridge of his nose, peering over the top. "We have things to work out. I've taken care of everything like I always do. Your girlfriend will be compensated if she agrees to keep her mouth shut." Blue gritted his teeth. Alfie continued in a greasy tone, "And the Glassers will be rewarded generously."

"He already gave me this!" Ingrid shook her pearls.

"You and I are still willing to do anything to succeed, right?" Alfie thrust his hands toward Blue.

"Are we willing to lie and take people down so we can rise to the top? That's a new low for you." Blue stared intensely at him, but Alfie shrugged like it didn't matter. "Is it true you're dating Elly? Would you stoop to dating a woman to stop her family from suing you?"

"Us!" Alfie jabbed his finger against Blue's jacket. "Everything I've done has been to better *our* careers and to satisfy *our* subscription base."

"Give me a break." Alfie had done a lot of things for his own good.

"I'd date Alfie in a heartbeat." Ingrid batted her eyes at him. "But Elly's the one with the broken heart. He makes her feel better."

Alfie coughed like he was choking.

James emerged from the hardware store next door and doffed his hat at Ingrid. "Hello, miss. Anything I can do to help?" He eyed Blue and discreetly tipped his head toward the street, where Deputy Brian was marching toward them. *Finally.*

"Yes, you can help me get inside the gallery." Ingrid rubbed her hands together. "I want to claim the painting I've been promised before the place goes out of business. If you would move this buffoon out of the way, I'd appreciate it."

James's eyebrows lifted. "Is there a reason you're not letting this charming lady into Paige's Gallery?"

Blue could think of a half-dozen reasons.

"At least Basalt Bay has one gentleman in it." Ingrid tucked her hand through the crook of James's arm, but he nearly tripped in his haste to get away from her.

"What's the trouble here?" Deputy Brian stopped next to Alfie, eyeing Ingrid suspiciously. "Ma'am, why have you returned to our city? And why are you anywhere near this gallery? Did you forget about your restraining order?"

"Well. I. Uh—"

"Don't worry, officer. It's just a misunderstanding," Alfie articulated smoothly. "If Blue will let us go inside this so-called gallery, we'll all sit down and talk like civilized people. Then Ms. Glasser and I will be on our way. Nothing for the law to be concerned about."

"I'll decide whether it's a matter I should be concerned about. My office might be a better place for this *so-called* discussion." Deputy Brian's glance ricocheted between Ingrid and Alfie. "Our town might be small, but it boasts two jail cells, should we need them."

"Is that so?" Alfie tugged on the neckline of his shirt.

"I'm not spending another night there!" Ingrid said in a screechy voice.

A man jogged across the street toward them, waving a piece of paper. "Here are my findings, Deputy." What findings? What was going on?

"Thank you, Forest." *Forest?* He must be the PI and co-owner of the gallery Sarah had mentioned. Deputy Brian perused the papers. "Alfred Denver, did you falsify tax documents and earnings to make it look like you made less than you have through *Blue's Art Clash?*"

"What?" Blue questioned.

"Well, I wouldn't say—"

"Have you embezzled funds from your business?" the deputy asked sternly.

"What?"

"No comment." Alfie thrust his hand over his hair.

"Did you pressure the Glassers into giving false claims about Blue Paxton, including the serious charge of sexual harassment?"

"Alfie?" Blue stared disbelievingly at his business partner.

"Did you tell them that they would face financial retaliation if they didn't cooperate with those claims and compensated if they said what you wanted them to say publicly?" Deputy Brian tapped his foot. "Did you?"

This was worse than Blue had imagined. Alfie started those terrible lies about him? Was their whole partnership a fraud?

"No, of course, I didn't." Yet Alfie's face turned beet red, a sure sign he was lying.

"He was in on it, too!" Ingrid pointed at Blue.

"I was not! If anyone was hatching a devious plan, it was you and Alfie." He met Alfie's cold gaze, and his partner's betrayal burned through him.

"Ingrid Glasser," Deputy Brian addressed her. "Did you attempt to run Blue Paxton off the road on Highway 101 on December first of this year?" Blue's backbone tightened. He lifted his chin. Had the deputy found proof of Ingrid's guilt? His estimation of Deputy

Brian's service to this community went up a couple of notches. "Did you plan to do bodily harm as a means of retaliation or vengeance against him?"

"No comment!" Suddenly, Ingrid bolted down the sidewalk, casting frantic glances over her shoulder. Forest sprinted after her. In less than a minute, he'd captured her and was hauling her back with her fighting him every step of the way.

Deputy Brian clutched Alfie's arm. "You're coming into the station for questioning."

"You can't do this!" Alfie's voice shook as if he realized how much trouble he was in. "Blue, help me! You can't just stand there after all I've done for you."

"What am I supposed to do? You're the one who did this."

"It's all a mistake."

"Right."

"After our chat, I may have to charge you and your accomplice." The deputy shrugged toward Alfie. "Looks like you might be spending some time in my jail, after all."

"Get me a lawyer! Blue, everything I did was for us."

"Sadly, it wasn't."

"Ingrid Glasser," Deputy Brian spoke sternly. "You are being detained on suspicion of conspiring to bring physical harm to Blue Paxton and violating the terms of your release by returning to Basalt Bay—and violating your restraining order by being within fifty feet of the gallery."

"But it was all Alfie's idea," she whimpered. "I only went along with it to help my grandmother. He said we'd make a wad of cash if I cooperated! Pay up, Alfie!"

"Shut up!" Alfie shouted, his frenzied look in sharp contrast to the well-kept businessman he usually portrayed.

All the way across the street and the City Hall parking lot, with Deputy Brian and Forest leading them, Ingrid and Alfie argued with each other and vented against the legal system, the deputy, and Basalt Bay. Ingrid shouted that Alfie was the only one who should be behind bars. Alfie ranted about how much trouble she had caused him and his plans for success.

"Are you okay?" James patted Blue's shoulder.

"I'm beyond stunned." His business partner was being led to jail. Where did that leave him and *Blue's Art Clash*?

"Understandably. If you need anything, just ask. And take care of Sarah, will you? She's part of our family here."

"I know. I will. Thank you for caring for her and for your kindness to me." He shook James's hand.

"You're welcome. We're here for you, too, son."

Son. Tears flooded Blue's eyes. "That means more than I can express."

When he entered the gallery, he found Gram and Sarah with their hands clasped and heads bent. Seeing his grandmother and the woman he hoped would always be part of his life praying together, praying for him, no doubt, he felt a strong tug of emotion. What had he ever done to deserve such love?

Nothing.

But that was the beauty of real love, wasn't it?

Chapter Fifty-three

Hand in hand, Sarah and Blue strolled to the water's edge below the project house after helping Francis settle into the second-floor spare bedroom. The weather was cool but not too windy to hinder them from enjoying a beach walk together. Sarah loved being close to Blue and having him all to herself. "What a day, huh?"

"What a couple of days! Whenever I think about Alfie swindling and using my name as leverage for his self-gain, I get disgusted all over again. How did I not see that coming?"

"Finding out what he was doing behind your back must have been hard."

"It irritates me still." Blue faced her and clasped her hands. "I'm sorry to mention this now, but I need to leave for a while." He was leaving? Already? "There's something I must do."

"Oh?" They'd hardly spoken since they acknowledged their love for each other. And his grandmother just arrived. "What's going on? Is there a problem?"

"Sort of. I need to go away for a week or longer."

Her heart sank. She'd been hoping—what, that he'd give up being a traveling podcaster and stay with her now that Alfie was in jail? Of course he wouldn't do that. Besides, hadn't she told him she would never ask him to alter his career? And she meant that. But with his grandmother in town and Christmas coming, she was hoping he'd stay longer and that they could get to know each other better.

He let go of her hands and ran his palms down her arms, and though she wore a coat, the movement chilled her. "I will count the minutes until I return and get to be with you again, but I feel like I must do this."

"I understand." She had to accept his leaving gracefully, but being apart wasn't as simple as she'd thought. "Where are you going this time?"

"To Bend." He linked their fingers, but she stiffened.

"Is this about Elly?" She tried to stay calm but was failing. Why was he leaving her and going halfway across the state to see another woman?

"Yes." He gazed at her intently. "Does that bother you?"

"Maybe." She pulled her fingers free of his. Blue had things to work out with the Glasser family, but the two of them had stuff to work out, too.

"I don't think she took our acquaintance as seriously as Ingrid said, but I need to talk with her about it." Couldn't he explain via a phone call or an email? "Ingrid implied that Alfie was dating Elly as a bargaining chip." He glanced toward the gray clouds overhead. "If that's the case, she needs to hear the truth from me."

Sarah inhaled deeply, trying to sort through her thoughts. Why was she so troubled about this? Blue had to do what was in his heart to do, and she wanted to be supportive of that. It seemed like he was honestly trying to resolve something about the past, which was an honorable thing to do. Was she fearful that he'd forget about her and fall for Elly once he saw her again?

"It's thoughtful of you to want to make things right," she said. "What else do you hope to accomplish by going there?"

"I'd like to make things right with Evelyn, too."

Ah. That made more sense. Before meeting him, she would never have guessed what a caring and considerate person he was. Now, she admired him more because of it, even though she'd rather he stayed close to her.

He swept some windblown hair off her cheeks. "What are you thinking about?"

"That your leaving is harder than I imagined." She wouldn't beg him to stay, but she wasn't going to pretend it was easy, either. "Will it always be tough to watch you go, like you're taking a chunk of my heart with you?"

"Possibly." He wrapped his arms around her, and she leaned her cheek against his chest, feeling warm and protected despite the chilly wind and wishing she could stay like this. "It's hard for me to leave you, too," he said softly.

"But it's worth it, right?" Leaning back, she held his gaze while a light rain fell over them.

"Our love?" He cupped her cheeks, looking deeply into her eyes. "Sarah Blackstone, knowing you are waiting here for me is worth every second of the heartache of missing you and longing to stay." He kissed her gently, his whiskers tickling her cheek, and her frustration about Elly faded. "You aren't worried about me not coming back, are you?" She was embarrassed to admit it. "Sarah?" He smiled in the way she loved, and she couldn't hold back.

"For a few seconds, I was worried about how you'll feel about Elly once you see her."

"I love *you*." He kissed her softly, and it was as if his lips whispered that he loved her with every brush of his mouth against hers. "I want to be only with *you*."

"It's nice to hear you say that." And his kisses were incredible, too.

He kissed her forehead. "We'll always be honest with each other, right?"

"And not leave things unsaid."

"Then believe me that whenever I have to leave you, I'll eagerly await the chance to drive back and hold you like a man wants to do with the woman he loves." She stared into his deep blue, shining eyes and knew he was sharing truths from his heart. "I'm not planning to cross any lines with you, Sarah. But I want you to understand how sincerely I feel about you and how close I want us to be."

She gulped. Intimacy wasn't a road she would travel before marriage, but she was very much in love with and attracted to Blue. If they were married—

"Let's keep walking." He nodded toward the rocky shore ahead of them. "That will distract both of us."

"You think we need a distraction?" A little cooling off, perhaps?

"Yes, I do." He led her down the beach, swinging their linked hands and smiling at her. "I'm glad Gram's staying with you and the other ladies. I think she's going to enjoy herself."

"I agree. She's a beautiful person like you."

His smile widened. "Did you just say I'm beautiful?"

"With your good looks, stunning blue eyes, gorgeous smile, and loving heart, you are a beautiful man, Blue." Warm feelings for him strummed through her.

"You're making me miss you more, and I haven't left."

"That's how I feel, too."

He stopped walking and pulled her to him for another hug. "I promise to call or text every day."

"I'll look forward to all your texts and calls." She glanced up at the darkening sky. Any second now they were going to get soaked.

Blue slid his cool index finger down her cheek. "We're going to make this work, right?"

"With God's help, we will." She recalled Francis saying he was considering moving to Basalt Bay. Was he thinking about marriage, too? "I don't want to force a discussion you aren't ready for, but what are we going to do about us?"

"I can think of something I'd like to do with you." His lips delicately brushed the corner of her mouth, inched across her cheek with infinitely sweet caresses, and lingered at her earlobe.

"I meant, what are we going to do about our love?" she asked breathlessly. "Our future?"

"Kissing you is a fantastic beginning to our future." He kissed her on the mouth hungrily as if proving the validity of his answer.

She played with a button on his jacket. "While you're away, will you do something for me?"

"Anything."

"Will you think about what you want our relationship to be someday?"

The tender look he gave her made her feel guilty for pushing him. But she wanted everything love and marriage offered, including children and a lifelong relationship with him. Would he understand and not freak out if she came right out and said that?

"Elly Glasser and I went out for a meal together." His admission scattered Sarah's romantic thoughts. "We were flirting and went for lunch. It was nothing, but I should have mentioned it."

"Why didn't you?"

"Whatever flirtation we had was over almost before it started. We didn't kiss or hold hands. We mostly laughed over gallery stuff." He heaved a breath and shrugged.

Even though she knew Blue was over forty and had dated other women, something about him flirting with Ingrid's sister annoyed her.

"I left Bend after I finished my last podcast there and didn't say goodbye, which wasn't very thoughtful. Elly disappeared from my radar after my assessment of her grandmother's paintings." By his forlorn expression, he felt bad about that. "I want to discover what my words may have caused their family and if I can rebuild any goodwill."

"That sounds admirable, Blue." Sarah appreciated his honest explanation and wanted to respond with understanding and grace, as she hoped he would do if their roles were reversed.

"Also, I have some soul-searching to do while I'm gone—not only about us, but about my career, the podcast, and the man I want to be."

"Thank you for sharing your thoughts with me. If I can do anything or you want to talk, call or text anytime." She kissed his cheek. "You're a good man, Blue Paxton. Your grandmother raised you well, and she's proud of you. So am I."

"That means a lot to me." He put his arm over her shoulder. "Thanks for looking after her while I'm gone. Gram is very special to me."

"It's my honor. She wants to try mosaics, so we'll bond over some craft time."

Just then, giant raindrops fell. Laughing, Sarah and Blue dashed up the soggy beach and trail until they reached the porch's shelter. They shivered and brushed droplets off each other's coats. Their gazes met for several moments, making her expect a whopper of a goodbye kiss. Instead, he held her gently to him like he thought she was precious. "I really am going to miss you, Sarah."

"I'm going to miss you, too."

His sigh had a melancholy sound. "I appreciated James, Forest, and the deputy's help today. I don't know how long I could have kept Ingrid and Alfie out of the gallery if they'd advanced on me."

"That's partly why I love Basalt Bay—how everyone helps each other. The way people embraced me when I arrived here homeless was nothing short of a Christmas miracle."

"I admit the kinder side of your town has surprised me." Blue stepped back a little. "I made some rash judgments about small towns based on a few lemons in the past."

"It's easy to do. But everyone deserves a second chance, right?"

"Or three and four?" He gave her a sheepish grin. "I should return to the inn and pack, but I hate to leave you."

He kissed her achingly sweetly, like it was their last kiss for a long time, and she tried to suppress the gloomy thought. Tears moistened her eyes, but she wouldn't let them fall. Blue was coming back soon. They were going to spend Christmas together, right?

After another embrace, he jogged through the rain toward his Mustang. Before climbing in, he turned back, waved, and called, "See you soon, my love."

She'd hold his endearment close to her heart and pray about their future in the coming days.

Chapter Fifty-four

Ten days later, Blue finished his final podcast from Bend, Oregon, had his Stang packed, including Christmas gifts for Sarah and Gram, and was waiting for Elly to return from making a bank deposit. He was all set to hit the road for Basalt Bay and the life he hoped to have with Sarah. Tomorrow was Christmas Eve, and he was excited to be heading home and celebrating the holidays with her and Gram. *Home.* Was he really considering Basalt Bay as his place of residence? Anywhere his two favorite people were waiting for him had to be the best place in the world. Why not call it home? He grinned.

All the tender feelings of family spending time together for the holidays and sharing in honoring Christ's birth had been filling him with anticipation and wonder for the last couple of days. His previous outlook on small-town life couldn't dampen the joy and expectation he was experiencing. Much of that had to do with the woman he planned to ask to marry him! He patted the small box with the delicate solitaire diamond in his jacket pocket. Still there. Safe. Should he wait until tomorrow night to propose? That would be romantic. Or maybe Christmas morning on the beach?

It sounded like there'd be a huge to-do on Christmas Eve with Sarah and her family, the Cedars gang, the project house ladies, and Gram and him all gathering for dinner and then going to church together. He was looking forward to everything, but mostly, he wanted to be with Sarah, kiss her, and ask her the question burning in his mind and heart. Would she say yes to spending her life with him? She'd asked him to think about their future. And boy, had he!

While he was in Bend, he'd spent most of his days volunteering in the Glasser Gallery. That had been a revelation! Never again would he take a gallery attendant's position for granted. Working in the gallery had been fascinating and enriching for his future podcasts, but it had been a lot of work.

Because of his volunteer hours, Elly was able to spend more time with her grandmother. Now, Evelyn was doing better and even talking about returning to the gallery part-time. Elly seemed a lot happier and less stressed. He had enjoyed some lengthy discussions with the artist and her granddaughter and apologized for any offense he may have caused them. Both gracefully accepted his apology, which lifted the burden he'd felt.

The door opened, and he looked up, expecting to see Elly. Ingrid marched into the gallery, her expression livid. Tension riffled up Blue's neck.

"What are you doing here? Get out!" she shrieked as she rounded some sculptures, heading straight toward him. "Are you swindling my family? Stealing from us?"

"Of course not!" He heard she was returning to do community service hours in Bend but hoped to be gone before her arrival.

"Are you trying to get back together with Elly?" Eyes wide, Ingrid gripped the edge of the counter, the only thing separating them.

"No. I've been helping here."

"Like I believe that!" She puffed out a noisy breath.

"Ingrid!" Elly bolted through the door and rushed over to her sister. "You're back." She cast Blue an apologetic look.

"I got here in time to stop this crook from taking what little money we have left!"

"That's not what's happening," Elly said firmly. "Blue has been helping us."

"I don't believe it!"

"You should." Elly slipped around the counter and stood next to him, facing Ingrid.

"I have a deeper appreciation for Evelyn's paintings now." Blue inched toward the opening beside the counter, hoping to get past Ingrid and leave, but she blocked his exit. "I even purchased one of a black rose with turquoise raindrops for my grandmother."

"You're lying!"

"It's true," Elly said. "He's been assisting Grandma and me. If he hadn't been here, I don't know what I would have done."

"He has ulterior motives. She might trust you." Ingrid jabbed her finger at Elly. "Not me. I will never trust you!"

"For that, I am truly sorry."

"Like I believe anything you say."

"Just listen to him, will you?" Elly pleaded.

"I don't want to hear anything he says!" Ingrid's lips bunched up like she'd taken a bite of something sour.

Blue recalled the podcast he'd done when he first arrived and attempted to rectify some of his previous comments about Evelyn's art. Since then, he'd tried harder to analyze her work more reasonably and with grace. He was certain Sarah and Gram would approve of his revitalized attitude and efforts to make things right with the Glassers. God might be pleased also since Blue had been talking with Him about it daily.

"He's been volunteering here," Elly said emphatically. "He watched the gallery so I could be with Grandma. You should be thanking him instead of being rude."

"Thank him for what? Getting me thrown in jail?"

Blue tensed at the accusation.

"You got yourself thrown in jail," Elly said. "You teamed up with that loser and did what he said, so own up to your mistakes and learn from them."

"Who are you? And what have you done with my mousy sister?"

"I'm standing up for myself." *Way to go, Elly!* "Blue and I talked about the past. I misunderstood about his leaving, but I wasn't heartbroken. And I was never going to date Alfie. You exaggerated all that!"

"Oh, please. He's brainwashed you! Blue Paxton is a dirty liar."

"No, he isn't!" Elly said. "Have you heard his podcasts lately?"

"How could I?" Ingrid huffed. "I was in the tin can referred to as a jail in the Podunk town Blue hates!"

I don't hate it anymore.

"Listen to his current work and see for yourself."

Blue appreciated Elly standing up for him, but Ingrid obviously wasn't buying it.

"I never want to hear *Blue's Art Clash* again! It makes me sick. So does he!" Ingrid picked up a rock from the counter with "Glasser Gallery" written on it and jerked her arm back like she was going to throw it at him. Instinctively, he pulled Elly out of the way, but she thrust out her hands toward her sister.

"Put down that rock! What are you thinking? Do you want to go back to jail?"

"I'm thinking Blue Paxton deserves to hurt for all the pain he inflicted on us." Ingrid scowled at him. "If I get thrown back into the dungeon, so be it!"

"Put the rock down this instant!" Elly shouted. Surprisingly, Ingrid lowered it. "Now listen to me." Elly shuffled over and set her palms on Ingrid's shoulders. "You never have to tune into *Blue's Art Clash* again because it doesn't exist. Tell her." Elly lifted her chin toward Blue.

"I'm done with Alfie's affiliation with *Blue's Art Clash*. I severed all legal ties, bought out his share of the company, and dissolved it." He grinned despite the daggers Ingrid was shooting at him. "I'm the sole proprietor of *Hello, Blue*."

"Poor Alfie," Ingrid moaned. "Wait. Does this mean you're done podcasting?"

"Aren't you listening?" Elly asked. "He's not done. He's starting over."

"As what? A new and improved moron?"

Blue wouldn't let her get to him. "My current format centers around my views and includes the valuable opinions of artists, gallery workers, and fans." He'd already received some positive feedback, and the show had only been live for a few days.

"I spoke on his podcast, too." Elly grinned proudly.

"You're doomed without Alfie." Ingrid shook her head.

"We'll see." Since the walkway was clear, Blue strode past Ingrid and proceeded to the door. He'd done his best to change what he could here. The rest was in God's hands.

Elly followed him outside and hugged him. "Thank you! What you did by volunteering and podcasting positively about our gallery has changed our business and our lives. Thank you for inviting me to talk on your show, too."

"You're welcome. I wish you and your family the best."

"You, too. God bless you."

As he drove out of Bend, Blue wanted to wrap his fingers around the small box nestled in his coat pocket and check on it one more time, but he had to stay focused on driving. If all went well, later today, he would kiss Sarah with all the love he felt for her and ask her to marry him since waiting until Christmas Day felt too long.

Every day he'd been away, he and Sarah had connected through texting or calling, sometimes several times a day, sharing about their lives, pasts, and childhoods. He told her about his feelings concerning Mom and Desi's passing and Dad's sunset obsession and abandonment. Both topics were challenging, but he got through them thanks to Sarah's understanding and compassion, and he felt better after discussing them. They spoke in depth about forgiveness, God's grace, and his need to let some hurts from the past go, even praying together over the phone.

Sarah shared more about losing her husband, discovering she was adopted, and why she loved Basalt Bay so much. She told him about growing up with her brother, Ryan, and how they'd never been close, and she always wondered why. Despite their distance, each conversation made him feel like they were getting nearer as a couple.

After a discussion with Elly, he called and told Sarah about it, and she was supportive and encouraging. Following his heart-to-heart with Evelyn, he wrote a lengthy email explaining how their conversation went, and Sarah wrote back, praising him for doing all he could to make amends.

When he was pondering a title for his new podcast, they tossed around names via texting—*A Chat with Blue; Chill Out, Blue; Art with Blue;* and the winner, *Hello, Blue.* When he contacted Gracie Parker about reconsidering keeping her watercolor paintings in Paige's Gallery, and she agreed, he immediately called Sarah and shared the good news.

Sarah also called him a few times at the end of her day, and he loved hearing about her work at the gallery and her interactions with Gram before he fell asleep. Each time they bonded like that, they were proving that they could not only make a long-distance relationship work, but theirs could thrive.

And he thanked God for it.

Chapter Fifty-five

Sarah lifted Micah up high so he could put a turquoise ornament on the seven-foot evergreen. "Yay! You did it. Good job!"

"More. More," he chanted in his cute toddler's voice.

"A few more ornaments, then we'll be done." She set him down, and he grabbed two decorated globes from a box. "Here you go." She lifted Micah again. He hooked the brightly colored spheres over the same branch, his eyes glowing, and Sarah felt so much love and joy over being involved in this little guy's life at Christmastime. *Someday, this could be like me with my son,* she thought nostalgically.

Lola strode into the dining room from her bedroom, which used to be Callie's room, and Sarah's grandmother's before that. "It's beautiful, but the tree has so many decorations it might fall over!" She held out her arms to Micah. "Let's give Auntie Sarah a few minutes to herself before her boyfriend arrives." Micah objected but Lola whisked him back into their room.

Boyfriend. Sarah smiled, her heart warming to the term.

Everyone in the house, including Francis and Kathleen, who were upstairs working on garden art mosaics, was giving her the holiday-decorated room to meet with Blue, so this time, she wouldn't have to worry about them being caught kissing. But she felt nervous about seeing him after ten days apart. He'd made some drastic changes in his life, professionally and personally. Did he feel any differently about them in the aftermath of those decisions?

When she heard his maiden *Hello, Blue* podcast and how humbly he apologized for offending anyone in his previous shows, her heart felt so tender toward him that she would have kissed him fervently if they'd been together. She loved a man who could honestly express his shortcomings. But what if he was so involved in his new business and all the responsibilities without Alfie that he didn't have time for her? Would he stay only briefly in Basalt Bay?

She groaned. He was coming to spend Christmas with her and Francis. She needed to stop worrying and enjoy whatever time they had together.

She smoothed her hands down her ivory sweater dress and touched the blue necklace Lola had given her for an early Christmas present. Lola told her how she and her mom used to make jewelry for family members, and that she made this one especially for Sarah. She fingered the sapphire-like jewel encircled by silver pieces and an idea came to mind.

What if Lola made jewelry like this and displayed it in the gallery? It was attractive, functional art, suitable for showing in an art collection. And it would give her a second source of income, since she'd gotten the part-time job at Bert's. Sarah would have to discuss it with Paige. However, considering she okayed a few of Paul and James's small wood-craft items, she would probably be okay with some unique jewelry being displayed in the gallery, too.

Sarah adjusted a gold package with a red bow she'd placed under the tree for Blue. A knock sounded at the front door, and anticipation rushed through her. *He's here!* She ran across the room, turned the knob, and pulled open the door.

Blue leaned against the doorframe, wearing a festive red scarf draped around his neck and holding two wrapped packages in his arms. He smiled warmly, looking so handsome, and she wanted to fall into his arms and kiss him until tomorrow! Why had she been nervous about seeing him?

He set the presents by the inside wall, his eyes shimmering, and stepped toward her. "Sarah?" he asked softly.

With a squeal of delight, she lunged forward and wrapped her arms around his shoulders, kissing him with all the longing she'd felt while missing him for the last ten days. His arms curled around her waist, tugging her closer, and he kissed her as exuberantly as she kissed him. "I've missed you and this," he whispered. He brushed butterfly kisses along her cheek until he reached her ear. "I love you, Sarah."

Her heart melted. "I love you, too. I've missed you so much."

He closed the door with his shoulder and, still holding her, nuzzled his nose into her hair. "Mmm. You smell delicious."

"It's Kathleen and Francis's baking."

"No. It's vanilla, a hint of flowers, and you." Holding her slightly away, he glanced around. "Are we alone?"

"Not entirely. But we have the room to ourselves."

"Good." He touched his lips lightly to hers, making her long for more. Then, holding her hand, he led her straight to the Christmas tree. "I can't wait another second to do this."

"To do what?" They'd already kissed passionately.

Clasping her hands, he gazed into her eyes. "Sarah Blackstone, I want you in my life always."

"I want to be with you always, too." Her heart pounded.

"I don't have the details of traveling, small-town life, and where Gram will stay ironed out, but you asked me to ponder how we can make this work. I've contemplated it a lot." His eyes appeared an even deeper blue tonight, and Sarah wanted to bask in his gaze for a long time. "I love you as I've never loved anyone before."

"I love you so much my heart aches with a need to be as close to you as I can get." She let go of his hands and hugged him tightly. He returned her hug, then dropped to his knee in front of her. "Blue?" He looked up at her with such an adoring, timeless expression, she could hardly breathe.

"I want to spend all my days and nights with you. Whether we're together in Basalt Bay or farther apart, texting and talking on the phone, I want to know you are beside me in my heart and thoughts, and I am right beside you." His gaze never leaving hers, he withdrew a small red box from his jacket pocket. She gazed back at him through tears.

"Sweetheart, will you marry me? Will you be my best friend and life partner for the rest of our lives?" He held out a lovely solitaire diamond ring.

"Oh, Blue," she whimpered. This was what she'd hoped and prayed would happen, but she could hardly believe it was happening now. She dropped to her knees in front of him and kissed him with all the love and yearning for him that she possessed.

"Sarah?" he whispered.

"Hmm?" Opening her eyes, she saw his questioning, half-humorous look. Ohhh. She hadn't answered him! "Sorry. Yes! Absolutely yes! I will marry you." She skimmed her fingers over his slightly rough cheeks, feeling the ticklish sensation of his whiskers against her skin, and held his gaze with her own. "Will you marry me, Blue? Will you be my best friend and life partner forever?"

"Forever and always." He slipped the ring onto her finger, kissed her hungrily, and then leaning back, gazed dreamily at her. "You're going to be my wife."

"And you're going to be my husband. This is like another Christmas miracle."

"For both of us." He helped her to her feet. Then they kissed again.

"I will always love you," Sarah said like she was saying her wedding vows to him. "You will have my honesty and deepest hope for a loving future together. And I will thank God for you daily."

"I will always love you." He clasped her hands, smiling tenderly at her, his eyes shimmering. "I will stand up for you, pray for you, be true to you, and share my heart with you. I wish we could get married today!"

"That might be a little tricky."

"Tomorrow then?"

She laughed. "That would be delightful, but I'd like to invite Sue Anne to the wedding. Ryan, too, if he'll come."

"I understand. I'm just eager to marry you."

"Me too!"

"I was thinking of proposing on the beach on Christmas Day but couldn't wait."

"I'm glad. A proposal here in the project house is special to me." Wanting to give him something, she picked up his present. "It's your Christmas gift. But I'd like to commemorate this moment with something I had made for you. I hope you'll like it."

"I'll love it." He peeled back the gold paper, revealing an acrylic painting of a red Mustang convertible with two passengers heading toward a stunning sunrise. Blue met her gaze, his eyes welling with tears.

"Do you like it? I asked Paige to paint this scene with a sunrise, symbolizing a new beginning, whether for you or—"

"Us," he finished. "It'll be a perfect reminder of our journey together. Thank you for such a thoughtful gift, Sarah. It's beautiful." He drew her to him, holding her close. "Paige is a great artist, and I love the details on the Stang." He glanced over his shoulder. "How about opening your gift, too?"

"Okay. But you've already given me the best gift ever."

"True." He lifted her hand and kissed her engagement ring. Grinning, he set the painting she'd given him on the dining room table, picked up one of the wrapped packages he'd set on the floor, and strode back to her. He handed her a heavy gift. "Merry Christmas."

"Thank you." She tugged on the paper and let out a soft gasp. "Oh, Blue. The monolith painting is gorgeous and unique! I love it!" She smoothed her hand over the flat stone. "Did you get this at the Rock Shop?"

"Yes, I did. I hope we'll have many Christmases to share laughter and love and exchange gifts." He kissed her softly. "These two pieces of art can be the start of our collection."

"'*Our* collection' sounds like a dream come true. I hope to see many sunrises with you, Blue."

"And I, you." They rested their foreheads against each other's.

As if they'd been awaiting a signal, Francis, Kathleen, Bess, Lola, and Micah burst into the room, surrounding them with hugs and congratulations. Callie and James, who must have been waiting on the porch, rushed into the house, shouting cheers.

Francis clasped Blue's and Sarah's hands. "I've waited for this with great anticipation and prayer. I love my grandson more than anyone other than Jesus. And now you, Sarah, and all the great-grandbabies you will give me, will be my loves for all the days I have left." She kissed Blue's cheek, then Sarah's. "I love you both."

Blue hugged his grandmother. "Love you, Gram."

Sarah hugged her also. "I love you, too. May I call you Gram?"

"I hope you will!" Francis beamed. Her resemblance to Blue really was adorable.

After the excitement subsided, and Kathleen, Callie, and Francis went into the kitchen to prepare a celebration meal, Blue whispered, "Care to step out on the porch with me?"

"I'd love to." Sarah grabbed her coat off a hook by the door, and they exited without any explanation. Everyone knew why they wanted to be alone, anyway.

Standing at the end of the porch, she rested her cheek against Blue's chest, feeling his heart beating. She already felt at home in his strong, comforting embrace. And soon, she would know this man completely, and she cherished the thought. God had blessed them with each other, even when an engagement and hope for a future together hadn't seemed possible or likely. *Thank You, Jesus, for healing our hearts and working in our lives so incredibly!*

"You're sure you want to marry me?" Blue asked teasingly.

"Definitely. Are you okay with living in Basalt Bay?"

"If you are here, this is my home." He pressed his lips to hers gently yet eagerly, making her pulse race. "Are you still okay with me traveling for work?"

"I support you doing the job you love. These days without you being here have been challenging. I can only imagine how it will be when we're married and—" This wasn't the time to talk about her hope of getting pregnant soon after their honeymoon.

"When we're married and—?" He stroked some hair off her cheek, gazing lovingly at her.

"How do you feel about us having kids?" What if he didn't want children? She should have asked before now!

"I'm okay with kids."

She exhaled. "That's a relief. I'm so glad."

"You heard Gram. She's always reminding me about wanting a great-grandchild." He chuckled. "I'm her only hope since I'm her only grandchild."

"Can we give her one soon, then?" She winked, and he laughed, his face hueing a handsome burgundy. "I'm almost forty, so I can't wait too long to start a family."

"Does this mean we can get married right away? I mean, the sooner we get started on a family, the better, right?"

"Aww, Blue." She kissed him slowly and softly, and by the way he kissed her back, he understood what she was trying to say.

"Do you think God planned for us to meet and fall in love like this?" She tilted her head, gazing into his eyes. "Did He see how well the broken and healed parts of our lives fit together, almost like a mosaic?"

"Yes! And He knew we both have something the other needs, like you can't resist my charming smile." He grinned.

"And you can't resist my need for honesty?"

"Sweetheart, I needed you to remind me how important it is to mix honesty with grace." He stroked wisps of hair behind her ears. "God used you to help me make some important decisions about my job and us."

"I love it when you say 'us.'"

"Us, us, us," he whispered and kissed her cheek. "I love you."

"I love you. And I'm ready to live with you and our family wherever that journey takes us."

"Does that mean you'll travel with me sometimes? Maybe spar with me on *Hello, Blue*?"

She wrinkled her nose. "I don't know about sparring. I am open to traveling with you so we can be together more if we always come home to Basalt Bay and each other."

"That's a promise I'll seal with a kiss or three or four." And he did.

Soon, they would be Blue and Sarah Paxton, to have and to hold for the rest of their lives. She was getting the fresh start she'd prayed about and hoped for thanks to God's incredible goodness … and a touch of Blue beneath a cluster of mistletoe.

Thank you for reading *A Touch of Blue*!

Look for Lola's story in 2025.

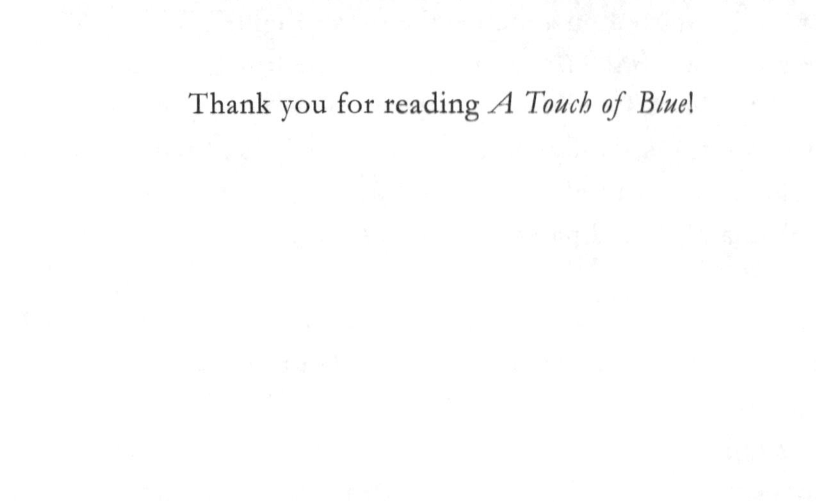

The Basalt Bay series is a spin-off from the Restored series that also takes place in the fictional town of Basalt Bay.

A special *Thank you* to …

Paula McGrew ~ for helping me deepen the characters and work through some challenges in *Blue*. I appreciate your assistance and encouragement in helping make this story come alive.

Mary Acuff, Kellie Griffin, and Jason Hanks ~ for reading *Blue* and sending me feedback and personal thoughts about the story. I'm so thankful every time you say yes to reading another tale.

Suzanne Williams ~ for taking time out of your busy life and helping me with another beautiful cover. I appreciate your artistry and wisdom so much.

Lord Jesus ~ for giving me story ideas and the heart to tell them.

Readers ~ for taking time to read this story. I appreciate you!

(This is a work of fiction. Any mistakes are my own. ~meh)

Christian fiction by Mary Hanks:

Liv & the Preacher: A Marriage of Convenience for a Good Cause Novel

The Preacher's Sons

Lake, Hud

Restored Series

Ocean of Regret, Sea of Rescue, Bay of Refuge, Tide of Resolve, Waves of Reason, Port of Return, Sound of Rejoicing, Shores of Resilience

Basalt Bay Series

Callie's Time, A Touch of Blue

Second Chance Series

Winter's Past, April's Storm, Summer's Dream, Autumn's Break, Season's Flame

About Mary Hanks:

When Mary isn't exploring the world through her characters' eyes, she is singing toddler songs and playing with her grandchildren. Vanilla lattes, gardening, and taking walks with Jason, her husband of 40+ years, rank high on her list of favorites. Telling stories is a huge part of Mary's life, and she hopes to continue writing heart-warming tales of grace, mercy, and love for a long time.

Thank you for reading the Basalt Bay series!

www.maryehanks.com

www.ingramcontent.com/pod-product-compliance
Lightning Source LLC
Chambersburg PA
CBHW032345310726
48973CB00007B/1866